A LESSON PLAN FOR
MURDER

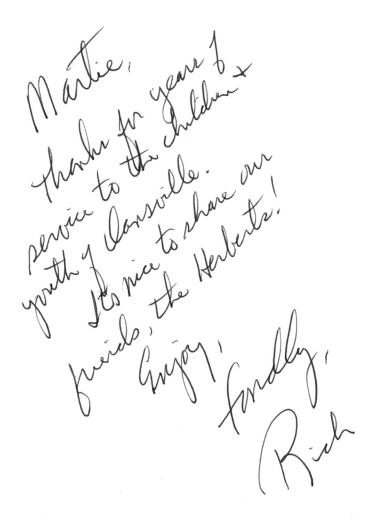

Martie,

thanks for years of
service to the children +
youth of Dansville.
It's nice to share our
friends, the Herberts!

Enjoy,

fondly,
Rich

A LOUIS SEARING AND MARGARET McMILLAN MYSTERY

A LESSON PLAN FOR

MURDER

Richard L. Baldwin

 Buttonwood Press
Haslett, Michigan

This novel is a product of the imagination of the author. All the characters portrayed are fictitious. None of the events described occurred. Though many of the settings, buildings and businesses exist, liberties have been taken in several instances as to their actual locations and descriptions. The story has no purpose other than to entertain the reader.

Published by Buttonwood Press
P.O. Box 716
Haslett, Michigan 48840

Publisher's Cataloging-in-Publication Data
Baldwin, Richard L.
     A lesson plan for murder: a Louis Searing and Margaret McMillan
     mystery /Richard L. Baldwin. – Haslett, MI: Buttonwood
     Press,1998.
          p.   cm.
     ISBN 0-9660685-0-5
          1. Police—Michigan-Newberry—Fiction.   2. Newberry
          (Mich.)—Fiction.   I. Title.
PS3552.A457 L47   1998   97-78341
813' .54   dc—21   CIP

PROJECT COORDINATION BY JENKINS GROUP, INC.

02 01 00 99 ◆ 5 4 3 2 1

Printed in the United States of America

*This book is dedicated to my father, Louis S. Baldwin, Jr.
Dad loved mysteries and read hundreds in his life time.
He encouraged me to take risks. Beyond love for his family,
he enjoyed a good meal, a good book, and
a challenging round of golf.*

Acknowledgments

To: **Louis Searing Baldwin and Margaret McMillan Baldwin**—
This is an example of what happens when you encourage your son
to take risks. I love you and wish you were here to read this book and
all to come. Somehow I believe you were helping me write it and
cheering me all the way.

To: **Patty Baldwin**—Thanks for your support, your love, your
belief in me, and your supporting me as I strive to reach my goals.
You bring joy to me each day. Sharing life with you is the closest I
can come to experiencing Heaven on earth. I love you!

To: **Scott, Patti, Benjamin Baldwin and to Amanda and Joe
Hoffmeister**—Thank you for bringing us tremendous joy. We are
proud of you and love you!!

To: **Gayle, Dick, Abby, Mac, and Stephanie Brink**—Thanks for
being in my life and caring about your brother, brother-in-law, and
uncle. I love each of you.

To: **Helen Baldwin**—Dad would've enjoyed this book, don't you
think? Thanks for being a loving step-mother.

To: **John, Annette, Mark, Lisa, Audrey, Elizabeth, Paul, Alicia,
Margaret, Dennis, Atticus, Mary, Ray, John, Kathy**—I'm proud of my
extended family and love each of you.

To: **Marge Fuller**—Thanks for those many supportive E-mail
statements along the way. May your teacher friends find an enter-
taining story in their Christmas stockings.

ACKNOWLEDGMENTS

To: Our cats, Luba and Millie—You've been wondering why I've been sitting at this computer for months? This is why.

To: Bill Kienzle—I've admired you since I read your first book. Thank you for meeting me on October 31, 1994 and accepting me, encouraging me, and writing me many letters of support over the years. I especially appreciate your advice to, "Never, never doubt yourself!!"

To: Sue Harrison—Thanks for helping me believe in myself and for taking some time to help me along the way.

To: Ron Lewis—Thank you for willingly offering advice and encouraging me to publish my story.

To: Lee Meadows—Thanks for inspiring by example.

To: Holly Sasso—Thanks for being a marvelous editor and teaching me some basic principles of writing. May your teaching bear good fruit.

To: Charlotte Fromholz, Jane Hattan, and Alisa Miller—Thanks for proofing with eagle eyes and offering important suggestions.

To: Theresa Nelson and The Jenkins Group Team—Thanks for producing this book and making my dream come true. First class job!

To: Diane Easterling, Doug McCall, Jennie McGeen, and Kathleen VanTol—Thank you for reading early drafts of this book, giving me honest feedback, and encouraging me to keep writing.

To: Dr. Karen Blackman, Emily Brusso, Dr. James Rawlinson, and Dr. Suzanne Sorkin—Thanks for expert medical advice.

To: Elaine Stanfield—Thanks for assisting with psychological profiles. People are interesting!

**To: Luce County Sheriff, Kevin Erickson; Chippewa County Deputy Sheriff, Bob Savoie; Charlevoix Chief of Police, Dennis

ACKNOWLEDGMENTS

Halverson; Mason Chief of Police, Roger Fleming; and Michigan State Police Sargeant M.T. Pendergraff, Owosso Post—Thanks for information and teaching me how experts protect citizens with compassion and professionalism.

To: Lt. Ed Moilanen, Michigan State Police Forensics Lab, Grayling, Michigan—Thanks for advice and introducing me to the exciting and fascinating world of the forensic crime lab.

To: Michelle Matteson—Thanks for information that will enlighten others.

To: Ben Hall—Thanks for words of encouragement during many Tuesday and Thursday rides together.

To: Penny Zago—I'm falling backward. I'll be caught. Thanks.

To: John Zago—The title is great. Thanks.

To: Gloria Anderson—You were one of the early ones who had an encouraging word. Thanks for countless suggestions and support.

To: Elizabeth Abeel—Thanks for asking, "Do you believe in your dream?" Yes I do! This is it, with more to come!

To: Margaret Goldthorpe—Thanks for confirmation and the telling and retelling of *The Finn Who Would Not Take a Sauna.*

To: Earl and Pam Kilander—Thanks for sharing dinner, opening some doors and pushing me into the emergency room.

To: Jim Line—Thanks for believing in me and introducing me to Sue.

To: Einstein—Thanks for saying, "Imagination is more important than knowledge."

To: Joseph Girzone—Thanks for writing in *The Shepard*, "Don't be afraid to use your imagination. God will enlighten you. You are the instrument of God. He will guide you."

ACKNOWLEDGMENTS

To: School teachers and administrators everywhere—Thanks for all you do to help children and young adults reach their maximum potential.

Finally, to you, the reader, I thank you and hope you will enjoy reading, *A Lesson Plan for Murder*.

A LESSON PLAN FOR
MURDER

Friday, October 9, Newberry, Michigan

Bill Blakeley, carrying his high powered deer rifle, walked into the back door of the secondary school complex in Newberry, Michigan. He proceeded through the janitor's area and down a hall past a few classrooms and up a flight of stairs to the second floor. He was heading to the middle school principal's office. He was aware that the board of education was planning to lay him off at the 8:00 p.m. meeting. The children had left for the day, but a few staff who saw him with the weapon immediately took cover. Blakeley had a reputation for angry outbursts.

"Bill! Bill, stop ya hear!!" shouted a teaching colleague, Frank Harrison who stepped out of his classroom to see Bill coming toward him.

Blakeley didn't stop. He marched on to complete his intended mission. He planned to aim the bullet in his rifle at the head of Luke Johnson, the middle school principal. Bill Blakeley couldn't take another layoff. He was lost in anger and frustration.

"Bill. I want to talk to you. Come here friend! Listen. Trudy called! She's got a message for you."

Hearing the name of his dear wife, Bill slowed and eventually turned to face his friend. "Trudy called?"

"Yeah. She loves you, Bill. If you do anything stupid with that rifle your only home is going to be inside a prison for life. Think of your wife and kids, Bill. Listen to me! Come on, Bill."

There was an eerie silence. A couple of teachers watched cautiously from down the hall. One went into the school office and dialed the number used in emergencies.

The call was answered by a dispatcher, "What's the problem?"

"A teacher, Bill Blakeley, at the middle school. He's got a rifle and he's very angry. Just got a layoff notice."

"We'll send a vehicle. Any shots fired?"

"No, you better hurry, please hurry!"

Back in the hall of the school, Bill could be heard shouting, "...laying me off, Frank. They gotta pay!"

"That rifle isn't the way to handle this, Bill. Get hold of yourself! Hand it to me!" begged Frank.

The sound of distant sirens snapped Bill back to reality for a moment.

"Hand me the rifle, Bill!"

As if in a fog, Bill walked over to Frank and handed him the rifle. "Good, Bill. Very good!" Frank walked into his classroom, ejected the cartridge from the chamber and hid it in a drawer in his desk. "Listen to me. We're going to walk back to your truck. You were just bringing in your rifle to show it to me because I asked to see it. There was no cartridge in the rifle. Got it?"

"I went too far, Frank. I'm in trouble. Big trouble!" Bill's large frame shrunk in despair.

"Listen up. Get hold of yourself. Let me do the talking. You didn't do anything wrong. You brought an unloaded rifle to show me. Understand?"

"Yeah, I think so." Bill took a deep breath. The two turned and walked out the back door and headed for Bill's truck with Frank carrying the rifle.

A Newberry police cruiser pulled up in the front of the school. Chief Morgan Fitzpatrick learned from the remaining employees inside that the teacher with the rifle and another teacher had just exited the school through the back door. Fitzpatrick immediately returned to his vehicle and announced the position of the two men into his police radio. The county sheriff, Eric Smithson, and a State Police vehicle were a block away. Within seconds these two vehicles and a Newberry police car came tearing into the parking lot behind the school. The officers slammed on their brakes, exited their vehicles, took out their revolvers, and crouched in a defensive position behind open car doors. The first on the scene, Sheriff Smithson, shouted, "Put down the weapon! Put it down!" In a matter of seconds, Frank and Bill were looking at four revolvers. "On the ground. Both of you, on the ground, face down, now! Now!"

Frank set the rifle on the ground. Both men went down on the asphalt pavement.

The four law enforcement personnel from the three agencies worked with precision to secure the weapon and handcuff the two men. Chief Fitzpatrick returned to the school to see that people were safe and out of harm's way.

"Bill was just showing me his rifle. What law are we breaking, man? asked Frank. "Thought this was America." Bill remained quiet as Frank had instructed.

No officer responded to Frank. The immediate goal was to secure the weapon, to take control of the two men, and to see that everyone else was safe. That accomplished, the two men were frisked. Bill Blakeley was taken in the sheriff's cruiser and Frank rode with Chief Fitzpatrick. All three vehicles filed away from the Newberry school toward the sheriff's office so the two men could be booked.

The office was only a few blocks away and in that time Frank, who knew Morgan Fitzpatrick as they were both in the local Kiwanis club, gave his story in detailed description. "Bill was bringing in his deer rifle to show me. Sure he was angry about the layoff notice, but the reason he brought the gun into school was to show me his rifle. Hunting season's only a few weeks away. The rifle's not loaded. You'll see that once the firearm's inspected."

Even though Frank was lying to save a teaching colleague, Frank was an honorable man, and Fitz had no reason to doubt his story. Fitz also didn't believe Frank was a threat to anyone. When they got to the sheriff's office, Fitz informed Sheriff Smithson that Frank was not a player in this unfortunate drama. Frank was freed from his handcuffs.

Bill, on the other hand, was put into the holding cell and read his Miranda Rights. He decided not to use the phone in the cell to call a lawyer; there was no need to. He would follow Frank's direction and feed the sheriff the story that he was showing the rifle to Frank in advance of deer hunting season.

The officers inspected the rifle and found that it was free of a cartridge. Sheriff Smithson and Fitz returned to the school to interview the witnesses of Bill's outburst, and to talk with the principal and superintendent. They learned that Bill had made no previous threats to anyone's life. He had expressed anger on occasion, but he wasn't a troublemaker.

On the way back to the sheriff's office, Chief Fitzpatrick called the Negaunee Dispatch, the agency that tracks law enforcement vehicles in the Upper Peninsula, and who had received the call in the first place. He reported that no shots were fired, and it appeared that no person had been in harm's way.

Sheriff Smithson and Chief Fitzpatrick discussed the case with the prosecuting attorney. Once all the facts were on the table, the prosecuting attorney said that while Blakeley appeared to have violated the Michigan Criminal Code by bringing a firearm onto the premises of a school, no charges were being filed against him. His gun was not loaded, and therefore he could see no reason to hold him.

The town eventually heard about Bill Blakeley's angry outburst in the school, with a gun, and that he was about to lose his job. The two men were released after Bill was given a severe verbal reprimand by Morgan Fitzpatrick.

The law enforcement officers closed the case and titled Bill's actions as non-criminal. Bill Blakeley was a free man and a lucky one at that after having a loaded firearm in a school with the intent to kill the principal.

Frank Harrison was relieved to realize that he had possibly saved a couple of lives. He regretted the lies, but he had done what he felt he had to do. Things could now return to normal. He returned to school, put the cartridge into his coat pocket and went home.

Late that same afternoon, Lou Searing, celebrating his fifty-sixth birthday, was sitting in front of his computer, in his writing studio, on the second floor of his beautiful home south of Grand Haven on Lake Michigan. Lou was wearing his Dockers with a favorite sweatshirt. He looked older than his fifty-six years. Maybe it was his baldness, and the hair that remained was grey. Maybe he had simply aged a bit more than others under the stresses and strains of his earlier career as a long time special education administrator. Or maybe wearing two over-the-ear hearing aids made him look like he was well into his sixties.

Lou had titled the mystery he was writing, *The Principal Cause of Death*. It was his second novel, and he was excited that it would be one of his best.

Once retired he not only pursued his passion for writing but also followed in the footsteps of his brother Bob. Bob Searing had enjoyed a distinguished career as a detective, and had solved some fairly complex murders in his thirty-five years with the Michigan State Police.

Lou's wife Carol arrived home from work and brought him out of his concentrated writing with a kiss and a rendition of the traditional birthday song. Carol traveled a lot as a preprimary home teacher. She worked with infants and toddlers with disabilities throughout Ottawa County. Her job took her into homes to work with families and children. It had been a long day. She would have liked to have gone out to their favorite restaurant, but it was Lou's birthday and she knew he'd enjoy potato soup. It would taste good on this cool October evening. The temperature and the clouds were giving the feeling that winter was coming early to the Great Lakes State.

The phone rang and Carol quickly picked it up. She knew that Lou didn't like to be disturbed when his thoughts were flowing. "Searing residence."

"Louis Searing, please."

Carol felt like this was a classic telephone solicitor call and she certainly wasn't going to bother her husband with such nonsense.

Lou would never purchase anything over the phone, and it would simply be a waste of time for both Lou and the solicitor.

"Who's calling please?" asked Carol in a polite way.

"This is Irene Richardson. I'm the coordinator of special education in Newberry. I knew Lou from when he was with the Michigan Department of Education. I would like to talk to him for a few minutes if I'm not disturbing your evening meal."

"Oh sure. He'll want to talk with you. One minute please."

Carol walked to the foot of the stairs and shouted. "It's for you, Lou. Irene Richardson from Newberry."

"OK, thanks."

Carol listened only long enough to be sure that the two were connected. She hung up and continued to stir the potato soup. She would take an occasional break and walk over to their large dining room window to look out over Lake Michigan. The view was breathtaking, and like a good movie, the scenes changed with different cloud formations, boats, and seasons. The frequent views provided the Searings with many hours of entertainment. Today the sky was cloudy and the lake was rough with whitecaps tumbling onto the shore.

As she looked through the large window she saw a reflection of herself. She saw a short woman with salt and pepper grey hair. The look on her typically happy face was one of concern. Carol was hoping the phone call would not pull Lou off to another investigation. She worried about his enthusiasm for tracking murderers. Life was too short for all the danger. She didn't want any harm to come to the man she loved.

"Hi Irene. Good to hear from you. How've you been?"

"I'm doing just fine. Sorry to bother you at the dinner hour, but something's happened up here and I think you should know about it."

"You've got me curious. Go ahead."

"This afternoon one of our special education teachers, Bill Blakeley, was told by the middle school principal, Luke Johnson, that he would be laid off. He seemed to take the news alright, but he

8

went out to his truck and brought his deer rifle back into school. He was quite angry."

"Doesn't sound good. Did he kill someone?"

"No, thank goodness. A teaching friend, Frank Harrison, got his attention and was able to talk him out of doing anything irrational. One of the teachers called the police. They came to the school and took Frank and Bill to the county building. We've heard that they were released and no charges were filed. Apparently there was no cartridge in the rifle."

"Sounds like a scary few minutes."

"It was. And people are still talking about it. Some say he did have a loaded rifle and was going to kill the principal. Others say he didn't have a loaded rifle, but was only going to threaten him. Still others think it was all show. My opinion is that the rifle was loaded and he was going to kill Luke. Thankfully, Frank stopped him and the police came quickly. Anyway, he's a free man."

"It sounds like you've had a lot to stress in Newberry this afternoon."

"Yes, we sure have. Let me tell you why I called."

"Please do."

"I wanted you to be alerted to a possible murder. You've been successful in investigating education related crimes. If I'm right, we've got a powder keg about to blow up here and I wanted you to know about it."

"I appreciate the heads up. Things have settled, I presume."

"Yes, I guess so. But, Bill gets angry and I have a feeling that he's eventually going to act on his frustrations. He's been laid off before, actually this is the fifth time in his career. You'd think he'd be used to it by now, but it makes him very angry, and you know what can happen when people go over the edge."

"Yes. I do. Well, thanks for briefing me. Feel free to call if something happens."

"Yeah. There's nothing to do, but I feel better knowing that you now know about this afternoon."

"I'm glad you called. Try to relax a bit this evening. There is enough stress in handling the day to day responsibilities of special education without having a teacher walking around a school with a deer rifle."

"Boy you got that right, Lou. It's crazy. It's simply crazy, and it's getting worse. Thanks for listening. Are you enjoying your retirement?"

"Sure am. I'm doing a lot of writing, playing some golf, and working on an investigation or two. Never a dull moment."

The two finished their conversation just as Carol was announcing that the soup was hot and ready. Lou came down to the dining area to join Carol and their golden retriever, Samm. The name Samm was short for Samantha who always lay quietly at the feet of Lou or Carol as they ate their meal together. She somehow knew that if she was a good girl, she'd get a romp on the beach after dinner.

"What did Irene have to say?" asked Carol before cooling her spoonful of soup.

"Oh, some special education teacher lost it when he got a layoff notice. Brought a deer rifle into school. Some think he was going to shoot the principal. She wanted me to know about it, that's all."

"You are getting so popular that now you get calls in anticipation of murders. What is this world coming too?" asked Carol, shaking her head.

"People have a need to share what they know and what they fear, I guess."

Carol had prepared a yellow cake with white frosting and a Jackson Pollack design of bitter sweet chocolate on top. The cake with vanilla ice cream seemed an appropriate way to usher in a new year. Lou successfully blew out the candles and privately wished for a long, healthy, and happy life with Carol, the most beautiful woman he had ever met.

The remainder of the evening was spent walking along the beach, writing, and taking happy birthday calls from adult children Scott and Amanda and their families as well as good friends, Marc and Mary Lou in Kansas City.

Thomas Franklin pulled into his driveway after a day of hard work at his car dealership. He owned and operated Franklin Motors in Newberry. He had been a car dealer for close to 30 years. He was a member of the Newberry School Board. He thought of it as his service to the community. His father taught him to always give back, to keep the energy flowing so to speak. He graduated with honors from Calumet High School in 1944. Franklin realized the wonderful opportunity he had in being able to attend school for free and in being taught by quality teachers who truly cared about his education and his development into an upstanding citizen. As a young man he vowed to carry out the example set by his father, to give back what he received.

After establishing his family and getting his business up and running, Franklin ran for the school board but was defeated. He lost to a popular dentist in the community. Not one to be set back with a defeat, he ran again in 1981 and this time was the top vote getter in the election. He had been on the school board for thirteen years and played a major role in school reform. In fact, it was Thomas Franklin who led the effort for fiberoptic cable that allowed students in Newberry to have access to instruction in a number of courses that the school district could not afford to provide for its students.

Because of the new technology, Newberry provided strands of math and science, college prep courses, and real life courses for those not going on to Northern Michigan University, or to other colleges downstate. Thomas Franklin was held in high esteem as the one who spearheaded the drive to see that a quality education was available for the youth of Newberry and for those in the eastern part of the Upper Peninsula.

Franklin walked into his large home on Truman Boulevard. He greeted his wife, Marian, with a kiss on her left cheek. The kiss was a daily tradition that dated back to the day after their marriage in 1946, two years after Tom Franklin and Marian O'Brien graduated from high school. Thomas Franklin was an affectionate man and a charmer who carried on the traditions of his own father.

"I'm not feeling well, dear," Tom said.

"What's the matter?" Marian asked with concern.

"Stomach. It seems to be unsettled. I feel like I might throw up. I don't feel very good at all."

"Shall I call Doc Polski?"

"Oh no, just an upset stomach I think. He'd just tell me to take a Mylanta and sip some tea."

"If that's what you think he might say, then maybe you should do that. I'll get the Mylanta and brew some tea."

Tom went up to the bathroom and sat on the edge of the bathtub. He tried to think thoughts that took him away from the upset stomach. The nausea seemed to subside a bit, so he went to the bedroom and lay on the bed. Marian brought the antacid and a cup of warm tea. She fluffed his pillow and with great concern made every effort to make him comfortable.

"Thanks, dear."

"You sip this tea and rest. Call me if you need me and I'll be up to check on you from time to time," said Marian softly. Tom rested for about an hour and then prepared to go to the Newberry School Board meeting. He managed to get himself to the meeting. He didn't let on to anyone that he wasn't well. After all, he had his pride.

The board meeting progressed normally until the subject of the three layoffs came up on the agenda. This was not a pleasant topic. Three families would be emotionally and fiscally hurt with the decision. Newberry people considered everyone in the community family. It was a tough decision, and the Board and local citizens looked to Tom Franklin for strength and direction.

Franklin accepted his responsibility as a leader, and attempted to explain, as humanly as he could, that the decision had to be made because the dollars were not there to support the programs. He stressed to the group that boards make decisions based on their priorities and he felt he must affirm his belief that these teachers should be terminated. The board listened to their leader and then voted five to two to layoff three teachers.

$$\backsim$$

At about 9:45 p.m., Bill Blakeley decided to call his father. He had always shared family news, good and bad. "Hello," said William Blakeley, Sr.

"Hi, Dad."

"How you doin my boy?"

"Got some bad news today. I'm beginning to settle a bit, but the last several hours have been very stressful."

"What happened?"

"I got laid off again."

"You've got to be kidding, son. What is this, the fifth time this has happened to you?"

"Yeah, something like that."

"The MEA going to be behind you this time or are they going to hang you out to dry like the other times? I can't believe you pay dues to that no good union. What have they ever done for you, my boy?"

"Not much, that's for sure. I've got no choice, I guess. The contract calls for dues to be taken from my pay."

"Stand up to 'em, son!" Bill, Sr. shouted. "My union at least was at my side when I got the ax. They fought hard for me. Demand that you get a fightin' team. Hear me, son. Gotta get tough with 'em."

"I know, dad. These are different times. The unions don't have much power."

"We need to get back to the days when management came to their knees when we made our demands. The fat cats couldn't make their money and drive their big cars if it weren't for our sore backs and calloused hands."

"Yeah, I know. I'm going to fight it this time, Dad. I'll be all right. If I don't change a few minds, I'll find another job."

"It must be hard on Trudy, Bryan, and Heather. That's what bothers me."

"They'll be fine. We support each other."

"I'm coming over to see you, son. Family has to stick together in rough times."

"That's not necessary."

"I didn't ask if it was necessary. We need to support each other. I'll be over tomorrow morning."

"Well, OK, if you insist. We always enjoy having you here."

"See you soon. My love to Trudy and the kids."

When Bill, Jr. hung up he knew he had lied. They didn't always enjoy having Bill, Sr. visit. Trudy thought he was a bad influence on Bryan. They were sure he brought his liquor. He would go to his room and take some swallows. They never saw it, but they smelled it and soon saw its influence. But, he was Bill's father and the Bible says to honor thy father and mother. His mother had died a few years earlier and Bill, Sr. was all that was left of his side of the family. The family would once again try to be friendly and hope that his visit would be short.

When Bill, Sr. hung up he went straight to the scotch. "Gotta drown the poor boy's troubles," he said to no one as he poured himself a shot and sent it down the hatch in one swallow. It would take a few more shots to put him in another less painful world, and he needed to get to that world. Bad news always drove Bill, Sr. to the bottle. Some people take their bad news to food, some to drugs. Bill, Sr. took it to scotch.

Bill, Sr. woke up in the morning sitting in the same chair that held him when he swallowed the last shot. He couldn't remember what time that was, and he didn't care. The TV was still on, and when he became conscious, the Saturday morning cartoons seemed to be on every channel.

Saturday, October 10, Newberry, Michigan

Tom Franklin awoke feeling a little better than when he went to bed after the school board meeting. He decided to have some tea and toast while looking through the *Newberry News*. The *News* was in an experimental phase. It had been a weekly paper but with a new editor and a sizeable grant the paper had become a daily on a two month trial basis. A study would determine if the effort should continue. Tom sat in the breakfast nook with Marian and glanced at the headlines. He quickly passed through the first section which highlighted the national and international news plus the editorials which he usually found boring. He got right to the local section. This held his interest because he knew just about everyone who was mentioned. You simply don't live in an area all of your life and not know who's having an anniversary, who died, who's having a baby, who's in jail, going to jail or who's being sought for a crime. He knew all about the city government and all about the schools because of his board position.

His eyes fell on the article entitled, "School Board Takes Action to Layoff Three Teachers." He read:

> On Friday evening, the Newberry School Board took action in a special meeting to layoff three teachers. Those affected were an elementary teacher, Lucille Simpson, who has been with the Newberry schools for one year; Bill Blakeley, a special education teacher who has been with the system for almost two years; and Malinda Harris, an art teacher who serves students in the elementary and the junior high school. All three teachers are the victims of a

decreased population of children in the Newberry schools and the failure of voters to pass a millage last month. According to the union spokesman, Mary Holland, "The layoffs were unfortunate but we hadn't effectively convinced the school board that teachers were more important than hiring an evaluation specialist or buying three buses before the three oldest vehicles in the fleet had put in all their miles."

One of two dissenting board members, Beverly Jones said, "I'm sorry this had to happen." Board member, Thomas Franklin, voted in favor of the layoffs, "We need to take action to keep within a budget approved by the voters, and if that means three teachers need to be released, I feel I have an obligation to set policy within available dollars. I'm sorry for all three teachers and their families." Superintendent Williamson said that every effort would be made to find employment for Mrs. Sherman, Mr. Blakeley, and Mrs. Harris.

Parents of the children in Bill Blakeley's special education classroom were at the meeting. One parent, Loretta Lafferty, gave an impassioned plea for not laying off Mr. Blakeley. She said, "Why are you doing this to our disabled kids? Mr. Blakeley is the only person who understands their problems and can effectively help them. If he goes, not only will these kids with disabilities suffer, but so will all the other teachers and ultimately, this community." Mrs. Lafferty pleaded to the board not to take this action.

The School Board President, Bill Owen stated that a behavioral consultant would be providing services from the intermediate school district and that with inclusive education becoming so popular, he thought such services would be sufficient. The School Board meets again in two weeks in the Newberry School Library on Newberry Avenue at 8:00 p.m.

"I don't know why that editor always needs to quote me when the School Board makes some unpopular decision?" Thomas said putting the paper down.

"Because you're a leader. Leaders always have to take the pressure of their decisions," Marian responded tenderly.

"I know, dear, but every board member made numerous comments during the course of the discussion, including our Superintendent, yet none of them gets quoted. It just always seems like I get to carry the bad news to the citizens. Maybe I'm getting paranoid, but I can't remember when I got quoted on a good news story. Whenever there is good news, like the students' scores on the Michigan Education Assessment Program testing initiative, it's Superintendent Williamson who is quoted. When our teams win district, regional, or state titles in sports or quiz bowl, it always seems to be Mrs. MacMillan who has the quotable comment to make."

"I do think you are getting a little paranoid, Tom. Next to Superintendent Williamson, you're the recognized educational leader in this community and you know it. I suggest you brighten up. If you feel well enough, I'll fix you some eggs over easy. How would that taste?"

"Sounds good. The doc says to stay away from the cholesterol heavy foods though. I don't seem to be taking his advice. You know, I was less than honest with you yesterday when I came home from work. I really didn't feel good and my stomach was off, but I felt some tightness in my chest and a little numbness in my arms and hands."

"Well, you better go see Doc Polski. That needs to be looked into."

"Yeah, I'll mention it at my next check up."

"When is that?"

"I think it comes due in a month."

"Better not wait that long. Give him a call this morning, dear."

"Nah, I'm okay. I was lifting some auto parts at work and probably pulled a chest muscle. I don't have the strength I once had."

"I don't want to nag you. I haven't done that in all our married years, but for my sake, please see Doc Polski soon. Please?"

"I'll see. All this talk about health and docs has taken away my appetite for eggs. Guess I'll just go back to bed for awhile."

〜

Bill Blakeley, Sr. arrived in Newberry on Saturday morning at 11:30 a.m. It was about an hours drive from his home in Rudyard, Michigan. Rudyard was a town adjusting to the closure of a nearby Air Force base. The town had no tourist attractions and travelers had no reason to leave the four lane to discover the quiet community. Rudyard sat about a mile west of I-75 as tourists drove north between St. Ignace and Sault Ste. Marie.

Bill, Jr. was working in the yard as his father drove up. Trudy was in town doing some errands. Bryan was in Marquette, at a sports day camp at Northern Michigan University. The coaches there were beginning to have their eye on him. Heather was at a girlfriend's house still sleeping. The pajama party had ended when the sun rose one more time on Michigan's beautiful Upper Peninsula.

Bill, Sr. shook hands with Bill, Jr. "How about a cup of coffee, Dad?"

"That would do just fine, son." What he was really thinking was that a shot from his flask would hit the spot and do more for his nerves than the slight hit of caffeine from the coffee, but sensed that his drinking was not appreciated by Bill, Jr., or Trudy, so he just kept the thought to himself.

"Let me give you a hand with your bag."

"I got it, son. It looks like I've got enough stuff to stay a month, but don't worry I'll be on my way tomorrow. I just want to be here long enough to give you and the family a little support in this unsettling time." Bill, Sr. pulled his bag out of the trunk of his 1992 Ford Taurus. He always bought a Ford. He was tempted in the late 1980s to get a Honda or Toyota, but he just had to buy American. He was a union man and the union guys had to stick together. Not to do so would be like running over to the enemy in a war, simply unheard of.

Bill, Jr. got the coffee for his father, "I'd like to finish up in the yard. It should only take me about an hour. If rain weren't in the forecast, I would just let it go, but I'd like to finish if you don't mind."

"Not at all. I'll just look at these papers here while I drink my coffee. You go ahead and do what you need to do."

"Thanks." Bill went out the door to finish his work while his father went to his flask to get a jolt to last him a few hours.

Bill, Sr. sat down in a comfortable chair and began to go through the accumulating newspapers beside the lounger. They were stacked in the order of the days of the week. He seemed to enjoy looking at the local news and seeing how it compared to Rudyard. It didn't take long to find the article about the lay off. His only son was one of three teachers in this predicament. All the emotions arose once again and he felt his heart beating faster.

Bill, Sr. noticed another article about his son being apprehended by the police for bringing a rifle into the school after the layoff meeting. He thought that once again Billy's anger was getting him into trouble. He was proud of his son for standing up for himself, but the energy in his emotions were not being effectively channeled. Someday, he knew that Bill, Jr. wouldn't be able to stop himself. It was simply a matter of time.

Trudy came in from her chores and greeted her father-in-law warmly. She secretly said a prayer for guidance to get her through the next couple of days without incident, or at least with less stress than was usually the case in these situations.

Bill, Jr. finished his yard work and they all sat down to a lunch that Trudy had brought from town: potato salad, sliced ham for sandwiches, and some soft drinks. The conversation focused around the layoff. Bill, Sr. questioned his son's intentions. "What are you going to do if you get laid off, son?"

"Got no choice, I guess. I'll just have to look for a job, and then we'll up and move again," answered the younger Blakeley.

Trudy felt a sense of déjà vu, as the meal discussion seemed to be the pattern in each of the previous situations when Bill, Jr. was laid off. In those days, Bill's mother and father would visit for a few days and, with each layoff, the ritual was the same. Except, when Bill's mother was living, there wasn't the drinking or the effects of the drinking on Bill, Sr.'s disposition.

"Think I'll head into town," said Bill, Sr. "Gotta see what changes there are, if any, in Newberry. I don't suppose there's anything I can get for you since you just came back from town, Trudy, but thought I'd ask."

"No, we're all set. Thanks."

Bill, Sr. pulled out of the drive and drove the two miles or so into town. He parked in front of Zellars, the local hangout for the older men. Coffee was always hot and available for those wanting to discuss the news of the day. Jocelyn was the waitress who kept the plastic coffee carafes full and hot. One had to be regular and the other was to be decaffeinated since Fred and John had orders from Doc Polski to only take in caffeine free foods and drinks. John had fallen into a state of depression over doc's news. He had lived on chocolate and coke-a-cola for the past forty years.

Bill, Sr. smiled as he walked into the restaurant greeting the Newberry locals. Bill was a friendly old guy. He could strike up a conversation with just about anyone. He could have been a fantastic salesman if only someone other than his wife, Beatrice, believed in him, or if he'd only believed in himself or some product so that he could push it onto others. "Mind if I join you?" he asked an elderly gentleman seated in the non-smoking section of the cafe.

"Help yourself young man." Young man was a relative phrase since there appeared to be no generation gap between the two men.

"Thanks. I'm visiting from Rudyard and was looking for a little company while I have a cup of coffee."

"Name's Olaf Johnson," the man said extending his hand to be shaken.

"Bill Blakeley."

"You related to the special ed teacher?"

"He's my son."

"We've got something in common then. My daughter, Maria, is a special education teacher in Ironwood. "I'll bet you're as proud of your boy as I am of my daughter?"

"I sure am."

"Maria's the first Johnson to get a college education."

"That's wonderful," Bill said recalling that that would not have been the case in the Blakeley family if he had been able to get that college football scholarship.

"What brings you to Newberry?"

"Just spending a day or two with the family. Nice day out there wouldn't you say?"

"Sure is for this time of the year. Seems everyone is getting ready for the hunters, snowmobilers, and the skiers," Olaf responded.

"Yeah, those folks keep the economy going."

Just then Jocelyn stopped by to fill up Olaf's cup and to ask Bill if he wanted to order a meal or have some coffee. He ordered a cup with no cream.

"There are some folks pretty upset about some teachers getting laid off. Guess your son was one of them." Bill nodded with head lowered. Olaf continued, "Any news like that in our town gets the people talking. This kind of thing makes news and gives the people something to talk about," offered Olaf.

"Whose responsible for this?"

"School board. They're elected to make the big decisions. Of course they don't act without the recommendation of Superintendent Jake Williamson," responded Olaf, feeling proud that he knew the ins and outs of the small town activity.

"Who's the responsible person in this town for my son's layoff? Where does the buck stop?" asked Bill.

"Stops with the President of the School Board, but in this district the School Board President doesn't act without the approval and blessing of Tom Franklin. He really runs the show."

"Tell me about him. I see his name in the local papers quite a bit."

"Local car dealer and community leader. Everyone respects him. He could probably get elevated to sainthood if the decision could be made by the citizens of Newberry."

"Young guy, old guy?"

"Tom's getting up there. He has diabetes real bad. He needs insulin on a regular basis to survive. He's got quite a bit of weight on him and he likes to eat all that bad stuff like eggs, beef, sausage, hot dogs. I don't know why he doesn't keel over with a massive attack. The genetics sure must play a big part in a person's date with death because by all health articles I read, he should of been gone a few years ago," Olaf sounded like a health expert. Actually, he had become well versed in health since his own heart attack a few years back.

The men continued their talk about Newberry politics. They got on well together. After about three cups of coffee, Bill thanked Olaf and got on his way.

Bill, Sr. attended to a few errands before making his way back to Bill and Trudy's home. Heather was home when he returned. She was beginning to prepare for a date. She excitedly told her grandfather that it would be her first date with Tom Franklin, III, the grandson of Thomas Franklin. She said that Tom was a nice guy, their school's sports hero, and pretty smart, too. Heather wanted to look just right and was intent on doing her hair and choosing her best outfit.

⌇

Early that evening a news flash spread throughout Newberry. Thomas Franklin, community leader for many years, had died of a massive heart attack. Telephones were ringing as neighbors called neighbors and talk spread through stores and restaurants. The news was that Marian Franklin checked on him late in the afternoon and he seemed to be sleeping peacefully. When she went to wake him up for a little dinner and he didn't respond, she called Doc Polski who immediately came to the Franklin home and pronounced Thomas dead.

Marian told friends how Thomas had come home Friday evening complaining of stomach upset, but had admitted the next morning that he had some chest pain and numbness in his hands.

Doc Polski didn't suggest an autopsy to the family. It was pretty obvious that Franklin had died of a massive heart attack. After all, what good would an autopsy do when the town figurehead was already dead?

The Franklin family immediately gathered at the family home. The Franklin's son, who had stayed in the area, was Thomas Jr., the postmaster in town. Mr. Franklin's second son, Hank, was on his way from Chicago, and his daughter, Elizabeth, was driving in from Cleveland. All three adult children were very successful in their own right. They adored and looked up to their father for all of his accomplishments, and for the respect he received in Newberry and the surrounding area.

The Blakeley family gathered for dinner. They were as remorseful as a family could be having only joined the community a bit more than one and a half years ago. It was hard to feel too remorseful given Bill, Jr.'s situation. Not much was said about Franklin's death that evening. "These things just happen, especially to older men who don't seem to exercise or eat in a healthy way," Bill, Sr. said. "Sure it's sad, but death is a part of life, and the hours and days just keep moving everyone to that final moment of life on earth."

Sunday, October 11, Newberry, Michigan

While the town read the Sunday *Newberry News* about Thomas Franklin, talked about him over every coffee cup, and prayed for his soul in every church, Bill, Sr. shook his son's hand and got into the car for the drive to Rudyard. Before leaving he had some advice for his son, "Fight this thing, Billy. They got their priorities out of sync. Keep talking to the parents of those disabled kids in your class. They can bring a lot of emotion to the issue. Board members have a lot of trouble saying no to parents of disabled kids. Stand up to this my boy. Fight a good fight."

"I'll do what I can, Dad. I'll meet with the parents of the kids in my class. I'll talk to my union representative again, and I'll ask for a meeting with Williamson, but I gotta face reality, too. I'm looking elsewhere and I heard there's a job opening in Charlevoix. I can't face the thought of another move and adjustment, but I may have no choice."

"Good to see you for a few hours, son. Give my love to Trudy and the kids. I'll be on my way."

"I will. Thanks for coming over. Drive safely."

With that, Bill, Sr. was out of the driveway and headed for M-28 back to Rudyard. He was glad he had come over. He firmly believed a family should support one another in stressful times.

Tuesday, October 13, Newberry, Michigan

The Beaulieu Funeral Home was packed for Thomas Franklin's visitation. The remaining town leaders were already talking of naming the library after Franklin or changing the name of the high school to Franklin High School. A few wanted to change the name of the main street to Franklin Avenue. The departure of Newberry's most influential citizen created a lot of emotion in the town.

Mildred Cunningham lived across the street and down a few houses to the east from the Franklin's. She carefully watched the comings and goings of the entire neighborhood, but especially the home of Tom and Marian Franklin. Not only was it a hobby, but it gave her some conversation at the weekly bridge club. She was always a hit when she could gossip about who was visiting and who stopped by for whatever reason.

At the funeral home Mildred greeted the Chief of Police, Morgan Fitzpatrick, whom she called Fitz. In her younger days she was a second grade teacher. Morgan Fitzpatrick was one of her favorite little boys. He was always playing cops and robbers, so it was fitting that when he grew up he would serve the community of Newberry by being the person whose responsibility it was to protect the citizens of his hometown. "Hello Fitz, or perhaps I should be more formal, Chief Fitzpatrick."

"Hello, Mrs. Cunningham. Please don't call me anything other than Fitz. How's my favorite second grade teacher?"

"Are you satisfied that Mr. Franklin's untimely death was a massive heart attack and nothing other than the heart giving in to a lazy man with a big appetite?" asked Mildred peering over her glasses and looking up to Fitz. Her snow white hair and wrinkled skin made her appearance as an elderly woman obvious to all who met her.

"Guess so. I have no reason to think otherwise. Doc Polski pronounced death as a heart attack, and that's good enough for me."

"I'm not challenging the wisdom and experience of our town's senior doctor, but it could be that something happened that caused him to have that attack sooner than he or anyone else would have expected."

"Sounds like you know something the rest of the town doesn't," questioned Chief Fitzpatrick, thinking to himself that it was like Mrs. Cunningham to get a scoop that others wouldn't even suspect.

"The afternoon he died, a visitor came to the Franklin home. The car pulled up about 3:00 p.m. Marian had gone to the post office or at least that's what she said she was planning to do when I talked to her around noon. She said Tom wasn't feeling well. She was concerned and hoped he would call Dr. Polski, but getting Tom to call the doctor was very difficult," Mildred's tone quickened as she relayed the news. "Anyway, while she was gone, a car pulled up and a man went up to the door. Mr. Franklin let him in. I'd say he was there for five or ten minutes."

"Did you recognize him?" asked Fitz.

"No, I never saw him before."

"What did you see that you recall? I mean was he old, young, bald, short, tall?"

"You know, I really can't help with that. I didn't have my glasses and really didn't care who was going up to the door. I know it was a man. I know he was alone. He didn't have a hat, he wasn't bald, but age is hard to determine. He was tall, normal build. Sorry not to be more specific, but I wasn't expecting to be grilled by the Chief of Police," Mildred said a bit frustrated now not to have an answer for every question asked by Mr. Fitz.

"Right now I have no reason to question Doc Polski's cause of death, and there was no autopsy. No one is suggesting any foul play, unless you are?"

"Oh, I really don't know. I just know that someone talked with Mr. Franklin before he died. I don't know if the interaction has any relationship to his death or not. I'm just telling you what I saw."

"I'll make a note of our talk and your comments. If in the future I have a reason to revisit the day of his death, I may give you a call."

The next day Chief Fitzpatrick saw Marian Franklin downtown at the post office. "Hello, Mrs. Franklin. When you can give me a few minutes, I'd like to ask you a few questions about activity at your house a few hours before your husband died."

Wednesday, October 15,
Newberry, Michigan

Bill Blakeley met with four couples: The Wixoms, the Thompsons, the Hockings, and the Laffertys at Zellars Restaurant. They agreed to meet with him to discuss his layoff and what it might mean to their children's educational future. There was a feeling of togetherness that existed in this group. The parents realized that the educational future of their children was very much in jeopardy. They were not a very happy crew as they assembled at Zellars.

The parents had already struggled tooth and nail to get the Newberry School District started on a program for their kids. Before Mr. Blakeley came to town, their kids were always in trouble or being suspended or expelled from school. There was almost a year of parent meetings and discussions with Superintendent Williamson before a proposal was taken to the School Board requesting and recommending a classroom program designed for children with emotional impairments. Once the School Board agreed to have a program, these parents gathered in the same restaurant to celebrate the opportunity that had just been given to them and their children. There had been hope and trust in the school. Parents were excited about a new teacher and the prospect of watching their children become the socially and academically adjusted kids that they had the potential to become.

Now, these same parents sat in Zellars and pondered the crash of their dreams. Bill Blakeley arrived several minutes late. He ordered coffee and sat among the seven people who could make it that evening. "Looks like we got a common problem," said Bill. "I've got no job and you've got no program."

"We've got to fight this with and for you, Bill. We've got to fight this for us. We've got to fight this for our children," said Scott Thompson with the enthusiasm of Patrick Henry declaring a couple of centuries ago, "Give me liberty or give me death."

Bill said, "My heart goes out to you folks. You worked so hard to get this program..."

He was interrupted by Loretta Lafferty, "Having a child with a serious emotional disability is very challenging. These kids really stretch the patience of the family, the school, the neighborhood, and the community. People seem to have emotions for children who are in wheelchairs, who use crutches, who are deaf, or blind, and for retarded children. However, kids who don't have any obvious outward appearances of being disabled, and who have trouble controlling themselves, don't generate feelings of sympathy. There's federal and state law. I've checked into this and our kids got rights. They simply can't do this to us."

"She's right," Bill counseled. "There're laws that protect kids with disabilities, but a lot of discretion is left to school districts to determine how to carry out the laws. They can provide services with a program like we have, or they can use consultants like they claim they will do, or they can work with other districts to create a program."

"Well, we don't want it changed and we pay taxes. I think we've got a lot of support from other teachers, parents, and leaders in the community," said Don Hocking.

Larry Wixom, who had been strangely quiet and calm, broke in to the conversation, "I contacted Mr. Franklin a few hours before he died. I was pretty upset and I told him that we would do whatever it took to get this program back. I told him that he had yet to see the power of a few people in action. I told him we would be at every board meeting until this program was reinstated. I told him we would file complaints and hearings against the Newberry School District at the rate of one a week until someone woke up to the need for this program. I told him in a very angry way, 'You will live to regret this decision Mr. Franklin. You will be faced with the reality of a lot of anger against you and the Board for this decision which is not based on what is good for children, but is based on money! I hope you can live with yourself for hurting the children, teachers, and the community of Newberry!'"

"You said that to Mr. Franklin?" questioned an astonished Loretta Lafferty.

"Gotta be tough in these times. When you're an advocate for the minority, and I don't care what minority you're advocating for, you've got to be forceful and show that you mean business and that action will follow," said Mr. Wixom.

"What did he say?" Bill asked.

"Oh, he defended his decision. Said he was assured by Mr. Williamson that services could continue and behavior specialists would help the kids. He said that with the inclusive education movement well underway it was time to get our kids out of special isolated programs and into the mainstream of general education."

"I told him it didn't work before and it isn't going to work now. These kids need intensive help from an educator who understands emotional problems. They need a teacher who can adapt the curriculum and work with general education teachers so that children can slowly get back into general education."

"Did he understand that, Larry?" Don Hocking asked.

"He seemed to listen to me. He said he'd meet with Mr. Blakeley to discuss it, but he didn't promise any change. He said that the school board is elected to make some tough decisions, and sometimes the decisions are unpopular, but they still need to be made."

"Did he contact you before he died, Bill?" asked Marie Thompson.

"No. I was home almost all afternoon. I went out for an hour or so, but there was no message on my answering machine when I returned," Bill said.

The conversation turned to what action the group was going to take to get the decision reversed so that their kids could get back in Mr. Blakeley's special class. After about an hour, some steps were outlined. Each of the parents would make an appointment with each board member and with Mr. Williamson to demand the reinstatement of the program. Each parent would attend each board meeting and use every minute of the allotted time, during the public participation portion of the agenda, to speak to their inappropriate action and to demand program reinstatement. Each parent would review the individualized education program to see if a complaint could be filed because some portion of the plan was not being carried out as agreed to by the parent and the school district. Each parent would demand a due process hearing so that the program change would be delayed until the hearing was complete. If they didn't win the hearing, they would appeal to the state, and if they lost at the state level, they would go to court. In addition, they would do whatever they could to keep federal dollars from coming to Michigan. Each parent would talk to neighbors and friends with the intent of getting the citizens to rise up against the Newberry Board for these actions which were damaging to the kids with disabilities. The plan was set. If the board reinstated the program, all of the above would cease. It was basically an ultimatum, give us what we, the parents of some deserving kids demand, or it will get very ugly around this quiet and peaceful town of Newberry, Michigan.

Thursday, October 17,
Newberry, Michigan

While all of this support was being generated on behalf of Bill Blakeley's program, Bill was getting his resume updated. He placed a phone call to Grand Valley State University's placement office. He would begin getting the placement bulletin so he could be thinking about where his next job would be. He knew that he would have no trouble finding a job. The basic decision he needed to make was where would be the best location for his family. He had been through this routine before, and he actually felt some comfort knowing the process.

Each year of teaching brought Bill closer to his thirty years of service which would allow him to retire with full benefits. He only had ten more years and he would be out at age 52. Since Bill had started teaching at age 22, he had never missed a year. He expected to start a whole new career at age 52. His Michigan public school retirement check would come in monthly, and until his social security check would arrive, he decided he would find something stimulating yet stable for that interim period of time.

Trudy had talked about her husband's future when visiting her parents. She explained that she thought Bill was leaning toward a second career in law enforcement. She felt that he knew how to handle bad actors since he had been doing it for twenty years. He was big in stature and strong, too. Bill's presence demanded respect. Add a cop's uniform and he'd be in position to be quite awesome. Since there will always be drunks, family disputes, drugs, greed, jealousy, anger, and people coveting what others have, there would always be a need for a cop. In fact, the more Trudy and her parents thought about it, the more they believed Bill would be switching to law enforcement before his thirty years were up.

⌘

Mrs. Cunningham's comments stayed with Fitz. He couldn't stop thinking that as obvious as Tom Franklin's heart attack was, maybe there was more to his death than what appeared on the surface. He had a flashback to a seminar he recently attended, in Marquette, that emphasized how more often than not something, or someone, could precipitate a health problem. The seminar stressed that what looks to be a simple stroke, or heart attack, could in fact be brought on by something or someone. Fitz was beginning to imagine the possibility of a murder.

Murder in Newberry was rare. A few murder suicides had occurred over the past several years. Marian didn't suspect anything other than a heart attack. Doc Polski said the same. The people in the town had no suspicions and anyone who knew Franklin's lifestyle would have predicted a heart attack several years before it actually happened. Nonetheless, Mrs. Cunningham's observation, as vague as it was, stuck to him like glue and he just couldn't live with himself if he didn't check it out.

Fitz called his friend, Harold Holcomb who had retired from the State Police a couple of years earlier. Harold, in his younger days, had been a detective. His mind was still sharp and Fitz counted on his years of experience to help him sort through his confusion over the case. The two men decided to meet at Pickleman's Restaurant later that afternoon. Harold was happy to be of service. He missed the excitement of the law enforcement world. Taking a three-month trip to Florida and doing odd jobs around the house were satisfying, but nothing could substitute for the old adrenaline rush of closing in on the final clues that would clinch a conviction for a criminal act.

It was four o'clock in the afternoon when Fitz met Harold at

Pickleman's. Betty, the late afternoon and evening waitress, a fixture of the popular restaurant at the intersection of M-28 and M-123, three miles south of town, stopped by the table, "You men going to order or is this just a place to meet?"

"Just a place to meet, Betty. We'll take a cup of coffee, though. Add it to my account and throw in a buck tip for your good service. I feel generous today. I don't want this to be expected on a regular basis, ya hear."

"Thanks, Chief. Naw, sometimes a kind and generous heart walks in here. Today it happened to be you. I appreciate it, Mr. Fitzpatrick. How's the Mrs.?"

"She's doin' good, but her arthritis is acting up. The weather station is thinking of contracting with her as a consultant. She can predict the weather with her knees and elbows."

"Yeah, I know how that goes. I haven't seen her in about a week. Say 'hi' for me will ya, Chief?"

"Will do, Betty."

"I'll leave you guys alone so you can solve all the big crimes of the world."

Picklemans was quiet. There was an hour or two between the afternoon coffee break and the dinner crowd. Harold began,"What's on your mind, Fitz?"

"Wanted to talk with you about some comments Mrs. Cunningham made to me at Tom Franklin's funeral home visitation. She said somebody stopped at the Franklin home the afternoon that Tom died. She didn't know who he was. She said she wasn't wearing her glasses but it was a tall man who entered the house for maybe fifteen minutes. She said Marian was not at home as she was at the post office."

"Is that all?"

"That's about it. I know it isn't much, but it's possible that something happened in that fifteen minute block of time that we should care about or look into."

"Did Marian say that Tom mentioned the visitor when she returned from the post office?"

34

"To my knowledge no one even asked her."

"Seems that if he did, and she thought it suspicious, she would have said something to you."

"I agree."

"Tough situation, Fitz. People come and go, knock on doors to visit, sell stuff, use the phone. If we thought every person knocking on a door and visiting for a few minutes was suspect in murder, we'd never find the time to watch for speeders on M-28."

"Yeah, I know. It's just that this community's icon died. And, a stranger, or at least a stranger to Mrs. Cunningham, who may not have been a stranger if she was wearing her glasses, was alone with Franklin before he died. I just wanted to mention it to you to see if you thought I should be concerned."

"Since you asked for my advice, I'd start a file on it. I'd interview Mrs. Cunningham and write up a report on her comments. I would interview Marian Franklin. I'd interview Doc Polski, and I'd write down the issues that Franklin was facing when he died that could even have the remotest connection to a possible murder. For example, the school board was dealing with the layoffs of three teachers, and wasn't he about to layoff some guy at his dealership? Things like that. I'd keep it low key and don't let people know that you suspect any foul play. If, in the future, something happens that causes you or someone else to be curious, you'll have a report on file to substantiate all you know about the situation. If nothing else, the leg work will show that you didn't just dismiss an observation as meaningless."

"Thanks, Harold. I can depend on you for good advice."

"Glad to help. Gotta get home to Joan. We're having the neighbors over for a birthday dinner celebration."

They waved goodbye to Betty as they walked to their cars and drove home to their wives. Fitz was pleased to have Harold's good advice, and Harold was pleased to know that his thoughts were still valued.

Ǯ

The group of Newberry parents of children who had emotional

disabilities formed a group called Parents for Justice. They decided
to meet weekly until the mess at the school was resolved. Resolved
for them meant a return to what had been arranged for their children; a special education teacher, Bill Blakeley, in the classroom.
Their leader was Mr. Wixom. Wixom was the one who confronted
Mr. Franklin before he died, and anyone who had the guts to take on
the town's esteemed leader was capable of guiding a few parents to
some justice. The group thought it best that the leader be a parent
and not Mr. Blakeley. It would look too self serving to have him lead
the attack.

The parents decided to meet in each other's homes. It was
cheaper, private, and would lead them to a stronger bonding. At one
of the earliest meetings, talk focused on community and state
resources to assist the struggle. A member of the group suggested
that the Michigan Coalition for Children's Special Education Rights
(MCCSER) might be sympathetic and would pour some dollars and
lawyers into the effort. The MCCSER's President, Ruth Wierenga
assured that the organization would remain at the parents' side and
offer whatever support, human or fiscal, to see that the special education program was reinstated.

The school officials sensed of what was brewing and predicted
that the situation was going to get very ugly. Superintendent
Williamson met with his Coordinator of Special Education, Irene
Richardson. They talked about several alternatives. One was to give
in very quickly and say that they had not carefully considered the
implications of their decision and would reinstate the program. This
would be a simple solution, save the district thousands of dollars in
legal fees, and keep the media out of the picture. They also feared
that the trouble might send a message through the community that
the school board was not in control, and could be forced to change
its mind under the force of a small group of radical parents. Once
the special education program was reinstated, then the success of a
few parents could fuel other groups who wanted their own pet pro-
jects to be funded. School officials were already feeling the heat
from a group of parents who wanted more technology in the high

school. Another group wanted values to be a part of the curriculum, while another segment of the population was getting more vocal about getting back to the basics.

Jake Williamson and Irene Richardson concluded that the decision to place the children with disabilities into the general education classes, with assistance from a behavioral specialist, was the best decision for the children and the school district. They decided to stay the course.

༉

Mrs. Cunningham was walking up the street to meet her lady friends for bridge. It was a weekly ritual she never missed, and she hadn't missed the bridge club on a Thursday afternoon since 1988 when she was hospitalized for minor surgery. The ladies decided to have the bridge game in her hospital room, but she was coming out of the anesthesia at the time and really wouldn't have been able to know a trump from a trick. If she could have been the dummy all afternoon, she would have fit the bill perfectly.

Once the ladies assembled and coffee was served, along with a few chocolate chip cookies for the non diabetics and graham crackers for the diabetics, it was time for bridge. It was also time to listen to Mrs. Cunningham. Everyone knew that her news for the week would be juicy, or interesting, or uncommon. After the cards were shuffled and dealt she began, "Nice funeral for Tom Franklin, don't you think?"

"Very nice. I thought Marian looked very nice and so did her children and grandchildren," said Wilma Wriggley.

And then it came up and took the club by surprise. "I think Tom Franklin was murdered," Mildred stated flat out.

"Murdered? How could that be? Doctor Polski said it was a heart attack and Marian even said he had chest pain and numbness. You can't have a better indication of a heart attack than that," Wilma exclaimed.

"Oh I know. I've heard all that. But he had a visitor that afternoon and I believe there's a connection between his dying and that visitor," Mildred said with conviction.

"You mean you think he was poisoned or something?" asked Edith.

"I'm not sure, I wasn't there, but you wait and see. Someday you'll remember this afternoon and your friend, Mildred Cunningham's words and you'll be saying, 'Guess she was right.'"

One of the bridge players was Edith Presley who claimed to be a cousin, far removed, of Elvis. Nobody took her seriously, but it was the same last name. Edith was one of those who claimed the King had a few genetic similarities to her family. She went to Graceland; she had been there twice. Edith has a picture of Elvis in her home and has been known to drive visitors away with her nonstop talk about this famous relative.

Edith's husband is Jim, the editor of the Newberry News. That evening she shared Mrs. Cunningham's prediction with Jim, who was always hungry for some good news. He called Mildred immediately and talked with her extensively about her accusation. After talking with Mildred, Jim decided it was fair to let the public know about the speculation surrounding the Franklin murder. The town would be talking about it soon enough anyway. When the next edition of the *Newberry News* came out and was picked up off porches throughout Newberry, the citizens read a shocking headline, "Thomas Franklin May Have Been Murdered."

Friday, October 16, Newberry, Michigan

It had been almost a week since Thomas Franklin died of a heart attack. Superintendent Williamson called the law firm under contract to offer advice and counsel on any matter that might find the school district in court. The lawyer, who Jake liked and confided in, was Rose O'Leary. "Masters, O'Leary, and Wilcox. How may I help you?" answered the receptionist from the Lansing office.

"Rose O'Leary please, Jake Williamson calling."

"One moment please, Mr. Williamson."

"Hi Jake, how is everything in the beautiful Upper Peninsula?" asked Rose.

"It's a beautiful day up here like most."

"What's on your mind, Jake?"

"Got a potential problem, or maybe by now it's more than a potential problem. I need your best thinking, Rose."

"I'll give it my best shot."

"The school board took my recommendation to layoff three teachers. One of the teachers is Mr. Bill Blakeley, a teacher in the classroom for children with emotional impairments. The parents are not accepting of the decision. They have contacted the MCCSER and have been advised to follow some costly and time-consuming procedures all designed to get the program reinstated.

"State and federal law give parents much more of a voice than they used to have, that's for sure," Rose responded.

"Here's my dilemma. They're all going to request a hearing, and I suspect that will mean about ten hearings. The Wixoms have already requested a hearing, and that, of course, according to law, requires that the child must stay in the last uncontested program, in this case, Mr. Blakeley's class. The parents come to each board meeting, and they take all of their allowed time for public comment. The citizens are sympathetic. I've learned that they may be circulating petitions to recall board members who voted for the layoff and, of course, they're after my job, too. After all, I recommended to the board that they take this action."

"Sounds like a challenge, Jake."

"It's close to becoming a big mess. I talked with Irene Richardson, our special education coordinator, and we agree that we have to take action that is both responsible and within our budget. This district has a lot of little advocacy pockets, and we think that if we give in we will find other groups demanding board action. They'll point to this issue and declare, 'You changed your mind for those parents, why can't you do the same for us?' They'll question why technology, basic reading, writing, and arithmetic are made to seem less important than a class for some trouble makers.'"

"Tough issues, Jake. I think I know what you face. How can I help you?" Rose asked.

"Well, I need your advice as we proceed. All of this special education law is complicated, and I have enough to do with running this district without dedicating my career to defending us from a group of upset parents. I talked with the Board President, Bill Owen, and we've decided to invite you to come up here for a few days and give us your best advice about proceeding. We would like you to meet with the board president, myself, my assistant for finance, and Irene. If we're heading for a war over this issue, I've learned that an effective offense is superior to an effective defense."

"Sounds like a good idea. I'll talk this over with my partners and get back with you. I'll let you know some possible dates and we can go from there."

"Thanks, Rose. I've got a feeling we're going to go through quite a lot in the next couple of months. Guess I need to start to lead a better life. I never thought that my name might be associated with a Supreme Court case."

"Let's hope it doesn't go that far, Jake."

"Oh, by the way, I have a meeting with our representative and our senator next week. Traditionally, upset citizens make a run to politicians, and I want our position to be very clear to these people. Representative Martinelli and Senator Lackey need to know that we are doing what the governor and the leader of their party has asked us to do. We heard his speech at Northern Michigan University urging us to consolidate, cut the high cost of education, and to look at ways to work with other districts. We're doing that, and not with an eye to hurting kids. I want the politicians to understand our side of this mess before they begin making promises to intervene."

"Good idea, Jake."

"Well, enough for today, Rose. Thanks for listening. I look forward to your call."

"See you, Jake. Have a great day, and keep up the good work you're doing in Newberry."

Rose had enough experience in special education law, and with Ruth Wierenga of the MCCSER, to know that this could be her most challenging case. If she did well with this, it would undoubtedly propel her name into the limelight as an attorney who can effectively work with school districts facing difficult conflicts with parents. She desperately wanted the success and national recognition that a case like this could mean. It could even set her on her way to her own law firm. She planned to put every ounce of her legal soul into this project.

ᔓ

The phone rang in Jim Presley's office ten seconds after he had opened for business at the *Newberry News*. "What do you mean with that headline, Jim. For crying out loud, does it ever occur to you to talk with us before you incite the public!!" Chief Fitzpatrick intoned angrily.

"Hold on, Fitz. I'll decide what goes in the *News*. Something's in the Constitution about a right to this, and you know it," Jim Presley challenged, trying to remain calm with an angry chief on the line.

"I know the right. I also know that responsibility goes with the right! Most people know you don't shout 'fire' in a crowded theater even though freedom of speech gives them the opportunity."

"Cool down, Fitz. I can explain. I talked to Mrs. Cunningham and..."

"Old lady Cunningham..., give me a break! I suppose if she told you Martians joined her for breakfast you would put 'Aliens Eat Breakfast in Newberry' on your front page," Fitz said, still perturbed with the editor's choice of words in this week's headline.

"As I was saying, I talked with her, and based on what I heard, I believe there is a justification to make the assertion that Tom's heart attack was brought about by the afternoon visitor. Further, I know you were informed of this a few days ago, and to my knowledge, you haven't done anything to investigate. It would seem to me that if a citizen reports a suspicion of murder to the authorities that there's an obligation to look into it."

"I suggest you leave the investigation of Newberry's crimes and possible crimes to me!"

"Precisely my point, Fitz. I suggest you leave the reporting of news to me."

"I still believe that sensationalizing one person's theory for the whole town and for the family without more evidence is unprofessional and is not in the best interest of the citizens of Newberry."

"You're entitled to your opinions, and I respect you and your opinions. I happen to think it's American to express ideas and to openly dialogue about them. I've such regard for you Fitz, that I expect my headline to be satisfactorily put to rest, or to lead to an arrest on a murder charge. You can be assured that whatever the outcome, I'll report it fairly and accurately in the *News*."

"I would ask you to print the following in your next edition," said Chief Fitzpatrick. 'Chief of Police Fitzpatrick contacted the editor of the *News* immediately upon reading the headline to say that there is no suspicion of murder in the death of Mr. Franklin. All information available to the police department would lead to a conclusion that Mr. Franklin died a natural death due to a heart attack, as determined by Doctor Polski. This town has no reason to be concerned with any violent act in the death of Mr. Franklin. The police have interviewed citizens who may have concerns which led to the headline, but denies any evidence which would cause anyone to suspect that Mr. Franklin died of anything but a natural cause.'"

"Consider it done, Fitz. Thank you for calling and confronting me in person. Please take this possible murder seriously. I don't want to believe otherwise, but I really do think that his death was untimely. I don't question that the cause of death was a heart attack, but I do challenge that he just up and died."

Monday, October 19, Newberry, Michigan

Chief Fitzpatrick once again sought advice from his law enforcement colleague, Harold Holcomb.

"Hi Harold, Fitz here. How ya doin'?"

"Good, Fitz. See where old man Presley got the people thinking, huh?"

"I gave him a piece of my mind. I swear the old guy never got any training in his profession."

"Aw Fitz, calm down. People take him with a grain of salt. All he said was that Franklin may have been murdered and maybe he was."

"You mean, you think it could have happened?"

"Oh, sure. Lots of things could have happened. In any possible crime, the only ones who know for sure what happened are the victim and the perpetrator. That's what makes detective work interesting. It's like a puzzle. You get a little initial information and then you need to get the whole story by diggin' and scratchin'. I loved it when I did it for a living."

"Wanta have some fun again, Harold?"

"What you got in mind?"

"I've got an entire town talking murder. I'm going to have to speak to it. If Franklin may have been murdered, then it's up to me to put that suspicion to rest. If you can help me with the investigation, that would be great. What do you think?"

"Sounds like the good old days. Why not? I'll need you to authorize me to act on your behalf for interviews and to obtain pertinent documents."

"Not a problem. Consider yourself deputized, Mr. Holcomb."

"Well, for starters I'm going to suggest that we contact Lou Searing. He's a retired state director of special education downstate, and he's highly respected by the State Police in the Lansing area. His brother is Bob Searing, one of the State Police's finest detectives. Lou and his partner, Maggie McMillan were successful in solving a murder in Kentucky. They did a great job. Word of their success has gotten around in the law enforcement business. He knows special education like the back of his hand and my guess is that this case will end up involving special education, if a murder really occurred."

"If you say this Lou Searing is someone who can help us, your word is good with me."

"Trust me on this, Fitz, you can't do better than Searing and McMillan when it comes to education crime. They're slowly but surely getting a nationwide reputation."

"How did they get into this business?"

"Lou was on a motorcycle camping trip with a good friend. They were attacked in their Smokey Mountain campsite in eastern Kentucky. Lou was wearing his leather coat and it saved him. The knife couldn't get through it and far enough into his body to kill him. Lou's friend wasn't as lucky."

"His friend was killed?"

"Yeah. Stabbed to death. Lou was determined to find out who killed him. He investigated and turned in a group of thugs who were on a crime spree. After that he was called on to help with a few education related crimes and that has become something he seems to specialize in now."

"You said he works with a woman?"

"Yeah, Margaret McMillan. People call her Maggie. She was an insurance claims investigator who was also stabbed by a guy she turned in for insurance fraud. Her investigation skills added to Lou's knowledge of education makes them a great team. Maggie uses a motorized wheelchair. She gets around great considering her disability. If we can get them into this case, you'll know if this was a murder or a heart attack. We couldn't find a better to team to work with us than Searing and McMillan."

Lou Searing was raking the first batch of leaves in their frontyard. While Lou was raking, Carol was working in her garden and filling the many bird feeders she maintained for her feathered friends. The cats, Luba and Millie, were on the porch standing on hind legs looking out at them and wishing they could be bird or leaf chasing. The phone rang. Carol took the cellular phone from her gardening apron. "Hello?"

"Is this the Searing residence?"

"Yes."

"This is Morgan Fitzpatrick, Police Chief in Newberry, Michigan. Is Mr. Searing available?"

"Yes. One moment please." Carol said, wondering if the teacher with the rifle finished the job.

Lou took the phone from Carol and covered the mouthpiece, "Who is it?"

"Chief of Police in Newberry. Says he wants to talk to you."

Lou removed his hand from the mouthpiece. "Hello. This is Louis Searing."

"Mr. Searing, this is Morgan Fitzpatrick, Chief of Police in Newberry. I have Mr. Holcomb on the phone and we'd like to talk to you about becoming involved in a possible murder investigation in the U.P.?"

"I might be. What's happened? This wouldn't have anything to do with that teacher who got laid off, would it? You know, the guy who brought the rifle into school."

"As a matter of fact it might. In a nutshell, a prominent citizen died a week and a half ago. The doctor says it was a heart attack, his wife concurs. There was no autopsy. However, a neighbor saw someone enter the home before the man died. The people in this small town are talking. I need to put rumors to rest or to go after a murderer."

"And, you think Maggie and I can help?"

"If there is any foul play, we think it could relate to special education. The victim was on the local school board, and one of the major recent decisions that has raised a lot of anger up here is the layoff of three teachers. One of the teachers is the special education teacher you heard about. His name is Bill Blakeley, and he's not a happy camper. His layoff has gotten the parents of the special education students very upset, and together they are fighting the school board and raising a lot of commotion in the community. Taking a special education program away from these parents' children isn't looking like such a great idea. You've got the special education knowledge and you've got the detective skills. When we put these two together, we think you and Mrs. McMillan are the best team to help us handle this case."

"Sounds like a challenge. I'll have to talk to Maggie to see if we can accept your request for help. I'll get back to you."

"Sounds great. Let me give you my number. It's area code 906 then 555-9123. Harold and I will look forward to your call."

Carol overheard the conversation and nervously asked, "Going to take on another case, Lou?"

"Oh, I don't know. I enjoy the work, but it consumes me, and I sometimes think I'd rather play golf. I can read how the popular fictional sleuths solve their cases from the comfort of my recliner."

A relieved Carol said, "Well, you know that I'll support whatever decision you make. Samm, the cats, and I will miss you and be concerned that you will get in harms way, but you do seem to enjoy working on these cases."

"Yeah. I guess I do. To be honest, it's more fun and challenging than when I was state director of special education."

ॐ

People were quiet around Bill Blakeley. He kept a low profile. He arrived at school on time. He kept to himself most of the day, and he left after school. He was aware that there was a lot of commotion in the town over his being laid off. Some teacher colleagues were supportive and others saw him as using parents to make a fuss so he'd keep his job. Trudy found herself in the same situation and it was uncomfortable. Living in a small town was hard enough without being in the middle of an ugly mess.

꒱

Bill Blakeley, Sr. arrived back in Rudyard without incident. He was glad to be home and back into his normal routine. Part of his routine was lunch with Stan Hovath. Stan was a retired Department of Natural Resources' worker. It was his job to catch poachers.

Stan and Bill ate lunch together about four times a week at the Pure Country Family Restaurant. The restaurant's menu was as American as one could expect. The only item on the menu common to the Upper Peninsula was the pastie: a meat, potato, and vegetable pie which was introduced to the Upper Peninsula by immigrants. The miners carried a pastie in their lunch pail when they worked the iron and copper mines.

Thursday was a lunch day for Bill and Stan. They met at 11:45 a.m., at the table by the window. Hilda always sat the customers, and she and all the regulars knew that this table belonged to Stan and Bill. It was like they earned it by allegiance to the restaurant, by frequency of attendance, and because of seniority and the community's respect for its elders.

"How was your trip to see Bill?" Stan asked.

"The school board wants to lay Billy off, but he's going to fight 'em this time."

"This is the second or third time ain't it, Bill?"

"Fifth time! Guy can only take so much of this. It disrupts everything. Too many people have their lives messed up. I only went through it once, and it still causes anger inside when I think about it!"

"I never got laid off at the Department of Natural Resources. Worked for 'em for thirty years and my job was never threatened."

"Of course you never got laid off. You state workers had it made and you know it."

"You a bit jealous? I mean, my job wasn't a piece of cake," said Stan not wanting to get into an argument with his friend. It wasn't difficult to get into an argument with Bill. He'd had a rough life. He seemed always to be upset when he thought of what others had in life and what he never got to experience because of his own layoff many years ago.

"I'm not jealous of you and your state job. You gotta admit that you didn't have any worries about losing your job. As long as Michigan has deer and as long as people don't want to follow hunting rules, you're going be working."

It didn't take a psychologist to know that Bill would have given his eye teeth for a good steady state job. He, too, could have put in thirty years of steady work, been protected by civil service, and he would be out by now enjoying full health benefits, a pension, and a check in his mailbox every month.

The serious give and take of their conversation was interrupted by Hilda. "Gunna be the special today?"

The question was a rhetorical one as Stan and Bill always had the special. It was ordered with little risk. They could count on a hot meal arriving in a matter of minutes. It would be cube steak or meat loaf, instant mashed potatoes, corn or green beans, and always coffee.

"Have we ever ordered anything else, Hilda?" Stan asked.

"Hey, you never know. If I bring the special, one of you would tell me to take it back and order something else!" Hilda said with a big smile. A few of the guys at the nearby tables were chuckling, as this exchange seemed to go on each day. There's nothing like a familiar routine for comfort, Bill, Sr. thought to himself.

ॐ

Meanwhile in Newberry, the parent group held its weekly Monday evening meeting. After cordial greetings and chit chat, the Parents for Justice quickly plotted and planned each step of their carefully devised strategy. They had everything on their side: emotion, federal laws, state laws, and the power of holding very expensive hearings over the heads of the administration.

The first order of business was to determine the status of their activities. Larry Wixom told the group that the individualized educational planning committee meeting for Eric had led to the hearing request, which was what he wanted, and a declaration that the program would have to stay in place to serve his son while the dispute was resolved. The Wixoms would hold the threat of hearings over the heads of the school officials if the officials thought anymore about closing down the program.

Marie Thompson said that she had contacted Representative Martinelli's office and they were shocked that the school board was going to close a program for disabled kids. The representative's assistant promised to look into the matter and get back with her as soon as possible.

Joan Hocking reported that she had called the State Department of Education in Lansing and asked if a school district could shut down a program without amending the Intermediate School District Plan. Joan was told that the Intermediate School District Plan would have to be revised and that could only be done with citizen input and a vote by the school board. The parents did not think it was time to call the federal government in on the issue, but they had done their homework and they knew who was who, and where to direct the call if, and when it became apparent that little or no progress was being made on the matter.

"I think we should make an appointment with Elizabeth Beller, the state director of special education," said Marie Thompson.

"I agree. We need to get her on our side and to find out what plans are in place for supporting the school district, if they have any," offered Don Hocking.

"I'll make an appointment," said Mr. Wixom. "It's a long trip to Lansing but let's face it, our children's education is dependent on getting our program reinstated. We can't do enough to make sure this happens."

"I agree. I think we should plan this meeting at the same time that the State Board of Education is meeting. We need to speak to them and to begin getting them on our side. They can either approve the Intermediate School District Plan or not approve it," Larry Wixom said.

The parents were right on schedule with a series of activities designed to bring chaos to the situation. After all, they believed chaos to be their best weapon. They would use every trick in the book, and they were prepared to fight this until Mr. Blakeley was back in the classroom full time and their children were given their rights to a free and appropriate public education at home in Newberry.

As the meeting was about to conclude, one of the parents brought up the headline in the News. "What do you think about the possibility that Mr. Franklin may have been murdered?" Don Hocking asked.

"Not in Newberry!" Tom Lafferty replied.

"I suppose it could've happened. Anything is possible," offered Scott Thompson, who the group counted on for an opposing view on just about anything.

"Mr. Wixom, you said you talked to Franklin before he died. What do you think about the murder theory?" Joan asked.

There was a thoughtful pause as the group watched closely for Larry's reply. "Anger is a very powerful emotion and it can cause people to do things they later regret. I regret talking with him that day and using the words I used. I was very threatening because I felt that my son was being threatened by his decision and his influence on the board. I'm asking that his death never be brought up again, by any of us, and that we only talk about how to keep our program in Newberry," he said. There was an eerie calm in the room. Mr. Wixom rose from his chair, found his coat and hat, and quickly exited. The rest of the parents were surprised, but none expressed their thoughts. The parents made plans to meet again, and went home to their families.

Tuesday, October 20, Newberry Michigan

Lou called Chief Fitzpatrick as he promised he would. "Margaret and I have decided to accept the challenge of this case. We've determined that I'll come up first and begin to work with you."

"That's great news. I'll call Harold and we'll look forward to seeing you and getting this thing straightened out."

Carol helped Lou pack. She had done this for years, and Lou had come to rely on her careful planning and packing of his bag. When she wasn't looking, Lou put a "Miss you, Love you" note under her pillow. He'd done this for years and he knew she'd be disappointed if she came up to a lonely bed without his little note.

If he were lucky, Carol would hide a small bag of M&Ms in his luggage, as well as a little love note tucked in his pajamas pocket, in his Dopp kit, or in some other conspicuous place. Carol made sure his jogging shoes and outfit were packed.

With his luggage in hand, Lou gave Carol a goodbye kiss and got in his car for the six hour drive to Newberry. He was wearing his usual Dockers and a sweatshirt. Since retirement, suits and ties were only good for weddings and funerals.

Lou made his way north, and after three hours decided to pull into the rest area just north of Gaylord. He glanced into the vending machine area and noticed Rose O'Leary, who Lou knew from his career in special eduction. She had presented at several special education administration meetings on special education law. Rose was often chosen to answer case law questions on a variety of important issues, including least restrictive environment or suspension and expulsion. The two warmly greeted one another and before long realized that they were heading toward the same destination.

"What's taking our famous lawyer to da U.P., eh?" Lou asked imitating the Finnish accent so prevalent in the Upper Peninsula.

Rose smiled at his attempt at Upper Peninsula humor and responded, "Going to Newberry on a consultation. What's taking our famous special education detective to da U.P eh?"

Lou chuckled, "I'm going to Newberry, too. It seems that school board member Franklin may have been murdered. The chief of police has asked Maggie and me to help him with the investigation."

"Staying at the Comfort Inn there?" asked Rose.

"Yup. A clean room and a breakfast. I get my money's worth there."

"Looks like we'll be neighbors," concluded Rose.

"Great. Maybe we can help each other. You never know. After all, detectives and lawyers do make great teams. I'm not kidding."

Rose liked the idea and became serious, "I'd appreciate your sharing any theories related to Mr. Franklin's death, and I'll let you know if I learn anything about the parents plans to soak the district for every penny they've got, or any other plan for that matter."

"Sure. Two heads are better than one, especially on this mess," answered Lou. "If you don't have plans to eat dinner with your client, would you join me? I'll be with a couple of police officers all afternoon, but everyone needs to eat some dinner and given a choice between a lawyer and a couple of cops, I'll choose the lawyer every time."

"Thanks. I'd enjoy that. I didn't realize you were a charmer, Lou."

"Its genetic. Got it from my dad. What can I say," he said with a smile and a wink. "I'll meet you in the lobby of the Comfort Inn at 7:00 p.m. If you can't make it, leave a message." With that both reentered their vehicles to continue the trip north.

That afternoon Rose O'Leary and Lou Searing met with the people of Newberry who would own them for at least a couple of days. Lou met with the police who hoped he and Maggie could unlock their mystery, and Rose met with administration personnel who hoped she could guide them through some troubling waters.

༽

Lou pulled up to the City Building which housed the office of the Chief of Police. Morgan Fitzpatrick, Harold Holcomb and Irene Richardson were present to greet him as he entered the door with a sign above it which read, "City Police."

"Louis Searing?" Fitz asked.

"Yes, sir. Chief Fitzpatrick?" Lou said extending his hand for the customary handshake. Fitz introduced Lou to Irene not realizing that the two knew each other quite well. The two hugged, and Lou explained, "Irene and I go back a long time. We've had similar special education interests for a number of years. Good to see you Irene."

"Always good to see you, Lou," Irene responded.

Fitz introduced Lou to Harold. The two shook hands. "Your brother Bob has a great reputation in the State Police. I had the privilege of working with him on a case about ten years ago."

"Thanks. The family is very proud of him. We spend many family holiday parties together discussing various investigations. I hope some of his talent has rubbed off on me," Lou said chuckling.

"Let me introduce you to my right arm," Fitzpatrick said. "My secretary is Mrs. Smith. You may be talking with her often during your stay and our investigation." They walked a few feet to where Mrs. Smith sat before a stack of papers to be filed.

"Sharon, this is Mr. Louis Searing from downstate."

"Pleased to meet you, Mr. Searing. Welcome to God's country."

"Thanks. You got that right. It's wonderful in the U.P."

"When you came in the door, I could've sworn that former Pittsburgh Steeler quarterback, Terry Bradshaw was coming for a visit," Sharon said with a grin. "I was pretty sure that Terry Bradshaw wouldn't be wearing an Alma College sweatshirt, though. Is he your twin brother?"

"No, but some people see a resemblance. Guess we share the same baldness, build, and take charge personality," Lou chuckled, hoping not to be taken too seriously. "Actually, he's much more muscular than I am, and several years younger, I might add. You're right in thinking that there's a resemblance. I've heard it before."

"I'm a big Green Bay Packers fan. I used to live in northern Wisconsin. In the Steelers glory days I used to throw darts at Terry's picture thinking it might jinx him on game day. We've got a team that's soon to look like the team of Vince Lombardi's era, but Pittsburgh drubbed us quite easily several years ago."

"I've always been a Detroit Lions fan. I remember the days of Bobby Layne, Doak Walker, and Lou Schmidt. Seems like yesterday," Lou said nostalgically. "Nice to meet you, Mrs. Smith."

"Well, come on in to our conference room, and we can begin talking about this possible murder." Fitz motioned Lou into the room.

During the next hour, Lou learned about the case. Irene did her best to explain what had happened the day of the layoff notice. "From what I've been able to learn over the past several days talking with people, Bill and his union representative were asked to meet with the junior high school principal immediately after school. Bill was told this at 2:45 p.m. on Thursday, October 9. He didn't know for sure why the meeting was being called. He said that the last time he got a meeting notice like this was when he was teaching in Battle Creek in the fall of 1992, and the purpose of that meeting was to lay him off.

"I've learned that the conversation went something like this," Irene said. "The principal said, 'I regret to inform you that we will be laying you off. The dollars aren't there to support your position. Your students will have individualized education planning committee meetings next week, and we will place them in general education classes with the support of a behavioral specialist from the intermediate school district.' He informed Bill that the board joined him in expressing their sincere sympathy for the action. The principal assured Bill of the administration's concern for his welfare, therefore the personal meeting instead of just sending a notice."

Irene continued, "The union rep, Mary Holland, then said something like, 'The union has been working with the school district to protect you and your position, but it appears that it is within their rights to take the action they are taking. You are the least senior special education staff person and there are no positions for which you qualify in the general education area.' The MEA promised to assist Bill in finding other employment.

"Needless to say, Bill was stunned. He described the feeling as one similar to what an inmate on death row would feel if the governor didn't grant a stay of execution," Irene said. "He had gotten this news before and he knew the disruption it would cause in his life. In fact, he had heard the message in a variety of ways on four previous occasions. He didn't say a word in response." Irene went on with the story as Lou created his own hypothesis. "Bill said that he could feel his heart beating much faster and he felt anger welling up inside. He hoped that he could contain it and express it in a manner that wouldn't cause anyone to get hurt. Mr. Johnson broke the silence with a final statement. He said something like, 'The school board will take action on this tonight. We're sorry.'

"Next Bill got up and walked out of the meeting without saying one word. He walked back to his classroom, gathered up his personal items and walked to a public telephone. He called Mr. Wixom, a parent of one of his students and said, 'Mr. Wixom, this is Bill Blakeley, Eric's teacher at school. The school board will make a decision tonight to lay me off. Your child's education and future are severely threatened.' He hung up and walked out to his car.

"This is where things get interesting," Irene said. "He got his deer rifle from the trunk, and he walked back into the school. His friend, Frank stopped him and was able to get Bill to give him the rifle. Frank was a volunteer fireman, and he had many friends on the small police force. He convinced the chief that Bill was harmless, and not a threat to anyone."

"Tell me more about Bill Blakeley," Lou urged.

Irene once again continued, "Bill's a middle school special education teacher. He's 43 years old. He's been a special education teacher for twenty years. He graduated from Grand Valley State University near Grand Rapids. He earned a teaching certificate with an endorsement in teaching children who were emotionally impaired. He's a strong man, standing about six foot three inches."

"He looks like he could be a walk-on defensive end for the Detroit Lions," added Harold, who had been quietly listening. "Not only is he tall and domineering, but he's a handsome man with a warm smile and always well dressed."

"The districts where he had worked liked him as soon as they saw him because he represented authority and would be effective in dealing with bad actors or kids with acting out behaviors," Irene added. "He commands respect by his presence and people's first impressions of him are very positive. He is a guy you can't help but like, except when he gets angry."

"Is Bill married?" Lou asked.

Irene continued with her description, "Yes, his wife's name is Trudy. She is also a teacher. They moved to Newberry in December of 1992 when Bill applied for a job teaching emotionally disturbed children. Trudy applied for an opening in the high school as a physical education teacher and cheerleading coach. She's very attractive and a good coach given her past experience as a cheerleader at Grand Valley State University. She's been out of college for twenty years, but Trudy looks like a typical aerobics instructor, tanned, slim, firm muscles, and full of energy.

" It might help you to know that before 1992, Bill and Trudy were teachers in the Lower Peninsula in the Battle Creek School District," Irene added. "Newberry was the seventh school district for Bill and any personnel director would have to wonder why there's been so much moving around. But, male special education teachers were hard to find, especially big men who can deal with tough kids. The letters of recommendation in his file are all respectable. While nobody held Bill up as a prize catch, he passed the college courses, never had a letter of reprimand in his file, and he had no skeletons in the closet. At least none that anyone knew about." Irene paused before continuing.

" Bill told me that the family looked forward to the move to the Upper Peninsula. Apparently, Trudy's father was born and raised in the Upper Peninsula, in the small town of Michigamme. Trudy's parents are getting on in years and had been in the hospital a few times recently, so she felt it important to move a little closer to them. They both thought the move to the Upper Peninsula would be good for their children, Bryan, who was 16-years-old and Heather, who was 14-years-old when they moved here. Also, the Upper Peninsula offered a quiet change from living downstate where crime was on the rise and the pace of life was hectic.

"In late 1992, they made the decision to move to Newberry. Bill said that Bryan and Heather weren't enthusiastic about the move. But, Trudy and Bill chose to leave friends, and a routine that was working, despite the kids objections. The Battle Creek coaches almost had heart attacks when they learned that Bryan would be moving. Bryan was not their best athlete, but he was very good and dependable in all sports. His absence would leave a hole in their already well established teams.

"In Newberry, Bryan was almost assured sports hero status. He was a shoo-in as the Newberry Indian's star football, baseball, and basketball player. The potential to be all Upper Peninsula, in three sports, helped Bryan agree to the change. Making new friends wasn't a problem. He, like his father, was easy to like, good looking, an athlete, and a fun young man to be around.

"Heather was assured of being on the cheerleading squad, instead of an alternate which she was at a Battle Creek middle school. Leaving her friends was tough to accept. Heather, like Bryan, was also popular. She was attractive and a good student also. In fact, Heather and Trudy would be perfect for a magazine advertisement where the reader might have trouble choosing the mother from the daughter. So, that is what I know about the family dynamics, where they were, why they moved up here, stuff like that. I think it's fairly accurate because most of it came from Bill himself."

Lou asked if anyone knew what happened after the confrontation with the police. Irene responded, "Again, from what I was told by Bill, he drove from the police station to his home. He took the mail from the mailbox, shuffled through the stack, and found the letter addressed to him from the Newberry School District. He put all the mail on the kitchen counter and opened it. He knew what he was about to read, and he said that it hit him again in the gut. Actually, I have the letter with me. Bill gave me a copy. I'll read it and then give it to you, Lou, for your records." Irene read, "Dear Mr. Blakeley: I regret to inform you that, due to reorganization plans within the Newberry School District, the special education program will be terminated. Individualized educational planning committee meetings will be held for each child in your class. All children are expected to be placed into regular education classes or will be assigned to a regional program in Sault Ste. Marie. At this time, there are no teaching opportunities for someone with your credentials in Newberry. You are hereby placed on layoff status. The personnel office will assist you in any way possible to find employment. I regret the inconvenience this will cause you and your family. Sincerely, Jake Williamson, Superintendent."

Irene put the letter down, "Bill told me that after reading the letter, he slammed his fist on the kitchen counter, barged out the side door, got into his car, and took off down the country road at a high rate of speed. He was very upset. He said that he began to calm down a bit so that he could devise a course of action. He said that the more he thought about it, the more determined he was to fight it. He confided that when change came in the other districts where he worked, he had gotten very angry, he said some things to people that he shouldn't have, but eventually he accepted the layoff and looked elsewhere for employment. He's angrier this time and ready to fight. It's just not fair to him, to his students, or to their parents, his wife and his kids." Irene paused in sympathy of Bill.

"The story continues," she said. "When he got home Trudy was there. He said that he shared the letter with her. She read it and responded in shock, 'This can't be, Bill. How can they do this to us, your students and their families?' This was the fifth layoff letter that Trudy had read, addressed to Bill, during his twenty years of teaching. She always understood and was always supportive of playing the cards that were dealt. She would adjust as she always did, but this time seemed to be different. She got angry, and so did Bill. They seemed as though they can't take it anymore. It isn't fair to them. Their kids were just adjusting to the last change and are also running out of patience with so many moves. This isn't supposed to be the life that teachers lead. This is what happens to military, or preacher's families. Bill said that he told Trudy that this time he was determined to fight it, and then he kicked the wastebasket in the kitchen. Bill said that the plastic container flew across the kitchen spewing paper trash left and right. Trudy said she always got scared when Bill got like this. He was so big to begin with that, when he got angry, which wasn't often, it scared her. She said that she didn't feel that he might hurt her, because he never turned any anger on her, but it scared her because she was afraid of what this pent up anger might do to others."

"Did he get in touch with more parents than this Mr. Wixom?" Lou asked.

"I was just getting to that," Irene continued. "The phone in the Blakeley home didn't rest idle all evening long. It was normally being used by Bryan and Heather, but that evening Bill was talking to the parents of his students. He called each of them during the dinner hour and acted, quite honestly, in a less than a professional manner. He said that he was still reeling from the layoff letter. He suggested that they all meet in the next day or two to decide how they, together, would fight the threats to their childrens' education and his job. He told the parents that this would be virtually the end of their educational rights if they didn't go along with him. He urged the parents to prepare themselves to ask for and endure due process hearings. In a nutshell, it was going to be ugly and he intended, for the childrens' sake, as well as his own, to fight this."

"You've given me a great background. Very helpful. I have a fairly good picture of the man, his personality, and how he reacts to stressful situations."

Once Irene finished, Fitz and Harold provided Lou with what they knew from Mrs. Cunningham's story and what Doc Polski had determined. Lou summarized, "So basically all we've got is a theory expressed by a neighbor. We know, if we can trust the neighbor, that someone came up to the Franklin house around 3:00 p.m. and was inside for about five to fifteen minutes." Lou continued, "The neighbor didn't recognize the person, but the description is of a tall slender man with a full head of hair. She described the car as a mid-size, but she doesn't recall color, number of doors, license plate color, or number. Mrs. Franklin has no recollection of a visitor at all. Dr. Polski simply says that the heart attack was the cause of death."

"That's what we know and at your leisure, you can read my file concerning my interviews, newspaper clippings, and board meeting minutes," Fitz said.

"Thanks, a great summary. Now I've got to get to work. I can only be here for two days, so here's my strategy. I want a detailed phone log from the Franklin home. I'll want to talk to Mrs. Cunningham, the three laid off teachers, and the parents whose children are in Bill's class. I'll also want to talk to Mr. Franklin's second-in-command at the car dealership. Finally, tell me where all the gossip gets aired around this town."

"Let's start with the last request," Harold answered. "Two places immediately come to mind. A group of men meet at Zellars every morning at about 9:30, and there is the bridge club we spoke about that includes Mrs. Cunningham and Mrs. Presley along with several others."

"Who leads these groups?"

Harold continued, "The men's group gets its direction from Herm Batchelder, and the woman's bridge club looks to Mrs. Cunningham, of course."

"Great. Harold, would you go to the phone company, or call them and ask them to fax us a printout of each call made to the Franklin home on the day of his death?"

"Will do," Harold eagerly responded, beginning to feel the adrenaline rush of the investigation. This was going to be like the good old days, he thought to himself.

"Fitz. Please set up interviews with the three teachers, Mrs. Cunningham, Mrs. Presley, the parents, and the second-in-command at the car dealership. I want all interviews recorded and private, in other words only with me." Lou had everyone's attention.

"Then I want photos and descriptions of the automobiles of all parents of the students in Bill's classroom, the three laid off teachers, Franklin's, and anyone else's who may have visited the Franklin home. For example, his best friend, the mayor, the superintendent of schools, the board president, et cetera. I realize he knows practically everyone in town, but I don't believe that this was done by some guy from Chicago. If he was murdered, my guess is it'll be traced to someone locally, someone who knows him."

"We're here to help you help us, Lou," said Fitz. With that, the afternoon was complete. Lou decided that the next day would be spent talking to people. If anything was going to break, it would be from people talking. After all, there was no autopsy, no body, no witness, and no weapon. If a clue existed, it was in the minds of Newberry residents, he was confident of that.

Lou was ready for a break, ready for dinner with Rose. He'd missed his morning jog in Grand Haven, so he drove to the Comfort Inn, changed into a running outfit, and spent the next hour getting his pulse up around 120 and letting his senses soak in Michigan's beautiful Upper Peninsula.

Lou's maternal great grandparents and grandfather spend some time in Dollarville, where his great grandfather was a prominent citizen and a merchant in the late 1800s. Dollarville was a few miles directly west of Newberry. Tens of years ago it was quite a lumber town, but now it is a curve in the road with some homes. Lou's relatives had come into the Upper Peninsula from Bracebridge, Ontario, Canada. Lou had a fondness for the U.P.

꒜

While Lou was listening, and writing down the information that, Irene, Fitz and Harold had to share, Rose O'Leary was doing just the opposite. She was doing all the talking and giving the school administration her best thinking on how to deal with Parents for Justice in a quiet way, or at least in a way that wouldn't be costly or end in legal battles.

Just as Lou had summarized what he had learned at the police station, Superintendent Jake Williamson summarized what he had learned from his legal counsel, "Well, Rose, it sounds like we may have a costly, adversarial, and lengthy mess on our hands. You've indicated that each parent has the right to a hearing on whatever change we are proposing at the individualized education planning committee meetings. They can then appeal the decision. If they lose, they can have a state level review, and then if they lose at that level they can go to court. We'll have to pay the costs of all of the local hearings, including the attorney's fees if they prevail. We'll have to revise our Intermediate School District Plan to make the Sault Ste. Marie program our setting for a categorical emotionally impaired program. Finally, the plan amendment has to be approved by the State Board of Education in Lansing, and the parents could appeal to board members to vote, 'No' concerning this change."

"Good summation, Jake. I don't like to be the bearer of depressing news, but my clients need to know every possibility. I don't like surprises and neither do you."

"I sure am tempted to put the program back. We'll spend more money fighting this thing than we'll save with the layoff of Bill Blakeley. I can't believe the Congress and State Legislature wanted to have parents hand tie school districts with blackmail and threats of running up hundreds of thousands of dollars in hearings and legal fees," said Jake, getting more perturbed with each passing minute.

"No question about it, they over did it. It appears that parents went from having no programs for their children, and no right to challenge decisions, to basically calling the shots," Rose said.

"Ok, this is depressing enough for one day. I've got other things to do in running this progressive school district than spending all afternoon with this fiasco."

"I understand, Jake. Before we adjourn, let me talk about tomorrow's activities. I'll be leaving the day after tomorrow and I'll want to spend time making sure that all of your notice requirements, evaluations, and your Intermediate School District Plan is in order. I don't want to give the parents and their legal counsel any ammunition by leaving our actions less than in complete compliance with state and federal law. I'll want to talk with your school board president and your principal to alert them to appropriate behavior in meetings and in any possible hearing. I'm sure that this evening I'll think of other business that needs to be in order," Rose said.

Superintendent Williamson thanked Rose and offered the following, "Rose, you're the best there is in this special education law business. I'm glad you are on our team, and I'm confident that our school board, and the citizens, will see our costs for your fine services as essential to upholding the dignity of this school district. I believe that we must challenge this attempt by a few to cease our control of a school district."

"I appreciate your vote of confidence, Jake."

"We'll see you about eight in the morning then. Do you have plans for dinner?" Jake asked.

"I'm having dinner with Louis Searing. You may know of him. He used to be the state director of special education."

"Oh yes, I've gotten many memos from him over the years, but I haven't met him. Irene speaks kindly of him though."

"He and his partner, Maggie McMillan, are fine detectives and your chief of police has asked him to come up and help the department look into the possible murder of Mr. Franklin."

"Yeah, there is some talk about that. I'll tell you this, if Mr. Franklin was murdered, I'd put my money on Bill Blakeley and I don't want that said out of this room. I've seen him angry and when all is said and done, we may be having the trial of the century right here in Newberry, Michigan. We'll probably even make court TV, and the U.P. satellite dishes will be glowing with drama. In fact, I challenge the people in this room to remember my comment."

Rose rounded up her papers, copies of state and federal statues, and rules and regulations. She filled her attache with papers from the *Education of the Handicapped Law Report* and copies of various court decisions from the sixth circuit. She piled all of her materials onto a wheeled luggage carrier and headed for her car. An attorney in the 1960s would be able to put all of her special education legal papers into a popcorn sack and still have room for a couple of handfuls of popcorn, but now special education law demanded its own stack in a law library.

Before going to the Comfort Inn, Rose decided to take a hike along the Canada Lakes Ski Trails. She loved the quiet setting and communing with nature. She pulled off the road and entered the small park. She put on her hiking boots that were stashed in the back of her car. She realized how odd she looked, a professionally dressed woman with hiking boots, but she didn't mind. The important thing was that she was where she wanted to be, doing what she wanted to do. Rose was happy.

The Upper Peninsula couldn't have been prettier. The fall leaves were crimson, bright yellow, and various shades of brown, the sky was blue, and Rose was alone in the silence of nature. It was a welcome change from the earlier afternoon of brain drain, negativity, and strategizing against parents of children with disabilities. It shouldn't have to be this way, but conflict is inevitable and parents and school districts need lawyers to defend, protect, guide, and eventually resolve those conflicts. She walked a ways into the woods and sat down on a log near a quiet brook. She often sought out the silence as a contrast to her usual hectic and stressful lifestyle. This brief commune with nature was refreshing to Rose O'Leary's soul.

꒜

Rose and Lou met in the lobby of the Comfort Inn at seven o'clock. "Well, where are we going to spend this pleasant evening?" asked Rose. Giving control to Lou, or to anyone for that matter, was not her style. She was more comfortable being in charge and making decisions which pleased her.

"I suggest we go to the Helmer House," Lou said. "I asked some locals where the best place to eat was, and they recommended that place."

"Sounds good. Your car or mine?" Rose asked, once again relinquishing control. Twice within a minute. Lou thought to himself, "Could be a record."

"You drive," Lou relented.

"That's fine. Where is this place?"

"It's about fifteen miles west and south of here right on Manistique Lakes Road."

The twenty-five minute drive was an opportunity to share their respective afternoons in general and to exchange small talk about their families, weather, politics, and the beauty of the Upper Peninsula.

The hostess seated Rose and Lou on the porch of the Helmer House Inn. Here, they had a view of the fall foliage. The birch trees offered a nice contrast to the dark browns and yellows that dotted the grounds and the shoreline of the largest of the two Manistique Lakes. The decor was victorian with white tablecloths and a candle that offered a nice glow.

After they were seated and had ordered their drinks, Diet Pepsi for Lou and a ginger ale for Rose, the conversation turned to a more serious topic. Right out of the blue, Rose asked, "Do you think Mr. Franklin was murdered?"

Lou was tentative in his response, "Not sure. I haven't much to go on. I haven't talked to any of the people involved yet. I'll do that tomorrow. If he was killed, the murderer couldn't have been luckier, the man was practically having a heart attack twenty-four hours before his death. The doc confirmed this and his wife swears he died of a heart attack."

"Well, my guess is that he was murdered," Rose said.

"What would bring a lawyer to that conclusion?"

"There's such anger surrounding this layoff thing. The anger is spreading among several people, especially between a teacher and a group of parents who are willing to bankrupt the district to either get revenge or to get a program reinstated, at any cost to Newberry or the State of Michigan.

"This afternoon I looked through Blakeley's personnel file. This is the fifth time he has gone through a layoff. The word in this small town is that when he got the notice, he was a very angry man. They say his anger is frightful to see unleashed."

"Elaborate please."

"He doesn't express it at home against his wife or children, and he hasn't expressed it against students in school, but when pushed a bit beyond his limits, he makes threatening comments and, from what I'm told, he takes it out with fast-driving and verbal outbursts."

"Sounds fairly normal to me, Rose. All of us get angry from time to time and take it out in acceptable ways: verbally, driving fast, slamming a fist into a pillow. Sounds like a normal guy to me," Lou said, not mentioning the rifle that was brought into school.

"I would agree, but I suggest you look at a letter in his file when you do your investigation. Look for the letter from a Mr. Olsen."

"Ok. Thanks for the tip. Got any others?"

"As a matter of fact I do. Watch Mr. Wixom carefully. Word has it that he talked to Mr. Franklin before his death. I don't know if the conversation was in person, or over the phone, but he's prone to violence and has a police record. He was in the Marquette Prison for two or three years for assault and battery about fifteen years ago. Word is he was furious when he got word that his son's program was being terminated."

"Not bad for a lawyer, Rose. We make a good team!"

After drinks, they both ordered whitefish that had been plucked fresh that morning from Lake Superior. Just as the entree was placed before them the conversation returned to the reason both were in the Upper Peninsula.

Rose began, "What do I get in return for my thoughts, advice, and tips?"

Lou responded, "I'll pay the tip for your tips," enjoying his play on words.

"Very clever my friend. I expected you to pay for the entire meal!"

"What? On my pension? You lawyers bill by the minute. I'm up here as a favor with no contract and you expect me to pick up this tab?"

"Hey, what happened to the charm I thought I saw this afternoon?"

"Charm goes when money gets involved, I guess," said Lou with a big grin.

"Seriously, have you any advice for me based on what you learned this afternoon."

"As I said, I haven't talked to anyone except Irene Richardson, Chief Fitzpatrick, and Mr. Holcomb. But, as an ex-special education director, who saw tens of conflicts, I'd reinstate the program for one year and appoint a special study committee to look at the situation and report to the board. Then I'd involve the parents, teachers, and community leaders and go into a cooling-off period. This district is on a collision course that will not leave anybody a winner. When I see these things coming, it's time to get back in the huddle and think about the options. To save face, I might bring in a third party to recommend reinstatement and study. It shouldn't look like the board is backing down and giving in to the demands of a few parents. This has ugly written all over it. My advice is to stay away from the hearings and the bad media attention that the board is getting for potentially hurting kids with disabilities. I know this doesn't bring a dollar bill into your purse, but you wanted a tip and that is my best one."

"Makes sense, Lou. I'll talk to Jake tomorrow and see if that's what he wants to do."

"I feel my charm coming back," Lou admitted. "In fact, I'm so honored to share this evening with you that I'll pick up the entire bill as long as you won't drive away until I finish doing all the dishes to pay the thing off."

Rose smiled, "You're very kind, Lou. To show my gratitude, I'll ask you to be my guest for dinner tomorrow night, only you do the driving, Is that a deal?"

"Sounds great. I had a hard time deciding between the whitefish and the pork chops, returning tomorrow night will allow me to try the pork."

When Lou got back to his room, he called Maggie and spent a half hour telling her what he'd learned, suspected, and planned for the next day. Later, he turned on the television and found a football game on ESPN.

Before trying to get to sleep, Lou called Carol to see how her day had gone and to let her know that he was safely in the Upper Peninsula and well into the case. Once assured that all was well on the home front, he told Carol he loved her, thanked her for a small bag of M and Ms he discovered in his luggage, and wished her a good night's sleep. With ESPN giving the end of the day scores, Lou began to nod off, and eventually he was asleep.

Wednesday, October 21,
Newberry, Michigan

Lou began his second day in Newberry by interviewing the teachers affected by the layoff. The interviews with Malinda and Lucille were short, and Lou concluded that there was no connection between their being laid off and the fate of Mr. Franklin. Actually, both seized the lay off as an opportunity to do other things. However, this was not the case with Mr. Blakeley. Lou learned that when Chief Fitzpatrick contacted Bill Blakeley for an interview, there was apprehension and resistance. Bill wanted his lawyer present and he was not at all cooperative. His lawyer thought it best to go ahead, but Bill demanded that she be present. Lou had hoped for the interviews to be private, but a person does have a right to have a lawyer present, and so the meeting was arranged between Lou, Bill Blakeley, and Jackie Thiebideau, one of three lawyers in town.

Lou began. "Mr. Blakeley, as you know, we are looking into an allegation of murder concerning Mr. Franklin and ..."

"Why you talkin' to me?" Bill asked in a defiant tone.

"I'm talking to you because I'm talking to the three people who have had a significant event occur in their life, a layoff, and a man who was a major force in that decision is now dead. And, Mr. Blakeley, I'm going to suggest that you relax and cooperate. It's in your best interest, and I'm sure your lawyer agrees."

Miss Thiebideau interrupted, "I'd like a moment of privacy with my client."

"Granted. Step outside."

A few minutes later they returned, and it was obvious to Lou that a change of attitude had been suggested to Bill Blakeley.

Lou felt like David confronting Goliath. He looked Blakeley in the eye and asked, "I assume you're ready to cooperate?"

"What do you want from me?"

"I understand that this isn't the first time you've been laid off from a school district?"

"This is the fifth time. How can you blame me for being upset about it? It's a devastating experience not only for me, but for my wife and our children. It's thrown our lives into chaos with uncertainty, confusion, and fear. So, no, this isn't a new experience for me. What is new is my commitment to fight this intrusion on my family and on the lives of the children I teach. There's fear and devastation in the lives of the families of the children I've spent so much effort trying to help," Bill offered.

Lou was getting more than he asked for. He searched every word for clues and information. It was his experience, and belief, that you simply drop significant questions and then you let the person ramble uninterrupted.

Lou was thankful that the lawyer didn't pull Bill aside and tell him to give only simple answers to the questions. Any lawyer worth his or her fee would never let a client ramble on this way, Lou thought. The only time that this would be allowed would be if the lawyer was convinced that the client is innocent. If that's the case it doesn't matter what the client says, as long as it's the truth. Lou began to realize that maybe Bill Blakeley had nothing to do with Mr. Franklin's death.

"Mr. Franklin died late in the afternoon on October 10. Please outline your activities that day, recalling specifically what you did and where you were all day," Lou requested.

"In the morning, after breakfast I began to work in the yard. My wife went to town to do several chores, and I didn't expect her till almost noon. Our children were away, Bryan was at Northern Michigan University and Heather was still at a friend's house sleeping in from a pajama party. My father arrived at about eleven o'clock from Rudyard. He came over to offer support to us. He and my mother always came, when she was alive, whenever there was a family event; good or bad. I greeted him, got him some coffee and then finished my yard work because bad weather was expected. My wife brought lunch and the three of us ate. After lunch, Dad went into town. I went to the library around three for about an hour, as I wanted to get information about state and federal laws to begin fighting this thing. Dad returned about four o'clock in the afternoon. Actually, Dad and I got home about the same time. Our daughter came home later in the afternoon. She was getting ready for a date with Tom Franklin's grandson when we got the news that Mr. Franklin had died. The four of us ate dinner in our home, watched TV in the evening, I made a few calls to the parents of children in my special education class, and the four of us went to bed around ten thirty or eleven."

"Did your father say anything about what he did from after lunch till he arrived back at your home?" Lou asked.

"He said he went to Zellars for coffee and met a gentleman there. He said that the two of them had a long and enjoyable conversation. He commented about some of the new buildings in town, so he must have walked or driven around."

"What kind of a car does he drive?"

"Ford Taurus."

"Color? Four door? License?"

"It's blue, two door, Michigan license but I don't know the number."

"Please describe your car."

"I drive a Chrysler LeBaron, four door, green."

"Is that the car you drove to the library that afternoon?"

"Yes."

"Did you check a book out that day?"

"No, I signed in at the desk to use it in the library. You can't take their law materials from the library," Bill offered.

"Please describe your father: his age, body build, health status."

"Aw, come on. I can see where you might think I might be

involved, which I'm not, but you can't be thinking that Dad is involved in this," Bill said.

"Once again, Mr. Blakeley, I will ask questions that help us understand who all the possible players are in this matter."

Bill looked at his lawyer as if to get a signal to respond. Jackie nodded and Bill replied, "He's about sixty years old. He's tall, about an inch or two shorter than me. He is slender. He seems to be in good health. He had open heart surgery a couple of years ago."

"So, you'd say he's in pretty good health?"

"Yeah, I'd say that. He has medication for his heart and he has some trouble moving about, you know, arthritis I guess."

"What were the schools that laid you off in the past?"

"Battle Creek in 1992, Stockbridge in 1990, Mason in 1985, and Mt. Pleasant in 1982."

Lou asked a few more questions and then thanked Bill and his lawyer for cooperating. When the interview was over, Lou felt that it had helped.

Lou's next interview was with Thomas Franklin's second hand man at Franklin Motors, Whitey Larson. He explained to Whitey why he was conducting the interviews, and he then began questioning, "When was the last time you talked with Franklin?"

"Well, I may have been the last person he talked to besides Mrs. Franklin," Whitey offered.

"Tell me about that."

"He called and said he didn't feel very good and that he was going to call Dr. Polski. He said the pain in his chest was increasing, and that he probably shouldn't have taken some drug that a guy had just given him. It was named something that sounds like a brand of hair goop," Whitey said, sort of apologizing for not knowing what he was talking about.

"Digitalis?"

"Yeah, that's it. Vitalis goes on the hair and Digitalis goes under the tongue, right?"

"Right. It is hard keeping all of the alis's straight," Lou said with a smile. "Who gave him the pill?"

"He just said a guy who came by."

"What else did he say?"

"That was about it. He called to ask about the sales that day. He always liked to know how many cars were being sold."

"Did he say anything more about this visitor?"

"As I recall, what he said went something like, 'Whitey, calling to get the sales count. Gee, I feel lousy. There was a guy here talking about a layoff, and when I told him I felt terrible he said I should have some digitalis and then he gave me some. I gotta call Doc Polski.' I told him we had sold two cars that day, and I suggested he call the doc right away. He didn't sound good, and I was concerned, but I thought Mrs. Franklin was with him, and I expected that he would call the doc as he said he would. I never thought anything was out of line."

"Maybe nothing was. This information helps. You have confirmed that he did have a visitor, and that the visitor may have given him a drug. You also clarified that the visitor was there to talk about a layoff. So, you have been very helpful and I appreciate your cooperation."

⌇

While Lou was probing and trying to pick up any clues that would confirm a possible homicide or convince the authorities that the death was natural, Rose was reviewing the files. She had the Intermediate School District Plan in front of her. She was making sure that her interpretation of law was accurate, and that case law was applicable to the situation in Newberry.

Rose O'Leary asked Jake to have lunch with her. He had nothing scheduled and gladly accepted the chance to talk privately with his lawyer. They didn't go to Zellars or Picklemans as all the locals would be curious and wondering who was with Jake and what was going on. They chose to go to the Helmer House. Rose knew she was overdoing the place, but she knew where it was, and it offered a peaceful setting for a meeting and a meal.

After they were seated, served coffee, and had ordered chicken salad sandwiches, Rose began, "Jake, I'm going to level with you. You're paying me for advice and I'm under an obligation, ethical and moral, to give you my best. That's what you are going to get, assuming you want it."

"Yes, I do."

"My advice is to give in on this one, Jake. I'll tell you why. This is not a win-win. This is a big loser for everyone. Because of the way that the special education system is designed, the Newberry School District stands to spend literally a couple hundred thousand dollars in hearings and legal fees. You stand to lose the respect of the community. The district will have to answer to state and federal offices and this will take time and paperwork. You will need to attend the State Board of Education meetings in Lansing. You would need to brief the state representatives and the senators who will see you, and the district as not being supportive of parents of children with disabilities. The entire thing will consume your time, your board meetings, and staff time for creating reports and notices and mailing materials. I can fight all of this for you, and will if you choose. You would probably win, because what you want to do is legal, and would probably stand the test of due process hearings, state reviews, and possible court action." Rose paused and looked at Jake with concern.

Rose continued, "It will be a battle. Besides all that I've mentioned you'd be up against a governing body, the State Board of Education. I've seen them invite parents to provide testimony, and then a member or two will speak negatively about special education administrators. It isn't worth the public relations nightmare. I'd do anything to keep this away from the State Board of Education!"

"Hate to give in, Rose. Know what I mean?"

"Yes I do, but I have a plan that might help. I suggest you brief your board president of the reality which I have presented, and if you'd like me present, or even to do the debriefing, I'd be happy to. Then I suggest you recommend the special education program be reinstated for the rest of the school year, and that you convene a task force to review the special education delivery system for Newberry students. You should involve the parents, teachers, and administrators. You should contract with a facilitator so the effort is not biased by your administrative staff. You should then keep Mr. Blakeley for the one year which could be extended if that is what the task force recommends, and the board concurs."

"It sure looks like this group of parents is running my school district," summarized Jake.

"Yes it does, and they are. But, the alternative is a nightmare, and I suggest you buy some time at practically no cost. It will be your idea to reinstate the program, so you will be seen as in control, and your advice will save the school district thousands and thousands of dollars. The parents can think they won and are in charge, but the board, your staff, and the citizens will see you as making a decision that is in the best interest of the entire community."

The chicken salad sandwiches were brought to the table and the conversation switched to, of all things, Jake's desire to be a clock repairman when he retired. He was taking a correspondence course out of South Carolina. He had collected all the tools of the trade and found the skill quite relaxing and challenging.

Rose wondered if he could bring in any money. After all, she wondered, how many clocks are there in the Upper Peninsula that need fixing?

Jake read her mind and explained, "Almost everyone wears a watch, and the average home has five to eight clocks that are subject to breakdowns. In a nutshell, where there are people, there are timepieces, and it's work that I can do that doesn't involve a board, a couple of unions, and an expensive public operation that is always under the tax paying public's scrutiny." Jake believed that his pension and his clocks would keep him a happy man till his earthly days were over.

"This little out of the way Inn has good food," Rose said.

"We're fortunate, here in the U.P., to have serious cooks that value preparing good food for the money. We don't have many fast food places up here. The mom and pop eateries take their family and friends seriously, and if a meal is going to be served to neighbors, it's expected to be tasty and homemade," Jake said proudly.

"If you think the pie is homemade, then I'll have to have a piece no matter how fast it travels to my hips," Rose said.

"It'll be the best piece of pie, aside from yours or your mother's, I'll assure that."

While they were enjoying the apple pie, Jake's with a scoop of vanilla ice cream, the two once again got serious and Rose said, "Anything I can do to help you with your decision, Jake?"

"I don't think so. I'll take your advice. I suggest both of us talk with Mr. Owen and Irene Richardson late this afternoon. If Bill concurs, and he will, I suggest we call a meeting of the parents and Mr. Blakeley to present our plan."

"Yes, and when you do, come across as a compassionate man who is not giving in, but who is deciding that it is in the best interest of the students not to disrupt their education at this time. They should see you as strong. Don't give them the impression that you are throwing in the towel. You should also work with your newspaper editor so that the article they print comes out positively for the school board and presents you as acting on behalf of children, not just the parents demands. Now, I also suggest that you don't go overboard, because your task force may recommend, in a year, what you are planning to do now, and then the quotes and articles may backfire on you. It will go well, Jake. I really believe you are doing the right thing for the children, for Jake, and for Newberry."

Jake picked up the check after being assured that Rose ranked the piece of apple pie right up there with the top ten slices of pie she ever ate. Their ride back to Newberry was quick and nothing more was said about the issue. Jake Williamson had gotten his money's worth by bringing Rose up to Newberry.

ॐ

Bill Blakeley took the mail from the mailbox. He was pleased to see a letter from the Charlevoix Public Schools. He had written to them asking about a position as a teacher in their juvenile detention facility. The juvenile detention facility temporarily housed delinquent youth who were too young to be placed in a county or city jail. Each facility throughout the state has an education component. The teacher hired to work there was usually a special education teacher.

Bill opened that letter as soon as he got into the house. It was a form letter, but nonetheless it offered promise. He was invited to fill out the enclosed application which would require him, once again, to update his vita and request that Grand Valley State University send a copy of his transcript to Charlevoix. The job description was inviting. It was certainly a job he could handle, and would, in fact, enjoy. He wouldn't have to deal with mainstreaming his kids, and he wouldn't have to be working with general education teachers. He could have his own class in this facility, and for the most part, be left alone to teach the kids who came to him for a few days or for several months.

His eye caught the salary range. With his years of experience, it would give him about a four thousand dollar raise. He was fairly certain that Trudy would be able to find a job either in Charlevoix or at a school district nearby. He believed that Bryan and Heather would eventually adjust. But, still it wasn't the way it was supposed to be. On the one hand, he felt that he should be thankful for a teaching credential and job openings, but on the other hand, ripping Trudy and the kids away from their lifestyles and friends wasn't fair. All he wanted to do was to dig his roots into a community, and to feel a part of someplace.

He wouldn't have any trouble convincing Trudy, Bryan, and Heather about the beauty of Charlevoix. There was water all around, and it was close to the popular towns of Petoskey and Traverse City. It wasn't nearly as isolated as Newberry. There was more culture and things to do. It would be further away from Trudy's ailing parents, which was one of the reasons they wanted to move to Newberry in the first place. But, this seemed to be the card that was being dealt, and they would probably play it.

~~

The Parents for Justice had gotten wind that the superintendent was considering reinstating the program serving their children. In a small town even a person's thoughts seem to get around with little effort. Phone calls of celebration and victory rang throughout the town. One of the calls was from Mr. Wixom to Bill Blakeley.

"Bill?"

"Yeah."

"Larry Wixom here. We've just learned that Jake Williamson is thinking of keeping your special education program."

"Now there's some good news for a change," Bill said with some enthusiasm in his voice.

"Yeah. It's sad what we had to go through to get them to finally listen to us. Looks like it's still a country where people can make a difference by working together for a cause."

"Good. I don't mean to dampen your joy and enthusiasm, but I may be taking a job downstate."

"You really know how to kill a little joy, Bill."

"Sorry, but you might as well hear it from me. The handwriting is on the wall. If they don't move the program this year, they'll probably try again. I want some security for myself and my family. If I get the opportunity for a better job, I'm going to take it, and I'd think you and the other parents would do the same if you were in my shoes."

"I understand. Our kids have had a variety of teachers and we're used to changes. We felt you cared about our kids, and we liked your style. The kids respected you, you know that."

"They're great kids. If I leave, I'll miss them, but their next teacher will do a good job. Part of their education is learning to adjust to a variety of people. Those challenges are going to happen when they leave school anyway, so they had better start making the adjustment now."

"The news of your pending departure will be heard by all very soon. Do you want me to try and keep it quiet?" Larry asked.

"What's fact is that I'm looking and applying. If I get an offer, and if the family supports making another move, I'll go. I don't have another job to go to at this time. I don't mind the rumor if it's simply that I'm looking for another job."

"I just wanted you to know what the parents know. The school district may take action at the next board meeting to reinstate your program."

"That's great news for you and the kids. I'm proud of how all of you came together and showed them that you meant business. Thanks for your call."

The phone hit the cradle, and Mr. Wixom was on the phone tree within minutes. Soon all would know that the teacher of the special education program was looking to make himself history in Newberry. The parents had reason to believe that the program would stay. Now they would have to see to it that he didn't leave or that the new teacher would be a good one, like Bill Blakeley.

⟶

Lou decided that he wanted to talk to Mrs. Cunningham, the elderly woman who had started the talk about a possible murder. He walked up to her front door. In his hand were photos of several cars, and he was hoping that, like a victim looks at a line up of people, one of which is the suspected perpetrator, Mrs. Cunningham would look at the line up of cars and say, "That's the one."

Lou was greeted warmly and invited into the living room. He could smell the coffee, and his senses told him that some muffins would accompany the fresh brew. "Would you like some coffee?"

"That would be great, thanks."

"I just finished baking some blueberry muffins. I'll bring a few in with the coffee. Cream or sugar?"

"No thanks, just plain black coffee and a muffin sounds great. Blueberry muffins are my favorite."

A few minutes later Mrs. Cunningham returned with the coffee and muffins. They sat down for the interview. "What I'd like you to do for me is to relive the afternoon that Mr. Franklin died. Tell me what you saw, heard, and what led you to the belief that he died by means other than natural causes."

"I'll be glad to. I was at home that afternoon. I called Marian Franklin in the noon hour. It was just a neighborly call which I make daily. She said she was doing fine. She said that Tom was not feeling well and that she was concerned. He was going to call Doc Polski. She said that she had some chores to do and that she would be out during the afternoon, for awhile."

"So, you got the impression that Tom was well enough that he didn't feel a need to call Doc Polski, or to go to the hospital, when you called around noon."

"Yes. You see, Marian is quite a motherly type. She would never leave his side if there was any pending crisis."

"Then what happened?"

"It was about three o'clock and I was walking from the kitchen to go upstairs, which brought me through this room, and I saw a car in front of the Franklin home. I didn't have my glasses on, but I could tell that the car was not a car that came to the Franklin's home regularly. I looked out the window and I saw a man, tall and slender, walking up to the door. The door was opened and he went in. Of course, I was curious. I did notice that the Franklin car was not in the drive, so I figured that Marian was out doing her chores. About ten minutes later the man came out, walked to the car, and drove away."

"Why didn't you get your glasses?" Lou asked.

"I wasn't that curious. How was I to know that Tom was going to die within the hour?"

"I'm going to name some people who may have walked up to the house, and I'd like you to respond to the possibility; or, better yet, if you think you saw that person."

"Bill Blakeley"

"Could have been, the man was about his size."

"Whitey Larson."

"No way, I can tell Mr. Larson by the way he walks."

"Larry Wixom."

"He isn't quite tall enough, but it could have been him."

"Jake Williamson."

"Nope. Jake's too short."

"Bill Owen"

"Could be, but..... No, it wasn't him. He comes by often to see Tom about board matters, but he always parks in the drive and not on the street."

"What an eye. You even know where people park!" Lou said with a chuckle, as he wondered if the lady in his neighborhood kept as good an eye on the comings and goings on Lake Michigan Drive.

"So, it could have been Mr. Blakeley or Mr. Wixom?"

"Of the people you mentioned, yes."

"Now, please look at some pictures of automobiles and tell me if you see the car that was parked outside."

One at a time Lou put a photo in front of Mrs. Cunningham. Each photo was taken from the rear, at an angle that she would have seen.

Mrs. Cunningham looked at each for several minutes and finally said, "To be honest with you, I paid more attention to the person and not to the car. I know that I didn't recognize the car, and I can't say for sure if any of these cars was the one in front of Tom and Marian's house that afternoon. The one that comes the closest is this one," she picked up and handed a photograph to Lou.

Lou turned it over and looked at the name, Larry Wixom. Lou added the Wixom car photo to the others and placed them in his attache case. "Is there anything else you'd like to tell me?"

"Yes, I think so. The women in my bridge club have a theory. We are just a group of ladies who have nothing better to do than try to run everyone's life. We think this is what happened, and for what it's worth, I'll share it with you. We secretly would like to be detectives and solve the unsolvable crime, I guess, and in Newberry this opportunity comes along about once every fifty or so years."

"I'd welcome your theory," Lou responded. "There may be a clue in your insight that would be helpful, and who knows, maybe when the investigation is complete, you'll be able to enjoy coffee and muffins and write a mystery as a group."

"We believe that Mr. Franklin was given something by the man that was with him around three that afternoon. We think the man was there because he was upset about the layoff of the Newberry school teachers. We believe the man is either a relative or a person from out of town who is acting on behalf of one or more of the teachers. We believe that the man may be affiliated with the Michigan Education Association. That last one is a bit far fetched, and we all don't agree on that, but Mrs. Wyble feels strongly about it, and I would feel that I didn't represent us all if I had not mentioned it. So, I have. We believe that Mr. Franklin was given something that would either contribute to a heart attack or that would not detract attention from Doc Polski's diagnosis of heart attack when he found the body. If the Woman's Bridge Club has the opportunity to put our collected savings on the outcome of this matter, we're willing to bet that we've hit the nail on the head."

Lou thought about what he had heard and replied, "Well, I'll say that your theory does make sense. I don't want to steal your thunder, but I've thought the same thing, and if this is what is found to have happened, I'll be sure to credit the Newberry Woman's Bridge Club with having the plot all figured out before the facts in the homicide are out and verified. How's that?"

"Sounds good to me. Did you like the muffins?"

"Mom's going to turn over in her grave, but to be honest, I have to say they're a bit better than the blueberry muffins she used to make." Lou's charm was at work once again. He knew he was lying and so did Mrs. Cunningham, but it sounded nice.

"Before I go," Lou said. "Let me get, as Paul Harvey would say, 'The rest of the story,' Not to put words in your mouth, but Marian Franklin came home and shortly thereafter the ambulance and Doc Polski arrived, and Tom Franklin was taken from the house?"

"Yes. I'd say it was about four o'clock in the afternoon."

"And, for the record, to the best of your memory you didn't see anyone come to the house after your phone call to Marian and before the man visited at around three o'clock? Nor did you see anyone else come to the house after the man left?"

"That's right."

The two exchanged some small talk over a quick second cup of coffee. Mrs. Cunningham had a cousin who lived in Spring Lake, near Grand Haven. They talked about the relative and the west-Michigan area. Lou thanked her for the delicious muffins and coffee, but he was more thankful for her information and the bridge club theory. He headed off to see the phone log and to talk to Mr. Wixom and Mrs. Franklin.

When Lou got back to Chief Fitzpatrick's office, the phone log was waiting for him. There were three calls made to the Franklin home and one call out between noon and four o'clock on the afternoon of Saturday, October 10. This was not counting the call of Mrs. Franklin to summon the ambulance and to Doc Polski to come help her husband. The first call was at 12:57 p.m., for four minutes, from Mrs. Cunningham, according to the phone number on the printout. The second call came in at 2:35 p.m., for four minutes, and was traced to the home of Larry Wixom. The third call came at 2:50 p.m., for two minutes, and was traced to a public phone outside the library. The fourth call was from the Franklin house to Franklin Motors, at 3:10 p.m., and it lasted three minutes. Finally, at 3:55 p.m., a call was placed to Doc Polski, and at 3:57 to the fire department for an ambulance.

After looking at this information, Lou asked Chief Fitzpatrick to call Mr. Wixom and ask him to come to the police station to answer some questions. With his police record, Lou decided that he would rather talk to him at the station than in his home. As far as Lou was concerned, Wixom was a definite suspect in the murder.

Mr. Wixom arrived at the station about fifteen minutes after Chief Fitzpatrick contacted him. Lou shook his hand and explained why he wanted to talk to him. "Mr. Wixom, there is a suspicion that Mr. Franklin didn't die of a heart attack, but may have been murdered, as you have no doubt read in the local paper. I've asked to talk with you to determine what information you may have about this, if any."

"I'll help if I can."

"Did you talk with Mr. Franklin the day he died?"

"Yes. I talked to him on the phone at about two-thirty in the afternoon on the day he died. We talked for about four or five minutes. I was upset. I won't deny that. I told him that the special education program was important to us parents and to the children. I told him that I thought it was cruel to make cuts in a program for kids with disabilities, when cuts could be made in the high salaries of administrators, travel budgets, and other things which we don't think to be essential"

"How did he respond to your call?"

"He didn't sound like he felt well, but he was kind and he listened. He did defend the action of the board, and he gave the line about tough decisions needing to be made. He said he felt a responsibility, to the citizens, to be fiscally accountable. I got upset and said that the parents and I would fight this all the way to the Supreme Court if necessary. Our kids are not going to be the losers in this terrible decision made by uncaring and heartless people."

"Then what happened?"

"He said he was sorry we felt that way and he would do what he could to assure a good program from the intermediate school district or in the Soo. I was mad and I said some things I regret before I hung up on him."

"What did you say that you regret?"

"I used some obscene words and I said he would live to regret what he did to defenseless kids with disabilities."

"Did you go over to see Mr. Franklin?"

"No sir. I made the call from home. I just hung up and went back to a wood working project in my basement. My neighbor, Dan Workman was there when I called."

Lou thanked him for coming right over and answering his questions. They shook hands and Mr. Wixom walked away. Lou knew, in his gut that Mr. Wixom, while he may have added to the stress on Mr. Franklin's life, did not participate in a murder.

The phone call from the library was the mystery that could unlock the drama. Lou recalled Bill Blakeley saying that he went to the library that afternoon. His theory was that Bill called Mr. Franklin and learned that no one was with Franklin. Bill asked to see him, and then he drove to the house, gave him a drug and left. All of Lou's investigations were pointing to the angry teacher who was laid off. He was likely the major force behind the event and had taken action to kill Franklin.

Lou stopped himself. He realized that even if Bill Blakeley did visit with Mr. Franklin, there was no evidence that anything happened when the two men were together. But, when Bill went through the day's activities, he did not say he stopped to see Mr. Franklin. Bill Blakeley would have more questions to answer, and maybe a lie detector test would be needed.

ℳ

Lou called Maggie and told her all that he was able to learn during his visit. When she learned that Bill had been laid off in other school districts, she suggested that she contact those districts. Maggie hoped she might uncover a pattern or more clues into the personality of Bill Blakeley.

Lou, too, was intrigued by the previous layoffs that had been a part of Bill Blakeley's life. There was no question that Bill took the news badly. His reaction was understandable. Lou realized Bill's predicament; no one enjoys being told they're not needed or will not be able to maintain a job that supports a family. Lou wasn't denying that it was a terrible bit of news to get and that many administrators must, on occasion, tell people that they will be laid off.

If Mr. Franklin was murdered, and it was related to the layoff of Bill Blakeley, Maggie surmised that a similar episode, in the previous school district, may have precipitated a similar angry outburst that could have led to a crime in Battle Creek and the other districts. Lou agreed.

Maggie called the State Police headquarters in Lansing and asked to speak to Sergeant Jim Shanks. She had worked with Shanks on a case involving insurance fraud. "Shanks, homicide," he answered.

"Maggie McMillan, Jim. How're you?"

"Just fine, Maggie. Good to hear from you. What prompts this call?"

"Lou and I are getting involved in a suspected murder in Newberry, up in the U.P. We're helping Chief of Police Fitzpatrick and one of your retired state troopers, Harold Holcomb, investigate a possible murder of a school board member. The prime suspect, at this point, is a special education teacher who was laid off. We think the guy lost it on hearing the bad news, and he may have let his emotions take over in a fatal episode."

"Yeah, that happens."

"The suspect taught in Battle Creek, and he was laid off in the fall or early winter of 1992. My question is this. Is there any computer program or any way to learn of any school official: superintendent, principal, board member, teacher who may have been murdered about that time?"

"Yeah, there's a data base. I can ask the secretaries to run a check on it and see what we can find. What's your phone and fax number? We should be back to you in a few minutes."

Maggie gave him both numbers and expressed her satisfaction with the offer to help, "Thanks, Jim."

"Good luck with your investigation."

A few minutes later a message was faxed. It read, "On November 29 of 1992, a principal of Battle Creek High School, Jack Olsen, was killed in a hunting accident. He was found dead while deer hunting. There was some suspicion of foul play and the case has remained open. This is the only murder or strange death of a Battle Creek school employee in the fall of 1992."

~

Maggie called and told Lou about the death of Jack Olsen. They agreed that they were beginning to see a pattern. Two layoffs and two deaths.

Lou had done enough for the day. As planned, he had a dinner with Rose that evening. Lou wanted to get another late afternoon jog in before having a pork chop dinner at the Helmer House. At least it would be easier to justify eating a pork chop dinner with baked potato bathed in butter if he had a forty-five or fifty minute run under his belt.

Lou thanked Harold and Fitz for the assistance they had given him all day long. He told both men that the day had been very productive and that he would spend the morning talking with the men at Zellars. He wanted another meeting with Bill Blakeley and his attorney in the late morning or early afternoon. The rest of the afternoon he planned to spend summarizing what he had learned since he arrived and what steps would be next. Lou decided that he would leave very early the following morning. He'd go home to Grand Haven and then rendezvous with Maggie for a planning session. They'd put all of their information together and plan next steps.

Lou met Rose in the lobby of the Comfort Inn. He drove, as agreed upon the evening before. They pretty much copied the previous evening; parked in the same spot, sat at the same table, had the same waitress. The only difference was they ordered pork chops, and Rose picked up the bill.

The conversation turned into a debriefing for each other's benefit. Rose began, "I gave your advice to Jake at lunch today, and he decided to take it. I have to be honest and tell you that I didn't give you credit for it. I feel a bit guilty, but having now confessed, I hope I'll be forgiven. It was excellent advice, and I'm glad he decided to follow it. We met with Irene Richardson and with the board president, Bill Owen, late this afternoon. Jake will suggest to the board, at their next meeting, that the program for kids with emotional disabilities be reinstated, and that Mr. Blakeley get his job back. Rumor has it, though, that Blakeley has gotten the message and thinks it in his best interest to look elsewhere. Apparently he has an opportunity in Charlevoix at a juvenile detention center."

"It's a compliment that you thought my advice was worthy of being shared. You aren't forgiven, because I only forgive behaviors that I think are sinful. Claiming my good common sense as yours is not a sin. I do think that ideas should be copyrighted. Then I could see you in court and get back some of the big bucks you get for all that legal goulash you pass out," Lou said with a chuckle.

"Glad you're so understanding. What happened in your day? Did you read the Jack Olsen letter in Bill Blakeley's file?"

"Forgot to do that."

"Well, thanks a lot. I give you great advice, and you don't follow it. At least I have enough common sense to steal your ideas, but you haven't the gray cells to remember taking a great clue and looking into it! How can a detective get the job done with your memory? You need a little note pad and pencil like the television detective. What was his name?"

"Columbo?"

"Yeah, Colombo. You don't need the cigar, wrinkled overcoat, and the old Studebaker, but you do need a note pad."

"I could use the dog. At least the dog doesn't make fun of me and challenge my intelligence," Lou said as they seemed to enjoy a little spontaneous one-upmanship.

"Seriously, I think the district will be much better off for changing their course, which, as you so accurately described, would've been devastating had they stuck to their guns," Rose said.

"It'd be nice if my efforts had been as fruitful as yours."

"What did you learn today?" Rose asked.

"Well, to make a long day rather short, I'm quite certain that if anyone is involved in the murder of Tom Franklin, it's Bill Blakeley. I believe that Blakeley called Tom Franklin close to three o'clock in the afternoon, and then visited him at his home before his death. Here's where I stop short of saying a murder happened. With no witnesses, no autopsy, and no means of documenting what was said or done, I really can't say if there was a murder or just a visit between two men. Tomorrow, I need to talk with Doc Polski, with Blakeley again, and with the men's coffee klatch. Following those discussions, I can draw some conclusions and then I've got to get back home."

"Well, if anyone can get a handle on this in two days of investigative work it is Louis Searing. I've a lot of respect for you. You do good work. But, I do recommend that you look at that letter in Blakeley's file."

The pork chop dinner was delicious. Not as good as the whitefish, but then the Upper Peninsula is not known for stockyards. Apparently, the farther you are from the source of the authentic food the less likely it will be at its best. Mexican food in Texas tastes much better than in Michigan. Lobster seems to taste better in Boston than in Kansas City, prime rib seems to taste better in Kansas City than in Miami and here in the U.P., whitefish seems so much better than any place else in the country.

Rose asked Lou about Maggie. "What makes her so good, Lou?"

"Maggie has the instinct. I think that's it. I called her with the information I'd gotten so far and her first response was to get information about the previous layoffs. Already she's looking for patterns. I seem to deal with the here and now. She's way out front."

"That makes the two of you a good team."

"I think so."

"I've never met her. Describe her, please."

"Maggie is about forty five. She's attractive. She has shoulder length and naturally curly brown hair, and a beautiful smile," Lou appeared sentimental about his partner. " She always wears slacks and often has on a turtle neck sweater. She's got good mobility, in that she gets around in her motorized chair and her customized van, but she is often content to remain at home and work on these cases from a base."

"Is she married?"

"Yeah, Tom McMillan is a retired oral surgeon in Battle Creek. He often travels with her. He has a hobby of playing famous golf courses around the country and the world. He's in his early 50s and still has a part-time practice. His time is devoted to golf and being with Maggie when she needs him for extended travel. Tom's a spitting image of Tom Selleck. He could have been a soap opera star in his early years."

"The reputation the two of you have is very good. Those who speak highly of your team rarely have met Maggie. People know you, but she's often a mystery."

"She's not trying to be. I happen to be more of the on-site person. She's the thinker, the strategist, and the one to help synthesize the information. You'll meet her. I'll make it a point to introduce you in the future."

"Thanks, I'd love to meet her."

They had a cup of coffee while conversing about nothing important. They thanked their waitress for a couple of evenings of good work; and, since Rose was more generous with her pocketbook, she left the waitress a very good tip. "I used to be a waitress when I was in college. Once you've done this work, you never leave a fifteen percent tip unless the service is really lousy," Rose said sympathetically.

Back at the Comfort Inn, Rose closed the evening, "Good luck tomorrow and in the future with this case. If a murder was committed, you'll find out who did it."

"Thanks Rose. Have a safe trip home." The two acknowledged that having each other to share and enjoy the evenings had made their visits more enjoyable. They wished each other a good night and called it a day.

Thursday October 22, Newberry, Michigan

The next morning, while Rose was crossing the beautiful Mackinac Bridge, Lou was looking into the file of Bill Blakeley to find the letter Rose mentioned. What he found was a letter that discussed Bill's limited capacity to handle bad news and to adjust quickly to a set back such as a layoff. The letter was not stamped "confidential." Lou didn't find anything surprising in the letter. It simply fed the perception of a man who had a problem controlling his emotions. Lou stored this information away in his mental computer. He thought that it might be helpful later on.

Lou called Doc Polski early in the morning. He said that it was very important that he talk with Doc concerning Tom Franklin. Doc Polski had been the region's medical icon for years. He had gone to the University of Michigan medical school. His entire education was paid for by the citizens of the eastern Upper Peninsula, as well as contributions by a very wealthy shipping family. A few decades ago, the region was without a doctor for several months.

It was during that crisis that the community leaders heard of a novel idea being tried in the barren areas of Montana and North Dakota. The community would pay for the college education of a medical student, and in return, the student, upon becoming a doctor, agreed to give ten years of service to the region. In Doc Polski's case, he fell in love with the Upper Peninsula, the people, and his wife of 41 years, and wouldn't think of being anywhere else on the face of the earth. Doc Polski agreed to meet Lou at Zellars about one half hour before the men's coffee klatch would arrive, and since Lou was going to meet with the men next, the arrangement was perfect.

After introductions, and a cup of coffee, Lou began, "You know that some people think that Tom may have been murdered. I'm here for a few days to try and help Chief Fitzpatrick and Harold Holcomb either dispel the rumors; or, hopefully, to find some clues that actually verify that a murder did take place."

"Yes, I've heard all about the rumors and the reason for your being here. It's all so silly. Tom had a heart attack, pure and simple. He was a patient of mine for years. I had told him time and again to start exercising, to start some sensible eating, and to slow down. He had mentioned some tightness in his chest a few months ago and I suggested we do an angiogram at the hospital in the Soo. He would hear nothing of it. He had all the classic symptoms of heart failure, and quite frankly, it was one of the easiest pronouncements of death I've ever had to make," the good doctor offered.

"Couldn't someone have done something that would have caused him to die early?" Lou asked.

"Oh sure, of course, someone could have angered him, scared him, given him some drug, or slipped something into his water or coffee. Mystery books are full of possible deaths, but at the time, it was my professional judgment that Tom Franklin died of a massive heart attack, or, as we say, cardiac infarction."

"I assume you prescribed digitalis when he said he was having some chest discomfort?"

"I suggested the idea and that he carry it with him, but he would hear nothing of it. You see, Tom Franklin was a very stubborn man. He wouldn't have hospital tests, wouldn't have me prescribe drugs, wouldn't watch his diet, or do any exercise. So, while I suggested digitalis, he wouldn't take any of it, so why waste a prescription when I knew he wouldn't use it? Oh sure, he could sue me for malpractice, but it's kind of hard for a dead man to testify that his doctor didn't prescribe digitalis when he knew it would possibly save his life. It was heart failure, Mr. Searing. In fact, I give Tom Franklin credit for lasting as long as he did. He, by all my medical journals and experience, should have had the main street of Newberry named after him about a year ago, if not two or three years ago."

"Thanks Doc. You've been helpful." The men parted company and Doc Polski offered to help if Lou had any additional questions.

The men's coffee klatch began to arrive predictably. They drank the same amount of coffee each day. The only thing that seemed to vary was the conversation. Nothing was spared. If it was happening in Newberry, the Upper Peninsula of Michigan, Michigan in general, the United States, the world or the universe it got talked about. If the group was to be typecast, it would fall to the conservative side. Most were Republican, and while some were far to the right, most were moderate.

Chief Fitzpatrick introduced Lou to the men after they had settled into their first cup of coffee. "Excuse me men, this is Louis Searing from downstate. He's helping Harold and me with an investigation into the possible murder of Tom Franklin. He told me he'd like the opportunity to talk with you for a few minutes. If you don't mind, I'd like you to answer his questions."

"No problem, Fitz. Nice to meet you, sir," said Herm Batchelder extending a warm greeting. Herm was the spokesperson for the coffee crew.

"Thank you. I'll only take a few minutes of your time. Do any of you men have any ideas about what happened to Mr. Franklin?"

Chuck Belski started with an opinion. "Got to look at the source of all the rumors. I got it that Mrs. Cunningham came up with the theory. We all know that the woman is nuts. You hang around this town long enough, and after a while you just attribute every crazy comment to that woman. I mean it was a couple of years ago that the world was coming to an end. Remember that?" The other men all smiled and nodded in agreement. "Then I think it was six months ago that she saw a flying saucer, outside of town, one clear night. She called the Air Force, the State Police and Oprah Winfrey. The woman is wacko." Once again the men smiled and nodded in agreement.

John Nelson was next to speak. "That's true; you got to take her words with several grains of salt, but it could be that while she has that reputation, she just might be on to this one. All of the attention is being focused on this Blakeley guy from what I can gather. Nobody is talking about Lester Romanski. All of us know that he was fired by Tom Franklin. Word had it that he had misused funds at the dealership, and when Tom found out, he fired ole Les on the spot and in front of other employees. Les was one angry guy and said to some friends that Franklin would pay big time for treating him like that. Remember?"

Once again the men nodded in unison but none were smiling. "Where is this Les now?" asked Lou.

"Haven't seen him for about a month or two. He went to the Escanaba area and got a job selling appliances for a discount store," Herm said.

"Describe this Les guy."

"He's about six foot two, 190 pounds, slender as opposed to having a gut," Fred said holding his own belly.

"What kind of a car did he drive?" Lou asked.

"Oh, it was a Chevrolet, late model, dark color. Franklin insisted that all his employees drive a General Motors car because that is what he sold. He gave his employees a great deal. He thought it was good advertisement, and giving his employees a good deal was a perk that he could provide. We all remember when he hired a guy about three years ago, and the guy wouldn't go along with Tom and decided to keep his Honda. Tom Franklin made his life miserable. I think he lasted about three weeks and then hit the trail for Minnesota," Terry Wilkins offered.

Jocelyn brought more carafes of coffee just as the men began signaling for more hot and fresh caffeine or non-caffeine as the case might be.

"Actually, some of us don't know why there's all this fuss. I mean, Franklin was on his death bed for about a year. He was always complaining about a pain here and there. He huffed and puffed just getting out of his car and into his office. He got more days for the shape he was in than anyone deserved. If he was shot or beat up, I can see why an investigation would need to be done, but that afternoon was his last whether someone laced his coffee or not. Actually, this may sound a bit cruel, but if someone did hurry Tom Franklin along, it was probably a favor," John offered and, once again, most nodded in agreement.

Lou thanked the men for their thoughts. He'd leave them to solve all the problems of the world, or at least those in Newberry. He told Fitz that he would share his thoughts after talking to Mrs. Franklin and Bill Blakeley. Fitz made the arrangements.

Lou pulled up to the curb in front of the Franklin house. He thought about turning toward Mrs. Cunningham's house and waving hello, but decided against it. He was fairly certain that his activity was being watched, and who knows, he thought, this visit might even be presented at the bridge club. Lou knocked on the door and was greeted warmly by Marian Franklin. "Hello, you must be Mr. Searing."

"Yes, I am. Thank you for agreeing to talk with me."

After listening to Lou's introduction and explanation for the questioning, Marian said, "I don't think there is anything to this, Mr. Searing. Thomas was not feeling well and had been complaining about these pains for sometime. He just wouldn't go to Doc Polski and, the few times he did, he never took his advice."

"I have a few questions. I'll only be a few minutes."

"Stay as long as you wish. I've got all day."

Marian presented the coffee along with a few sugar cookies. The two were seated in the family room with what appeared to be a thousand books all neatly arranged around a couple of very comfortable leather chairs and brass lamps. "This room is wonderful," Lou said. "I could curl up in one of these chairs with a good book, a fire in that fireplace, and be in Heaven."

"Yes, we like it in here. That's exactly what Thomas would do. He loved this room. I suppose if he would have taken an evening walk instead of sitting in this chair after every meal, he may have lived a little longer, but we all have choices to make."

"Please, if you would, take me through the afternoon that Mr. Franklin died. I realize that the memory may be difficult for you, but it would help me in this investigation."

"Well, Tom came home from the garage about noon for lunch. We had a light lunch because he complained that he wasn't feeling very good. I could tell he didn't feel well, and I was concerned. I'm always concerned, but after awhile his poor health just became a way of life. While I was afraid and worried, there wasn't much I could do but be there for him."

"I imagine that was difficult," Lou said sympathetically.

"Yes, it was. Anyway, I got a call from Mrs. Cunningham who lives down the street. She calls once a day, at least, to chat and see how I'm doing. I told her I had some chores to do in the afternoon, and we talked about Tom and the weather and so on. I went to town about two-forty and did my chores. I got back at about three-twenty. Tom was in the chair you are sitting in when I came home. I looked into this room and thought he was napping, which was normal, and I didn't need to disturb him and tell him I was home. I was just grateful that he was resting."

"What position was he in?"

"The chair you are in is a recliner and it tilts back. He had the chair tilted back a bit and he was just lying there with his feet on the little stool that kicks out when you lean back."

"Go ahead."

"About twenty minutes later I went in to see if he was OK, and I could tell he wasn't. I walked over to him and could tell that he wasn't breathing, so I immediately went to the phone and called Doc Polski, and then I called for an ambulance."

Did you find anything around the house, like a note or a phone number or any materials that were strange?"

"No. Mrs. Cunningham said someone was here while I was out, but that happened all the time. Tom was a very popular man with people coming here on automobile business, community business, and school business. Visits in the afternoon were rare because he's often not at home. Visitors usually knew Tom's schedule and came in the evenings and on weekends. Anyway, I didn't see anything that might have been left by a visitor or anything in Tom's papers that may have indicated who was here. I wasn't looking with an eye toward someone being here to kill Tom. I think it's out of the question. But, if there was anyone who wanted Tom dead, it would be Les Romanski. Tom told me that he fired Les, and apparently Les vowed to get revenge. I simply don't buy the teacher theory. Education folk get mad, like we all do from time to time, but they wouldn't kill anyone. For what it's worth, that's my theory," Marian said.

"Thanks for your help. I know it's not easy to talk about this."

"No, it isn't, but I'm getting along. Thanks for trying to settle this. Everyone talks in this small town, and anything you can do to put the peoples' minds at rest is appreciated."

The two parted, but not until Lou complemented Marian on the sugar cookies and the coffee. If it weren't for his jogging, he'd gain a few pounds just eating the muffins and cookies given to him during his visits.

～

Lou asked for a conference call with Bill Blakeley and his attorney.

"Thanks for giving me a few more minutes, Mr. Blakeley. I'll get right to the point. Did you go over to the Franklin house the afternoon he died?"

"No."

"Did you call him that afternoon?"

"No."

Lou didn't quite know how to take these one word answers to his questions. The last time they talked Bill had offered long answers.

"Did your dad call or see him that day?"

"No."

"That's all I need to know, Mr. Blakeley. I understand you will probably get your job back."

"The family and I will be on our way. We can't go into town without people talking and pointing. It's not a way to live. We'll be pulling up stakes and heading elsewhere as soon as I can get a contract signed."

"Where do you hope to go?" Lou asked.

"Charlevoix."

"That's a wonderful town. Good luck to you. We'd appreciate it if you would keep Chief Fitzpatrick informed about your whereabouts. You're not going to be charged with anything. In the future, we may need to ask a question or two."

"I'll do that," Bill agreed.

༚

Lou proposed to Fitz and Harold that they go somewhere for lunch to talk. Fitz suggested that they pick up a pizza at the Pizza Hut on the edge of town and go to his house. They wouldn't be disturbed, and could talk without concern for anyone listening or overhearing them.

With a cheese and pepperoni pizza on the table, the three men sat at the kitchen table as Lou prepared to share his evaluation of two days of interviews and serious thinking. "Well men, this is what I think as of today. Realize that Maggie and I still have much work to do, so I'm not one hundred percent sure of my theory, but for what it is worth, Thomas Franklin was murdered. The visitor who stopped in around three o'clock was involved. That visitor is either Bill Blakeley, Bill's father, or Les Romanski. The visitor got Tom Franklin to take an overdose of digitalis, or some other drug claiming to be digitalis, and that's what put him away. The only pieces that need cleaning up now are who made the call from the public phone at the library, and was Les Romanski, or someone acting on his behalf, in town. I also sense that it could be Bill Blakeley's father. We don't know what happened during the couple of hours that he was away from his son's house, except for a stop at Zellars and a visit with someone there.

Just then the phone rang and Fitz answered, "Morgan Fitzpatrick."

"Chief, Olaf Johnson called. Says he's got some information that might help you," said one of Fitz's officers.

"Ask him to come over to my house, if he can."

"I'll call and tell him. If he can make it, I won't call you back."

Fitz told Lou and Harold about the call. No call came within the next five minutes, so Fitz felt certain that Olaf would appear any second. Olaf's car pulled in the drive and Fitz was at the door to let him in. After greetings and handshakes, Lou said, "Well, what do you have for us?"

"The afternoon that Tom Franklin died, I was having some coffee at Zellars and a stranger came in and asked if he could join me. I said of course, and we probably spent the better part of an hour talking about this and that. I don't remember his name, but I'm pretty sure he is the father of that special education teacher that was laid off awhile ago."

"Did he say anything about Tom Franklin?" Harold asked.

"No, he didn't say anything about him that I recall, but he did ask about the layoffs and about who was responsible. I said that Tom Franklin had a part to play as people respected his position in the community."

"Did he say what he was going to do when he finished talking to you?"

"No, just that he had some things to do. He did ask me where the closest public phone was, and I told him that I was sure Jocelyn would let him use the phone in the restaurant. He said he didn't want to impose and would find one around somewhere."

"Thanks for coming forward Mr. Johnson," Lou said. "We'll consider all the information we get."

Fitz walked Olaf to the door and he was on his way. "Not much there," Lou said. "But we may want to talk with him further at some point. You know, I've still got to keep Bill Blakeley, Jr. in the loop of possible suspects, even though he answered 'no' to critical questions. He said he neither talked nor visited with Tom Franklin that afternoon, and maybe he didn't, but it's very easy to lie when you're facing life in prison. So, to sum it up, I think Tom Franklin died by ingesting some drug that brought on the heart attack. I think it was given to him by either Les Romanski, or someone acting on his behalf, or by Bill Blakeley, Jr. or Sr."

"Your visit was very helpful," Harold said.

"Sure was," added Fitz. "Did you suspect Wixom?

"Yeah, for awhile he was number one on my list. His prison record and his anger about his son's program led me to think he did it. I called his neighbor after I talked with him, and I'm convinced that the two of them were working in Wixom's basement all afternoon."

"So, my friends, I'm ready to get home to Carol. While here, as you know, Maggie suggested looking into past layoffs. Once we get information about that we'll add it to this case. I'd like you, Harold, to check out this Romanski guy to see if he's involved. It's time to call it a day. The weather looks good for my drive downstate."

"Any advice for Mr. Presley when he calls? He's going to want a story. He knows you have been up here and will probably expect a headline from me," Fitz said.

"Oh, just tell him the mafia is involved and they will shorten the life of any editor that even implies that Thomas Franklin was murdered. That ought to challenge his editorial policies," Lou said with a smile.

"Seriously now. Any advice?"

"Tell him the truth, I guess. Say that a preliminary investigation does not produce enough evidence to draw any conclusions or to make any arrests on suspicion of murder. However, further questions need to be asked, and additional information needs to be gathered. Feel free to give him my phone number in Grand Haven, and I'll talk to him. I'll surely speak highly of your work."

"Thanks," Fitz said humbly.

Instead of waiting until morning, Lou decided to head on home. He'd arrive before bedtime. Lou pulled out of town and headed for the Mackinac Bridge and points further south. He felt good about what he was able to learn. It was certainly a challenge but he felt that he and Maggie were beginning a solid border around a big jigsaw puzzle. There were many pieces scattered all over the table, but he knew that slowly but surely they'd put the whole thing together. The truth would be out there for everyone to see soon enough. Driving

101

along Lou thought about what he would soon be learning from Maggie regarding the Battle Creek accident. Maggie would want to ask questions in Stockbridge, Mason, and Mount Pleasant. Lou was having another one of those intuitive hunches. He felt sure that a pattern was emerging and soon it would bring Bill Blakeley, Jr. up as the prime image of the puzzle.

Friday, October 23,
Grand Haven, Michigan

After a long jog along the beach and a relaxing breakfast with Carol, Lou met with Maggie.

It was time to turn their attention to Battle Creek and the death of Mr. Jack Olsen, the high school principal. "I decided to get information from three sources: the newspaper, the current superintendent, and the police reports. The easiest was the *Battle Creek Enquirer*," Maggie said. "I called the library and asked for a photocopy of the newspaper for November 30, 1992. I also requested that they search a few future editions for any follow up articles. I called the current superintendent in Battle Creek; and, after explaining my need to obtain information, requested a copy of Bill Blakeley's layoff notice and all other pertinent information in his file. Finally, I called the Battle Creek Police and the Department of Natural Resources to obtain reports on the deer hunting accident.

"While you were in Newberry the material arrived," Maggie continued. "My review of the newspaper accounts and the police report revealed that no one was ever charged with a crime in the hunting accident. Jack was with a hunting party that included several friends. No one saw him get shot, but friends went looking for him when he didn't return to camp at an agreed upon time. No one called in to report the accident.

"School records showed that Mr. Blakeley was laid off three days before the accident. There was a letter in the file from Mr. Olsen that indicated that Bill Blakeley did not take the news well. I paid special attention to the sentence, "I was concerned for my safety and that of staff in our high school because of Mr. Blakeley's verbal threats and his anger. It's normal to be upset when getting news of a layoff, but Mr. Blakeley's behavior was not normal. In all of my years in dealing with staff on a number of personnel issues, I have never encountered this type of behavior from a professional educator."

Maggie and Lou decided not to talk to anyone in Battle Creek. Their major concerns were addressed by Maggie's investigation. There was proof of the death of another school official in the school system that also laid off Bill Blakeley. And, the death was around the time of the layoff. All Lou and Maggie had to do now was to accept this as a coincidence, or verify it as a connection. They decided to look back at the previous school district where Blakeley was laid off to see if the pattern continued. They would resume the investigation on Monday, with a look into Bill's past in Stockbridge.

⤳

The *Newberry News* came out as expected on Friday, and the Franklin matter didn't even make the front page. An insert on page four simply said that Chief Fitzpatrick, with assistance from Harold Holcomb, and a respected detective from Grand Haven, had been looking into the possible foul play in the death of Tom Franklin. The article stated that no report from Chief Fitzpatrick had been issued, and none was expected in the near future. It appeared that Newberry could get back to business as usual.

Monday, October 26,
Stockbridge and Newberry, Michigan

Stockbridge, Michigan is a small rural town in the southern part of Ingham County. The locals there have their choice of driving to Lansing, Jackson, or Ann Arbor to find shopping malls or cultural activities beyond garage sales, estate auctions, school band and orchestra concerts, or school plays. People chose this rural community because they wanted to live there. The Stockbridge school system had trouble passing a millage, and the teachers there were among the lowest paid in the county. Lou estimated that the failing to pass a millage was probably why Bill Blakeley was laid off in 1990.

Maggie McMillan arrived at the school administration office located in the middle school. She parked her van in the parking spot reserved for people with disabilities. She maneuvered herself onto the lift and was slowly lowered to the pavement. The efficient hydraulic system returned the lift into the van, and all Maggie needed to do was close the door. She used her hand controls to guide her motorized chair into the school.

Once inside, she introduced herself and then asked the secretary for the personnel records on Bill Blakeley. There was hesitation by the secretary and superintendent to provide this confidential information. Maggie produced a letter from Chief Fitzpatrick indicating that she was acting on behalf of the Newberry Police Department and investigating a possible homicide. The letter was sufficient to have records opened to Maggie. Her main purpose in looking at the records was to get the date of the layoff notice.

The layoff letter was dated May 27, 1990. Attached to the letter was another letter written to Superintendent Wiggins from Bill Blakeley. The letter was full of anger and spoke of revenge. Attached to these letters was a note stating that the superintendent had called the Chief of Police in Stockbridge, who alerted the Ingham County Sheriff to Bill's threatening letter. The note also contained information provided by both law enforcement agencies stating that each would routinely keep an eye on Blakeley, and the superintendent was to call whenever he was going from school to home or vice versa, or when his travel was to any place other than these two destinations. The superintendent's wife and children had been asked to visit her parents home in Howell for a few days while the situation was given some time to cool off.

Maggie asked the secretary if the superintendent of 1990 was the superintendent today. "No," she responded. " Mr. Wiggins left last year and is now a superintendent in Missouri, but I can't remember the city. I think it is near St. Louis, but I could be wrong. I just began working here a couple of months ago."

"Would you know anyone in the system now who was working here in 1990?"

"The person who comes to mind is Wanita Fuller. She's been a principal at the elementary school since the beginning of time. Oh my, please don't tell her I said that. She'd kill me! I mean, she was my principal when I was in elementary school, and that was at least a century ago. I don't think we studied the Civil War 'cause it hadn't happened yet!" the secretary chuckled.

"She's still the elementary principal?"

"Yup. Never misses a day. Healthy as a horse. She loves kids and wouldn't think of doing anything else. She is now seeing her third generation of kids come through her school. She often says to kids, 'I remember your grandfather when he went to school here.' Can you imagine that?"

"That's remarkable. Could I visit with her?"

"Oh sure. I'll call and tell her secretary that you're on your way over. The elementary school is one block west. You can't miss it. Her office is right inside the front door. Tell her Priscilla says 'Hi.'"

"Thanks for helping me, Priscilla."

Maggie moved her wheelchair easily down the block thanks to solid sidewalks and entered the Stockbridge Elementary School. She went right to the office as the sign on the door directed visitors to do so. The woman walking up to her was Mrs. Fuller. "You must be Mrs. McMillan?" Wanita said.

"Yes. Priscilla said to say 'hi'. She was helpful in guiding me to you."

"What brings you to the 'Bridge'?" Wanita asked.

"I'm helping the police in Newberry investigate the possible murder of a prominent citizen there.

"You must be here to ask some questions about Bill Blakeley."

"As a matter of fact I am, but why would you conclude that?"

"Oh, it's a long story. I suppose you'll want to hear it. After all, it's why you're here. I knew someone would eventually come around asking some questions. I just didn't know when. Looks like the time is now." She looked knowingly at Maggie.

"Can you tell me about it now, or would another day be better?" Maggie asked realizing that Mrs. Fuller didn't look like she wanted to talk about it.

"I really would rather wait. But you must be thinking, 'I'll bet she doesn't buy green bananas,'" she said with a smile. "I'm getting up there in years and you probably want what I know as soon as possible."

Maggie wouldn't have passed a lie detector test if she said she wasn't anxious for her story, but she could tell this wasn't the right time.

"You see, I took my cat to be put to sleep this morning, and I just can't get old Snugs off my mind. She was my companion for fourteen years, and you just don't say 'goodbye' to a family friend without having it be on your mind for a few days. You know?"

"Sure, Mrs. Fuller, that's tough. I've had to do that and I understand your grieving. You're right, this isn't a good day for talking about anything other than trying to see the positive side of life and what's good. Tell you what. How about you and me going to The Milkshake? Isn't that the name of the dairy on the edge of town? I'll buy you an ice cream cone. I haven't bought an ice cream cone for a teacher in a long time," Maggie said.

"That might cheer me up."

"Good. There's nothing like a chocolate cone to make the day."

"Chocolate or strawberry. Either flavor is delicious," Mrs. Fuller said with a smile on her face. "Well, let's go to The Milkshake and I'll have a double scoop of strawberry. Since I've lived this long, what is a little fat and some cholesterol? You'll probably get some nonfat yogurt."

"No way. To celebrate meeting you I'm going to have a double scoop of Mackinac Island fudge ripple," Maggie said feeling the saliva glands kick into overdrive with the mention of anything chocolate.

Maggie and Wanita went to The Milkshake in Maggie's van and nothing more was said about her beloved cat, Snugs, or Bill Blakeley. It was an unseasonably warm October afternoon and they had a great time filling their faces with everyone's favorite treat.

Maggie took Wanita back to the elementary school. She expressed sympathy once again for Snugs. She knew the pain involved in taking a cat to the vet and leaving it there for an instant and painless death. She made plans with Wanita to return in the near future, to talk seriously about Bill Blakeley.

Wanita suggested they eat at the Sausage House, a well known German restaurant in town. The place often got attention and was talked about on radio station WJR in Detroit as a favorite German Restaurant of the late Fat Bob Taylor, a radio personality who had a beautiful singing voice and could be heard opening various sporting events in the Detroit area with his rendition of the "Star Spangled Banner". The two agreed to meet on November 6, and Maggie headed home.

A LESSON PLAN FOR MURDER

༯

The Newberry Board of Education was in session on Monday evening. The Board President, Bill Owen, read a proclamation naming the Newberry High School after Thomas Franklin. The school would be called Franklin High School. After the formal opening activities were complete, the first item on the agenda was the reinstatement of the special education program.

Superintendent Williamson spoke, "Mr. President and members of the board, I'm recommending that the special education program be reinstated in Newberry. I have discussed this with the district's legal counsel and with our special education coordinator. I believe that my advice to you earlier was not in the best interest of our students with disabilities. While it is true that we are in a financial crisis, like most Michigan school districts, I do think it is best that we maintain the special education program, and further, I recommend that the school district ask a task force to study our special education options and needs and report back to this board in six months."

"I move to accept Mr. Williamson's recommendation," said board member MacMillan.

"Second," offered Beverly Marsh.

"Discussion?"

"I'm in favor of doing what's right for our kids with disabilities and I expect to vote in favor of the motion, but since we made this decision for fiscal reasons, what programs will go, now that we are about to reinstate the special class?" the newest member of the board, Willis Monahan asked.

Superintendent Williamson responded, "That's a fine question, and I have given it some thought. I think we will have to take a look at our funds for field trips and perhaps our athletic budget will need to be stressed, but I expect that we can find the dollars."

Board President Owen then said to the people in the audience, "Is there anyone present who would like to comment before a vote is taken?"

Mr. Wixom rose and came to the board table. He was recognized and spoke, "On behalf of the Parents for Justice, I'm here to speak in favor of the motion and to express our appreciation for the superintendent's recommendation to reinstate the program for our children. We expect that all of you understand that we had no choice other than to use our rights to maintain our program. We believe it is critical to the future of our children. We stand ready to assist this board, the administration, teachers, and other parents in Newberry to work toward a fiscally sound school system. We'll work in any capacity on millage campaigns, and we'll look forward to participating on the task force. I would also like to add that if a teacher vacancy occurs in our children's program, we'd like to participate in the selection process. Thank you again for caring about our children and for reinstating the program."

"Question."

"All in favor say, 'I'." All voiced a positive "I".

"All opposed, say 'nay'. There was silence.

"Motion passed."

Mr. Wixom and the parents got up and went out of the board room. They hugged one another, and felt very good about what they had been able to accomplish.

Still there was a lot of pain and anger in the few days that followed the turn around decision by the Newberry Board of Education. Bill Blakeley, Trudy, Bryan and Heather were hoping that they would soon be on their way to finding a community where some roots could be sunk once and for all.

Sunday November 1, Newberry, Michigan

Bill Blakeley was watching *America's Funniest Home Videos*, when the phone rang. Trudy answered it. "This is the superintendent of schools in Charlevoix. Is Mr. Bill Blakeley there?"

"Yes. Just a minute." Trudy covered the mouth piece of the phone and said, "Bill, this is the superintendent in Charlevoix. He wants to talk to you."

"Hello. This is Bill Blakeley."

"Good evening, Bill, my name is Al Forrest calling from Charlevoix. First of all, I apologize for bothering you at home on a Sunday evening, but I felt that I would be able to reach you easily at this time."

"Oh, no problem, Dr. Forrest. Thanks for calling."

"We have reviewed the applications for the opening at the juvenile detention facility, and we are very interested in talking with you.

"That's wonderful. Thank you."

"Would you be able to come to Charlevoix within the week for an interview and to see our community?"

"Yes. I could do that. When would you like to see me?"

"Ideally, we would like to have our interviews next Friday. We are planning to interview three candidates, but I'll tell you that we're very impressed with your application and credentials.

"Well, thank you."

"I must make this clear. This is not an offer but only an opportunity to be interviewed for this position."

"I understand. I'm honored to be one of your candidates, Dr. Forrest."

"I will send you a letter in the morning confirming our plans to see you next Friday afternoon at 1:00 p.m. We'll send you information about our community, and we'll pay you for your mileage and a night's lodging here in Charlevoix."

"Thank you."

"You're welcome. Thank you for being interested in Charlevoix. Once again, I apologize for calling you on a Sunday evening."

"Anybody calling with good news is welcome to call at any time of any day," Bill said, feeling very good about being wanted once again.

Trudy and the children were waiting for him to come into the family room with some news. In the background the host of the show was asking the studio audience to vote for one of three home videos. Bill came into the room with a smile on his face. "I think they want me in Charlevoix. I have an interview next Friday." Trudy gave Bill a warm and tight hug. "That's great, Bill." Trudy was ready to get out of town and get on with a new life. Bryan and Heather were unemotional, but both knew that they would soon be leaving for a new school, new neighborhood, new friends, new teachers, and new coaches. They were less than honest when they said they were happy for their father.

As was customary, Bill called his father to report his good news, "Hi Dad, got some good news this time."

"What's that, Billy?"

"Got a call from the superintendent in Charlevoix, and I'm one of three candidates they want to interview. I'm going to have an interview next Friday."

"Good for you. I'm proud of you. Do Trudy and the kids feel good about it?"

"Yeah. Trudy is happy about it. The kids are apprehensive, and I understand that. They've been carted around. It's tough making new friends and getting adjusted to new schools, teachers, and coaches. They'll be OK."

"Well, good news, son. Whatever happened to your Newberry class?"

"The board reversed their decision and reinstated the class. I've got my old job back, but we've got to be on our way. Hardly a day goes by in school or in town where a negative comment isn't made to me, Trudy, or one of the kids. This isn't a way to live."

"So your union came through for ya, huh?"

"No, they didn't do a thing for me. The parents of the kids in my class did it all."

"I don't understand that weak union! Just a bunch of softies. No back bone. My union was tough, and when they went to bat for me, management stood up and listened."

"Yeah, Dad. Oh well, I just called to give you our good news. Maybe I won't get the job, but I think I will. Dr. Forrest sounded like it was mine for the asking unless I do a lousy job in the interview, and I won't."

"Thanks for calling. I'll be thinking of you next Friday. Give me a call when you get back. I'll be curious to know if you get an offer."

"Will do. You doing OK, Dad?"

"Oh yeah. Doin' fine."

The father and son talked a bit more about the weather and the kids and then brought the conversation to a close. It was comforting to Bill to know that he had a parent who cared what happened in his life. His mother was always involved and wanted to know what was happening to Bill. Now that she was gone, Bill felt close to his dad, and felt some comfort in knowing that he cared about the joys and sorrows of the Bill Blakeley, Jr. family.

Monday, November 2,
Grand Haven, Michigan

About a week went by. Louis Searing was home when his wife, Carol, summoned him to take a phone call from Harold Holcomb.

"Hi Harold. How ya doin'?"

"Doin' good, Lou."

"What's on your mind?"

"Just wanted to brief you on a little development up here."

"Good, I've got some information for you and Fitz, too. You go first."

"We believe that Les Romanski was in town on Saturday, October 10. Our source said he was visiting an acquaintance, a friend he got to know when he was at Franklin's Garage. This friend was seen in the library Saturday afternoon around three o'clock. He drives a mid-size Chevrolet and he's about six foot three inches tall."

"Well, that's interesting. What does this friend say about his whereabouts on Saturday afternoon?" Lou asked.

"We can't find the friend. I mean, he lives here in town, but he's disappeared and nobody knows where he went. We contacted the place where Romanski works in Escanaba and we're told he's not there."

"Did you or Fitz ask Mrs. Cunningham if this friend could be the visitor?"

"No, we haven't done that yet. We're guessing that when we do talk to her she won't know the friend, and the car won't help since photos didn't help when you met with her."

"You're probably right. You know, if you do catch up with this friend of Romanski, you may have him pull up in his car, park, and walk up to the door of the Franklin home. Then ask Mrs. Cunningham to watch from her window and see what reaction you get. In fact, if Blakeley is still in town, you may wish to do the same with him and Wixom, too, just for comparison. I probably should have thought of this when I was there, but I didn't."

"I might do that. What have you got for us?"

"I don't have any big break, or I would've called. You should know that in Battle Creek and in Stockbridge we've found a pattern related to Blakeley's angry reactions. As you know, the Battle Creek Central High School Principal was shot while deer hunting a couple of days after Blakeley's layoff. Maggie will soon be talking with a principal in Stockbridge who knew Blakeley when he taught there. I'm expecting to learn quite a bit when she returns. I think we're beyond coincidence with this case and investigation will show that someone in the Stockbridge school system also died around the time of the layoff there. If I had a lot of cash, I'd bet I'll find the same thing in Mason and in Mt. Pleasant. I can't wait to look into this at the other schools, no matter how repulsive. One or two more school district deaths, and Mr. Blakeley is going to be solidly at the top of the suspect list. We're close to a full bingo card and taking home the Kupie Doll."

"It's all pretty convincing. However, I've seen judges throw cases out for nothing but circumstantial evidence. But, stranger things have happened. You can't send a guy up for murder, or should I say, five murders, because some man or woman died near the time he was laid off," Harold said.

"Yeah, I know. Thanks for checking my enthusiasm."

"Well, my friend, keep up the good work. We'll let you know if we learn anything new, and you do the same."

"Will do. Regards to Fitz."

"Talk to you soon." There was a new twist to the drama in Newberry. Lou mused, if Bill Blakeley didn't murder Thomas Franklin, it would pretty much dampen his theory of a serial killer being laid off. On the other hand, if Bill Blakeley was the murderer, the string could go back a few years. It looked possible to Lou that he and Maggie would uncover the ticket for closing more than one strange death around Michigan cities during the past decade.

さう

Bill was unaware that he was the topic of more than one conversation that Al Forrest had on Monday morning while contacting a variety of people who knew the three candidates he planned to interview on Friday. It was Al's policy to always call the superintendent of the district for references on a currently employed candidate. Not only did he want to talk about the person, but he wanted to personally tell the superintendent that one of his or her staff was being recruited. That's what he would like to happen when other districts are interested in a Charlevoix teacher. Al dialed the number for Jake Williamson.

"Superintendent's Office."

"Is Mr. Williamson there please? This is Al Forrest, Superintendent of Charlevoix Schools calling."

"Just a moment please, Dr. Forrest."

Within ten seconds Jake was on the line, "Hi, Al. Sorry for the short delay. How are you, my friend?"

"I'm doing OK. Facing all the same problems you are, I'm sure. We're all in the same ball game."

"Boy you got that right. Oh well, it puts bread on our table and brings meaning to our lives. I guess that's one way to look at it, right?"

"Right. Say. My reason for calling is to ask about one of your special education teachers, Bill Blakeley."

"He's interested in coming to Charlevoix?

"Yes, he's applied for a teaching position at our juvenile detention facility, and we're impressed by his credentials and experience."

"We were impressed, too, and I don't regret hiring him. He has done a good job, and has a nice family. His wife is an excellent teacher, and the kids are good kids who are doing well in school."

"Sounds like a good catch."

"Yes and no. Gotta be honest with you just as I would hope you would be with me. The man is scary when he gets angry. Never had any abuse with kids or staff, but we had a situation where his anger got out of control. If you don't plan on making him mad, you've got a great guy and teacher."

"Would you recommend I not hire him?"

"Oh no, not at all. You use your good judgment. We had to layoff three teachers, and he was one of them. That's where we witnessed his anger. He was a bit out of control when he received the news. A couple days after the layoff, a member of our school board, Thomas Franklin, died. Most concur that it was a heart attack, but some say that he was murdered. Some even believe that Bill Blakeley is involved."

"Well, we're not about to hire a man accused of murdering a school board member. You think I'm nuts? That's why I place these calls and why we help each other to steer clear of crazy people."

"Hold on, Al. I'm leveling with you. I'm telling you everything I know, but I'm also going to tell you that he's a good man. He takes his teaching very seriously. The parents of his students hold him in high regard. He has no skeletons in the closet, no drugs, alcohol problems, no abuse, or sexual harassment claims. I'm sorry he wants to leave us. Whoever gets Bill Blakeley will have a good teacher," Jake said, giving quite an endorsement to the man he thought might be involved in the murder of Tom Franklin.

"His resume shows that he's been in a lot of school districts in his twenty years of teaching. Was that a concern when you hired him?" Al asked.

"To be honest, I didn't pay much attention to that. We needed a teacher for difficult to manage kids with emotional problems. He was credentialed. He was big and strong. His wife was also a teacher, and we needed someone with her background and experience. Not only that, but their son is great in sports. This family was a real catch for Newberry. I could have cared less if he had been in 19 school districts in 19 years."

"Well, we're in a similar bind. We need a teacher for some tough kids, and he stands out in the list of candidates."

"Al, I know this. Bill has no criminal record. He's never even been caught speeding. If you hire him, he'll do a good job for you."

"Well, we'll look at the three candidates and draw our own conclusions. Thanks for your candid comments. I'd do the same for you."

"Thanks. Am I going to see you at the superintendents' conference next month in Traverse City?" Jake asked.

"I'm planning on it."

"I think I'm going to run for president this year. Can I count on you for support?" Jake sounded like a politician.

"Absolutely, and I'll talk you up among some of my friends in this area."

"I appreciate it. Good talking with you.

"Same here. Thanks again, Jake."

The two leaders hung up their respective phones. Jake was feeling a slight bit guilty for feeling relief that Bill was on his way out of town. Bill was a potential trouble maker because of the anger. The anger scared him and was a characteristic he didn't need in a staff person, even if his son was certain to take Franklin High School to the football championship in the Upper Peninsula next year.

Al was feeling a bit let down. He had hoped that Bill Blakeley would come highly recommended. In one sense he was, but being mentioned as a possible suspect in the murder of a school board member didn't sit well with the superintendent of any school district, especially his.

With Lou and Maggie, not much happened during the rest of the week. There were no leads, no phone calls. In fact, Lou and Maggie were concerned that the lull meant they wouldn't come upon the clue that would open up the case.

Friday, November 6, Stockbridge, Michigan

Maggie McMillan was looking forward to her luncheon with Mrs. Fuller at the Sausage House Restaurant in Stockbridge. She was anxious to learn more about Bill Blakeley's experience in the town and especially the reason Mrs. Fuller brought up his name so quickly when she learned why Maggie was in town a week ago.

Maggie met Mrs. Fuller at the restaurant as planned. Wanita saw Maggie as a friend immediately. She admired her independence despite a disability. The women settled into the comfortable atmosphere of the unique restaurant. Maggie knew that she would have to order something German in this place. If she didn't, it would be like going to the Upper Peninsula and not having a pastie. They both took a few minutes to look over the menu. A young waitress approached and smiled warmly as she offered the ladies service.

"Hi there, Gretchen." Mrs. Fuller greeted.

"Hello, Mrs. Fuller. How are you today?"

"Oh, I'm still kicking. How are you doing?"

"Pretty good. I'm working to save some money to go to Michigan State."

"Wonderful. I always thought you would graduate from college someday. What's got your interest?

"I seem to go from one area to another. At the moment, I'd like to get admitted to the College of Veterinary Medicine. Growing up on the farm gave me a real love for animals. I've always enjoyed taking care of them."

"Whatever you decide to pursue, you'll do just fine."

"Thank you. Have you decided what you'd like?" Gretchen asked.

"What do you recommend?" Maggie asked.

"Bratwurst and German Potato Salad with German Chocolate Cake is popular," Gretchen said smiling enthusiastically.

"Sounds good to me."

"I'll have the same," Mrs. Fuller said. Gretchen walked away to turn in the order.

"Gretchen was one of my favorites. She's very intelligent, has a good head on her shoulders, fine parents, and a strong work ethic. She was voted most likely to succeed when she was a senior, and she seems to be fulfilling that prophecy."

"She seems like a nice young lady," offered Maggie. "Well, I've been patient and curious for a whole week. I'm anxious to learn what you have to share about Mr. Blakeley."

"Well, Mrs. McMillan. I've been thinking about what to share and how to share it. I want to help you, and I will, but, I'd be less than honest if I didn't say that I think I am taking a risk in telling you what I know. I've lived a good many years, many more years that most of my friends, and I'm beginning to feel guilty for hanging on so long. I still like life and I don't want to jeopardize a day of it by talking about Bill Blakeley." Mrs. Fuller was looking very serious.

"Well, I don't want you to share anything that makes you uncomfortable. I hope you trust that I need your information to solve these murders, if they were, in fact, murders."

"I tend to trust a person who buys me an ice cream cone and who seems so caring, but telling you about Bill Blakeley may bring him back to our community with an evil vengeance."

"Let me assure you that I'll do whatever it takes to ensure the safety of this community. Would you rather talk to my partner Mr. Searing, or Lieutenant Shanks of the State Police?"

"No, Maggie. I trust you. I've lived long enough to know when I can trust someone, but I wanted you to know that I did consider the possibility that talking to you might backfire on the community of Stockbridge."

"Please trust me. What do you mean, bring evil back to Stockbridge?" Maggie asked quizzically.

Just as Mrs. Fuller was about to launch into her explanation, Gretchen approached the table with their German Potato Salad and some fresh hot coffee.

When Gretchen was finished and had moved away from the table, Wanita said, "We tried for a millage in 1990. We seem to have a lot of trouble getting a millage passed in this district. We told our citizens that not passing the millage would result in some layoffs. We were upfront about specific layoffs in special education and that the sports program could be cut. The administration thought that would do the trick. I mean, who would not vote for services for children with disabilities, and who in this neck of the woods would tolerate a cut in sports?"

"Sounds like a couple of threats that could pass a millage."

"We sure thought so. Anyway the millage failed and failed by a big margin. Almost two to one."

"Wow. That's quite a message."

"You betcha, and we got the message. We had a meeting of the board of education, and in order to stay in budget and not go into debt we had to layoff the least senior special education teacher, who was Bill Blakeley, and the newest gym teacher and coach. The superintendent at the time was Wilbur Wiggins."

"Wilbur Wiggins?" asked Maggie with a smile. "Don't you often wonder about parents and what goes through their minds when they name their children. But, who am I to judge, maybe Wilbur was named after a kind old uncle who made some great and glorious contribution to the family name. I'll bet he learned to fight as a kid, which probably prepared him well to be a superintendent."

"I should have made a book of all the unique names of kids in my school during my career as a teacher and a principal. I remember Sugar Caine. How about Angel InHeeven? One of my favorites was Luke Warm," said Wanita with a smile.

"Oh, come on now. You're not serious?"

"Oh, yes I am. I've got copies of birth certificates to prove it."

"Anyway, Wilbur Wiggins was superintendent."

"That's right. He called Bill Blakeley into his office to give him the bad news, and Bill lit into him in a rage of anger. I was in the room at the time because I was an assistant to the superintendent. He made verbal threats on Wilbur's life and became a crazed man. I really was fearful for not only Wilbur's life, but mine, and anyone in town for that matter. We had to call the police chief and the county sheriff. Mr. Wiggins' wife and kids went to Howell to stay at her parents because we were so afraid that he would do something terrible and would kill all of us. I mean, we were very scared. It bothers me terribly to talk about it, even today."

Gretchen brought their bratwurst, and Maggie suggested that they stop talking about Mr. Blakeley and talk about something pleasant as they enjoyed their meal. They talked about children and grandchildren. They talked about their careers and their plans for the future. Most of all they thoroughly enjoyed their lunch at the Sausage House Restaurant. Gretchen kept the coffee hot and the water glasses full. They were treated like royalty. Maggie knew that when she paid the bill she would leave Gretchen a ten dollar tip. She felt that any young adult working to go to college to help animals deserved a break. It would probably make her day.

Maggie could tell that maybe it would be better to continue the discussion outside of the restaurant, so she suggested they go back to Mrs. Fuller's office. Wanita thought that would be a good idea. After saying goodbye to Gretchen and thanking her and the chef for a delicious meal, they drove separately to the elementary school and settled into Wanita's office. She closed the door after asking her secretary not to disturb them.

"So, where were we?" Wanita asked.

"Wilbur told Bill about the layoff, and he went into a threatening rage that caused Wilbur to call the police and sheriff, and to send his family to Howell for a few days," reminded Maggie.

"Oh yes. Well, thankfully, nothing happened except that Wilbur and I didn't sleep for almost 48 hours. I recall a phone call from Mr. Wiggins informing me that Mrs. Young had just died. Mrs. Young was the business manager for the school district. She had not been ill. Everyone knew that she was a diabetic, but she had it under control and was very conscientious about taking her insulin and doing whatever was necessary to remain in the best of health."

"Did the autopsy indicate how she died?"

"Yes, the autopsy indicated death was the result of insulin shock, and the doctors think she must have taken too much insulin. Too much of the stuff can produce serious complications, even death," explained Wanita.

"I take it you believe Bill Blakeley is involved?"

"Most of us do, yes. He was treating the layoff like somebody had to pay. A person doesn't act like a raging lunatic and not have it result in something. He was never charged or even identified as a suspect, but I know he did it and no one will ever convince me otherwise. I try to be a good Baptist and not judge my neighbor, but I'll die believing that Bill Blakeley caused that death."

"How could he have caused death by insulin shock?"

"I know I'd never see my suspicions in a police report. Murder is very rare in Stockbridge. Nobody would step forward to press charges and especially not against Bill Blakeley, not after the outrage he expressed when he was laid off. Murder was never officially a question because diabetic shock seemed natural."

"I understand, but how would Bill Blakeley have caused a death by insulin shock?"

"Mrs. Young had to have an injection daily and at around five in the afternoon. She lived alone and knew Bill. I mean, in a small town, if you live here for a year or more, everyone knows everyone. I don't really know how it happened. I just know that, in my opinion, Bill Blakeley did it."

"Well, what eventually happened with the case?"

"There was no case. As I said, there was no suspicion of foul play. The woman died of insulin shock. It happens all over the country with some degree of regularity. The doctor didn't suspect foul play. Her son, who lives in Idaho and is her only living relative, had no reason to question that insulin shock was unnatural as her cause of death, so he didn't raise any questions."

"But, you think she was murdered?"

"Clear as a bell. Here was a woman who took very good care of herself. She was conscientious about her health. She was in excellent health for a diabetic, yet she died of insulin shock? Come on."

"Well, maybe she didn't know that a larger dose would kill her and she felt she needed more."

"A slight possibility, but all diabetics are given very precise instructions on administering this stuff, and the side effects for not following the directions exactly. Not only do I think Blakeley did it, but I have a theory on how he did it."

"What's that?"

"He knew when she took her insulin. He waited for the right time and then got into her home when she wasn't there and switched the insulin bottles. The insulin bottle he brought in was either poisoned or was a much larger dose. She came home, injected the insulin, went into shock and died."

"He knew her schedule for coming and going and for taking her medicine?" asked Maggie quizzically.

"Piece of cake. She worked at the administration offices and always worked till four-thirty or so and sometimes later. She lived alone in an apartment building. All you had to do was ask her about diabetes and she would answer any question about it including when she administered her insulin and how. She seemed to want people to know about diabetes and how it is treated and to assure people that she was getting along alright."

"Where did she live?"

"In the Stockbridge Apartments."

"Where are they?"

"They're located at the south part of town. Mr. Santimore built them and he rents them out to people. He's been renting for about twenty years."

"Is he still there?"

"Sure."

"Do you know him?"

"There isn't a person who lives in this town that I don't know."

"Can I have a talk with him?"

"I'll give him a call and see if he can see us," Wanita said as she reached for the phone.

Wanita called Greg Santimore and said that she and a friend would like a few minutes of his time. He was watching *All My Children*, a soap opera that hooked him a couple of years ago when he had a bad case of the flu. He encouraged the women to come over. In a few minutes Mr. Santimore met Maggie and Wanita. After introductions, Maggie began, "Mr. Santimore I'm assisting in the investigation of a possible homicide up in the U.P. There may be a connection here in Stockbridge. Can I ask a few questions?."

"I don't know how I can help, but ask me anything you wish."

"Do you remember when Mrs. Young died of insulin shock?"

"I'll never forget it. She died right here in one of my apartments."

"Please try to go back to that day in your mind. Can you remember anything?"

"Yeah. I was here at the complex all day. I was working outside doing some painting and yard work."

"Did anyone call or visit?"

"Not that I recall. Well, yeah. Some guy asked if I could let him into Mrs. Young's apartment. He had a uniform on and said that Mrs. Young had asked him to deliver something. He asked me for the key and I let him in."

"You didn't think that strange?"

"Naw, happens all the time. Small town. A lot of my tenants don't have families, and they work all day. They see me as kind of a fatherly type, or at least the young ones do. I'll let delivery people in, and I accept UPS stuff for them."

"Can you remember anything about the man? Did he have any characteristic that sticks in your mind?"

"He was kinda tall. I don't mean real tall or anything, but as opposed to short, he was tall. He wasn't young, but he wasn't old."

"Was it Bill Blakeley?"

"I didn't know Bill Blakeley, but if he was under thirty years old, it wasn't him."

"At that time, he would have been in his late thirties."

"It could have been him. I couldn't be sure. It all happened so fast, and I didn't pay much attention. I'm confused. Maybe the guy was younger. I don't know," Greg said, acting a bit frustrated at not being able to help.

"You're helpful, Greg. Do you remember what happened next?"

"I let him in, and I told him to just close the door when he was finished. The doors lock when they're closed."

"How long was he in there?"

"I don't recall, but it was probably less than five minutes. I saw him drive away. In fact, I think he waved at me on his way to the vehicle."

"Do you recall the vehicle?"

"Nope."

"Was it a truck, car, van, jeep?"

"No idea. It's a miracle I even remember the guy or that someone came to her apartment."

The three of them talked for a few minutes longer, but nothing surfaced that would help Maggie. A pattern was emerging. In Newberry, and in Stockbridge, the victim was visited by someone within an hour or two of death. But that wasn't the case in Battle Creek, at least Maggie didn't think anyone saw Jack Olsen take a shell from a deer rifle. Maggie thanked Greg for his help, and then she and Wanita drove away.

Back at the elementary school, Margaret thanked Wanita for the afternoon. "You've been very helpful, Mrs. Fuller. I shall have a fond memory of our lunch at that German restaurant. If there is a pattern involving Bill Blakeley, Mr. Santimore's memory is critical and he's provided helpful information."

"I enjoyed the lunch too, Maggie, and I'm glad Greg could help. What happens next?"

"Now we're going on to Mason to see what we can find. I'll keep you posted as our investigation progresses. You've been very kind and helpful. Thanks," Maggie said with sincerity.

Monday, November 9, Mason, Michigan

Mason is another small town in mid-Michigan, the county seat for Ingham County. The town is located about twenty minutes south and a little east of Lansing. Lou made an appointment with Cynthia Hamm, the director of special education. Cynthia had been the director of special education for about twelve years and had been Mason's director for a couple of years before Bill Blakeley was laid off. In fact, she hired Bill Blakeley.

Lou arrived at the appointed hour, and walked into the Administrative Offices of the Mason Public Schools. The directory on the wall told him that the special education office was in room three, which the receptionist said was down the hall on the right. He entered the office and was greeted by Helen Phillips, Mrs. Hamm's secretary. "You must be Louis Searing?"

"Yes, I am. Right on time for my appointment I might add."

"Yes, you are, and she's ready to see you. Can I get you some coffee?"

"Thanks. Just plain coffee, no sugar or cream."

"Go right in and I'll bring it to you."

Lou did as directed, and met Mrs. Hamm inside. He recognized Cynthia from special education administrators meetings, but hadn't known her name or known that she was the director in Mason. "Mrs. Hamm, I'm Louis Searing."

"Hi. Pleased to meet you. I recognized your name from countless memos I received when you were the state director. I've heard you present at many of the Michigan Association of Administrators of Special Education meetings. Is Helen bringing you some coffee?"

"Yes, she is, thanks."

"How can I help you?" Cynthia asked.

"I'm investigating a possible homicide in the Upper Peninsula. One of the suspects is a special education teacher by the name of Bill Blakeley."

"You've got to be kidding!" she responded obviously quite shocked.

"I haven't enough information to suggest to the authorities that he be arrested and charged, but he's one of the people who may, and I repeat, may be involved. I am looking at employment records and talking with people who knew him in his previous districts to see if there's a pattern in his behavior that will either cause me to believe he may be involved or to convince me that I'm on a goose chase."

"Well, I may be the one to convince you that you're chasing a goose," Cynthia said. Just then Helen came in with the coffee.

"That's fine. All I need is information, or, as Jack Webb used to say on *Dragnet*, 'Just the facts ma'am, just the facts,'" Lou said with a smile.

Cynthia wasn't smiling. "I can't get over what you have said. Bill Blakeley is one of the last people on earth that I would ever think capable of hurting anyone. I'm absolutely certain that you're barking up the wrong tree."

"Well, I may be. Please help me and help him."

"I'll certainly do that. What makes you think he may be involved in killing someone?"

"I won't divulge all I know, but as our discussion evolves, you'll see why I at least suspect that Mr. Blakeley may be involved."

"What do you want from me?"

"First of all, I'd like to see a copy of his layoff notice from his records in 1985."

Cynthia called Helen into her office and asked that Bill Blakeley's personnel file be brought to her. In about five minutes, Helen walked in and handed the requested file to Mrs. Hamm. The file was opened and Cynthia found the letter. She read it and handed it to Lou.

Lou read the letter and noted the date of the layoff notice, April

1, 1985. "Since you were the director of special education at the time, do you recall how he took this?"

"Oh yes. I know all about it. He came to me because I think he was comfortable with me. He trusted me. I hired him when he got laid off from the Mount Pleasant district. He was very angry and upset. I was able to calm him down. I explained how the layoff came to be and that I was sorry, but that I would do everything I could to help him find another job."

"Did you?"

"Oh yes. While he sat in my office I called the special education directors and coordinators in Ingham County and encouraged each to consider him for a job. A couple of them seemed interested. So, when he left, he felt that in spite of his being laid off he would get a job that would allow him and his family to stay in the area."

"Where did the Blakeley family live at that time?"

"Dansville."

"Where is that exactly?"

"It's about seven to ten miles east of here. So, instead of coming to Mason to work, he would eventually go to Stockbridge to work."

"Put your memory hat on for me. Did anybody who was an employee of the Mason School District die within a couple weeks of his being laid off?" This was Lou's key question, and a "Yes" answer would reinforce a pattern.

"Oh my goodness. I have a pretty good memory, but who died ten years ago? That's asking too much for this fifty year old brain."

"I understand. Why the layoff of Bill?"

"We were ahead of the inclusion movement. Mrs. Anderson was a counselor in the high school. Her daughter had a child with a disability. They lived in Canada at the time. Her daughter's school district had a strong inclusion philosophy. In fact, it was getting national attention. Mrs. Anderson became a real disciple for inclusion and convinced the superintendent and me to give it a try. Well, we did and discovered it worked so well that we didn't need one of our special education teachers. Bill had the least seniority at that time, so we had no choice but to lay him off," explained Cynthia.

"When he was angry in your office, did he make any threats against anyone that you can recall?"

"He was a very angry man, and I'm thankful for my background as a clinical psychologist and my ability to counsel him. In answering your question, yes, he did threaten the superintendent and me."

"How did you respond to this?"

"I put my psychologist hat on and worked with him to deal with his anger. In fact, I arranged to talk with him on several occasions during the two or three weeks following the layoff."

"If you heard his threats and it took your professional counseling to help him, why are you so sure that he couldn't be a suspect in a homicide for another layoff situation where he might not have had someone with your skills to counsel him?"

"Because, I know he's not capable of carrying out his threats."

"I don't understand."

"He defends himself and his self worth by making threats and scaring people in order to have people think of him as a powerful person. You see, he can't perceive himself as being without a job and a means to care for his family. To overcome this, he has to show others in authority, or peers, that he is someone. The behavior isn't socially acceptable, which is why you are looking at him as a murder suspect, but he didn't do anyone any harm," Cynthia said with professional conviction in her words.

"This is very interesting, and I thank you for sharing it with me. I trust that you will be available to help Mr. Blakeley and me as my work continues?"

"I'll help you if I can. In fact, let me give you my home phone number in case you want to talk some evening. Call anytime before ten. I'm a very early riser. Ben Franklin and I believe in the phrase, 'Early to bed, early to rise, makes a person healthy, wealthy and wise.' I'll claim 'healthy' as I'm certainly neither wealthy nor wise," said Cynthia beginning to lighten up a bit.

"Thanks for your thoughts today, I'll be back." With that, Lou felt satisfied with his first contact in Mason. He had the basic information he needed, the layoff date. Next, he was on to the Lansing

Public Library to read the editions on microfilm for the few weeks following April 1, 1985. While Lou wasn't a statistician, he was beginning to believe that he and Maggie were moving a bit beyond chance, especially if he found an employee in the Mason Public Schools had died.

Lou called the library in advance of his trip into Lansing. He learned that the library did have the past editions of the *Lansing State Journal*, that he could review them, and that someone would be available to help him. In fact, the librarian said that if he wished, he could request the time period for the newspapers he wished to review, and they would have the canister waiting for him. Lou was most appreciative. When he arrived, he found everything in place and ready for viewing.

It only took about ten minutes of reading for Lou to find the obituary for Mrs. Leona Anderson of Mason. She died on April 3, 1985 and had been an employee of the Mason Public Schools. Her husband, Gerald, preceded her in death. She was survived by a son, Arnold, who lived in Sacramento, California, and a daughter, Sherry (Anderson) Wellington, of Kitchener, Ontario, Canada. Lou concluded that this woman was the same Anderson that Mrs. Hamm talked about who had a daughter with a disability in Canada. He decided to look at additional editions of the *Lansing State Journal*, but he expected to find no other deceased Mason school employee, and, in fact, he didn't.

Lou hoped to keep working in Mid-Michigan. He decided that instead of driving the four hours, two hours each way to Grand Haven, he'd stay in a motel in the Lansing area. He'd call Cynthia in the morning and hopefully, with Chief Fitzpatrick's help, visit with the Mason Police.

Lou called Carol that evening to touch base and find out if any interesting mail had arrived. He assured Carol that he'd be home tomorrow. At least, he hoped he would.

Tuesday, November 10, Mason, Michigan

The next day, Lou called Cynthia. "Good morning. Can you give me a couple of minutes?"

"Oh sure. The daily crisis can wait."

"You only have one a day? When I was state director, a day didn't go by when I didn't have at least a dozen," Lou said chuckling.

"Yes, I can imagine. What do you need?"

"I wanted to get back with you and ask you about Mrs. Anderson. Do you remember when she died?"

"It was about eight to ten years ago, I think."

"How did she die? Do you remember?"

"Yeah, I think it was a suicide. People were talking about how sad it was. It's coming back to me, now. The car was left running in her garage, and she died of carbon monoxide poisoning. Yeah, that was it."

"Suicide, huh?"

"She had a lot of trouble with depression. She was getting some help from a local doctor, and people just figured she had lost her will to live."

"Any note found?"

"Oh, I have no idea. I just remember that she died of carbon monoxide poisoning, and it was believed to be suicide."

"Thanks, Cynthia. Once again, you've been helpful."

"Are you thinking Bill was involved?" Cynthia asked with concern.

"Don't know. Just gathering the facts."

"I don't recall the sequence of events, but I'm pretty sure that Bill was gone from the district when that happened." Lou chose not to

132

give Cynthia his new found information; it would throw her into a defense posture once again.

"I'll let you get back to your crisis. Thanks for being there for me."

"Call again when I can help."

"Thanks."

The next stop was the Mason Police Department to look over a report of the incident. Lou called Chief Fitzpatrick, in Newberry, to grease the skids so to speak. There is something about one chief talking with another chief that allows doors to open so much faster. With that contact made, Lou approached the Chief of Police for Mason. "Chief Fred Milbourne?" Lou asked.

"Yes. You must be Louis Searing?"

"Yes sir. Pleased to meet you," Lou said as they shook hands.

"Chief Fitzpatrick has asked me to provide you with whatever information you need to complete your investigation."

"Thank you. I appreciate your support. To start with, I'd like to ask some preliminary questions, and then we'll see how it goes from there."

"That's fine."

"Were you, or any member of your force, working in the police department in 1985?"

"I was. In fact, no one has been here longer than I have. I'm the only person in the department who was here in 1985."

"Were you the chief in 1985?"

"No, I was an officer."

"Did you know Bill Blakeley when he was a teacher here in Mason or in Stockbridge?"

"The name doesn't sound familiar."

"In 1985, a high school counselor named Mrs. Anderson died of carbon monoxide poisoning..."

"I remember that. I was part of the team of officers that looked into her death. In fact, I found her slumped over the steering wheel of her car, dead. I can't forget it, because she was the first dead person I'd discovered as a police officer. It was difficult because she was my counselor when I was in high school at Mason High."

"Yeah, I can imagine that would've been difficult. I'd like to see the incident report written about the death. Is that possible?"

"Oh, sure. I'll get the records. I'll be back in a minute."

As promised, Fred returned within the minute holding a manila folder that looked to contain only a few papers. Fred handed it to Lou. "Thanks. If you wouldn't mind, I'd like to take a couple of minutes to read this and then, if I haven't taken too much of your time, I'll probably have a few more questions to ask."

"No problem. Make yourself at home. Can I get you some coffee? We don't have any decaf here."

"Sure, I'll take a cup," Lou said with a smile. Fred gave him a thumbs up, and left the room to get the coffee.

Lou read the report on Leona Anderson, but there was no mention of any foul play. The report looked innocent, an older woman, in a depressed state, decided to take her life. Having finished the report Lou summoned Chief Milbourne.

"Going to ask you to go back into your memory on this one, Fred."

"I'll do my best."

"Tell me what you remember when you received the call about this case."

"It was about nine o'clock in the morning. I was in a patrol car. I heard the dispatcher indicate that Mrs. Anderson was unaccounted for at the high school and she was not answering her phone at home. The dispatcher gave me her address and I drove out there."

"What did you see when you arrived?"

"Nothing. The house was closed up. I knocked on the door and there was no response. I walked around the house and looked in the windows. I didn't see anything unusual. There was no sign of breaking in. I tried to open the garage door, but it was locked. I called the dispatcher and reported what I had seen and done. At that time, a second patrol car arrived. Officer Daly and I asked our Chief for direction. He had confirmed from the high school principal that she had no relatives in the area who should be called for a key or for information about her whereabouts. He had also called the area hospitals to see if she had been admitted during the night. Negative. We don't like to cause damage to a home, but we thought she could be on the floor and still alive from a fall or a stroke. We needed to gain access. A window is easier to replace than a door. I smashed the back door window of the garage so we could unlock the door. As soon as we got into the garage, we saw her slumped over the steering wheel."

"Then what?"

"We opened the car and checked for any signs of life. Nothing. She was a rosy color, a sure sign of carbon monoxide poisoning."

"You found the car running?"

"No, the key was in the on position, but it had run out of gas."

"Did you take fingerprints?"

"No. We had no reason to suspect anyone else was involved. It looked like a typical suicide."

"Did you find a note from her?"

"No."

"Just about everyone who commits a suicide leaves a note of some kind. There is something about leaving this world, even in a state of depression, where the person has to have the last word. Do you know what I mean?"

"Yeah, but we didn't find any note."

"Was there an autopsy?"

"Yeah, isn't it in our report?"

"I didn't see any autopsy report."

"As I recall, there was evidence of quite a bit of alcohol in her system. We interviewed a good friend who admitted that she had been hitting the bottle quite a bit in the weeks before her death. I guess the medical examiner figured alcohol had contributed to the suicide."

"Did you consider that someone could have forced her to drink the alcohol and to get into her car?"

"I guess that could have happened. As I said, we didn't find any evidence of a break in. The neighbors didn't see anyone come to the house. She had attempted suicide in the past, and had a drinking problem. The autopsy showed no bodily bruises which would have

been evidence of a struggle. In the last 15 years, I've seen a few suicides, and this case was a classic, Lou. When I teach this stuff at the
Police Academy, I use this case as an example. Mrs. Anderson was-
n't murdered, Lou. It was a textbook suicide."

"I'll take your word on it, Fred."

"Do you suspect a murder, Lou?"

"Very possible."

"Why?"

"Oh, there are many reasons. In my line of thinking, someone
wanted her dead. Knowing she had depression problems, they
either broke into her home and drugged her to sleep, threatened her
in some way, or drugged her into a state that would have allowed her
to breathe the fumes but not be able to get to a phone or out of the
car. This person could then start the car so that she would quietly
die and it would look like a suicide. The fact that there was no note
is a big clue to me that she didn't plan to do this.

"Were neighbors interviewed to see if there were any vehicles in
the area late at night or if anyone suspicious was hanging around?"

"Yeah, we talked to her neighbors. They didn't see or hear anything. When we began this meeting, you asked me if I knew Bill
Blakeley. Do you suspect him of killing Mrs. Anderson?"

"I really don't know, Fred. I'm making my way through an investigation. I still have at least one more situation to look into before
I'm ready to fit all the puzzle pieces into a picture that will allow me
to draw some conclusions. You've been very helpful, and I appreciate it."

~

When Lou got back home, he had a phone call from Harold
Holcomb. Lou called back immediately.

"Hello. Holcomb here."

"Harold? Louis Searing returning your call."

"Hey. Thanks for calling back. I wanted to keep you informed of
some things."

"I don't like surprises, so let me have it."

"Well, first of all, Bill Blakeley and family have moved to Charlevoix. He was offered a contract and accepted it. Word has it that he wasn't the first choice, but they needed a teacher with the right qualifications and he had them. So, a piece of history has left Newberry."

"I had a feeling he would go if the opportunity came to him."

"Yeah. So did I. The second bit of news is that Fitz and I are quite certain that Romanski wasn't a factor in Franklin's death. We found him and his friend. It was simple. They decided to go fishing and didn't tell anyone. We were able to substantiate his whereabouts on the ninth, and he wasn't around Newberry. Case closed on Romanski."

"Well, one more suspect that can be checked off of our list. I guess that's good news."

"What are you learning down state?"

"We're on to a pattern and that is about all I can say. In three of the four school districts where Bill Blakeley worked, someone on the staff died within the week of Bill getting the layoff notice. In all three cases, the cause of death was related to a medical condition: heart attack in Newberry, diabetes in Stockbridge, and a depression suicide case in Mason. The only death that doesn't fit the pattern is Jack Olsen's. He died in a hunting accident."

"Patterns are important in our work, Lou."

"I know, and we have one more district to investigate. To add to this drama, we've learned that Blakeley was highly suspect in Stockbridge, but in Mason, the director of special education, who knew him and hired him, swears that there is no way he would be involved."

"We appreciate all of the work you and Margaret are doing on this case, Lou."

"I know, and we're enjoying doing the digging. By the way, please thank Fitz for introducing me to Chief Milbourne."

"I'll tell Fitz 'hello' and thank him for you, too."

"Thanks for the update, Harold. Oh, by the way, whatever happened to the special education program?"

"They hired a teacher from Northern Michigan University. She seems to be doing a good job. The district saved quite a bit of money in hiring a teacher with no experience. The task force has been formed. They haven't met yet, but I'm expecting they will recommend keeping the program in Newberry, and the board will probably concur. I guess the entire mess didn't really have to happen, but it did."

"Thanks, Harold. Gotta run."

"Keep up the good work, Lou. Regards to Maggie."

꒳ꙩ

Maggie called the Gratiot Isabella Intermediate School District Director of Special Education, Brian Conway. Brian was a friend of Lou's. They both enjoyed the game of golf. "Hello, Brian Conway."

"Hi Brian, this is Maggie McMillan. I'm working with your friend, Lou Searing. We're investigating a possible murder in the Upper Peninsula."

"What can I do for you?"

"We need your help."

"No problem. Do I get to wear a deputy badge?" Brian asked chuckling.

"Sure, if that's what it takes to get a little support."

"I'll try to get serious. What do you need?"

"There was a special education teacher laid off from Mount Pleasant in 1982. His name was Bill Blakeley. He probably taught a special education class for children with emotional disabilities. Would you please seek his records from personnel and find out the date of his layoff notice?"

"No problem. I know the personnel director for Mt. Pleasant Public Schools."

"We figured you did, that's why we're asking for your help. I'd like you to look through his records and see if you can find any disciplinary reports, evaluations, or anecdotal information."

"When do you need this?"

"As soon as possible, but not if you have more important things to do. In addition to this request, we'd like to know the name of someone who worked in the district in 1982, who may have known several people in the system. I'm referring to a principal, board member, someone in central administration for example."

"I can do that, too."

"Finally, I need to know where I can find microfilm for past editions of the Mt. Pleasant newspaper. Usually it can be found at the local public library."

"Am I getting paid by the hour?" asked Brian laughing once again.

"No, but Lou says he'll give you two strokes when spring comes around and you two can get back out on the Pine Lake Country Club course in Alma."

"Only two strokes? He beats me by at least seven strokes every time we play," laughed Brian. "Lou enjoys the Alma course. He played there when he was on the Alma College golf team."

"Lou's given me something to negotiate with. His maximum is three strokes. Is that agreeable?" Maggie gambled.

"Sure. I'll need some luck, but that should even the match a little. I'll get back to you with the information you want."

Two hours later, Brian Conway was on the phone. "Hi, Maggie. I've got some answers to your questions."

"Good work, and fast too."

"Bill Blakeley was laid off on May 4, 1982. The person to talk with is Dick Thompson. Dick was the principal in the building where Bill taught. He has been in Mt. Pleasant Schools for about 25 years and he's the district's unofficial historian. *The Mount Pleasant Morning Sun* past editions are microfilmed and are available in the public library."

"Excellent, Brian. We may let you keep your deputy badge with that kind of performance."

"Hey, when my friend needs something, I'll be there for him. You know that. Especially when I get three strokes at Pine Lake!"

"Appreciate it. Do you know Dick Thompson?" Maggie asked.

"Not well, but we've met, and he knows who I am."

"Would it be an imposition to ask you to set up a meeting, lunch for example, at the Embers in Mt. Pleasant? Lou and I, and the two of you, could have a little talk, and maybe we'll get some clues to our investigation."

"No problem, I'll call back and confirm. I'll try for tomorrow. If that's not possible, I'll arrange it for another day. Is your calendar wide open?"

"Yeah, this is a priority. You set it up and we'll be there. Brian, where is the Mt. Pleasant library?"

"Downtown. It's called the Veterans Memorial Public Library, and it's downtown at the corner of University and Michigan."

"Great work, Brian. Many thanks. Lou and I will see you and Dick Thompson tomorrow or whenever."

Maggie had no sooner hung up when the phone rang again. She answered it and found herself listening to Bill Blakeley, in a very disturbed tone. Using obscenities he told Maggie to stay away from him.

"I'm afraid I don't understand," Maggie spoke calmly into the phone.

Once again Bill shouted obscenities and threatened to sue if he wasn't left alone.

"Is there something you expect me to find?" Maggie asked. Maggie was glad this verbally violent man was at the other end of the phone and not in her presence.

Then came the threat, "If you like living, you had better change your ways, 'cause I've got your number! If there is something you've always wanted to do in life and you haven't got around to it, you sure better get about it," Bill said in an irrational tone.

Maggie remained calm, "How is your new job going, Bill?"

"Listen! If I hear one more time that you, or that Searing guy, are asking questions about my past, you're lights are going out!"

"Who is giving you this information, Bill?"

"None of your business! One more word from you, and you won't know what hit you."

"You are sounding like a guilty, scared man," Maggie attempted to rationalize.

"That's it! Get a will!" The phone slammed against the receiver. Maggie was taken back by the outburst, but as an insurance claims investigator, she was used to handling people who were disturbed. She'd never handled anything like Blakeley's verbal blast. Maggie was certain that his contact was Cynthia Hamm, the only person who didn't see Bill Blakeley as a threat, and the only person who he seemed comfortable talking with, let alone accepting therapy from.

Once Maggie briefed Lou about the call, he realized that they should not trust Cynthia Hamm. They had no proof that she had contacted Blakeley, but he was sure it wasn't Mrs. Fuller.

Lou called the supervisor who oversees the special education program at the juvenile detention facility. He relayed the information about the threatening and angry phone call Maggie had just received from Bill Blakeley. Lou wanted information about what was going on there with Blakeley as a new teacher. "He seems relatively calm and is working well with the kids. He seems like a good teacher," was the response.

"Has he shown any signs of anger?"

"No, none at all."

"So, his behavior is acceptable and normal?"

"It appears to be."

Lou thanked the supervisor for the information and immediately called Chief Fitzpatrick, "Hi Fitz, Lou here."

"Hey, Lou. How are you doin?"

"Just fine till a few minutes ago when Maggie was the target of a Bill Blakeley outburst. Now I understand why people are so upset by him!"

"Yeah. He's scary. No question about that."

"I'd like to suggest a conference call between you, me, Maggie and the chief of police in Charlevoix. We'd like Blakeley monitored for a couple of days."

"Sure, you want to set it up?"

"Yeah. I can do that."

"I'll be in the office. I'll call Chief Brewbaker in Charlevoix and let him know a conference call is being set up."

"Thanks that'll help. Talk with you soon."

The AT & T conference phone operator rang up each party, and in a matter of minutes, all four were on the line. "Thank you, Chief Fitzpatrick and Chief Brewbaker, for talking with us."

"No problem. How can we help?" asked Brewbaker.

"Maggie just completed a call with Bill Blakeley who works at the County Detention Center in Charlevoix."

"I know him," interrupted Brewbaker. "He's the new teacher at the center. We take some kids there when we pick them up for violations. I've met and talked with Bill a couple of times."

"Yeah, well, Maggie and I have been working with Chief Fitzpatrick in Newberry. We're investigating a possible murder, and Bill Blakeley is a suspect even though we are working with nothing but circumstantial evidence at this time. We've been looking into Bill's past employment in districts where he's been laid off. It seems that he's gotten wind of this and called to threaten Maggie's life."

"That's the Bill Blakeley that has scared school people wherever he's been," Chief Fitzpatrick said.

"Mr. Brewbaker, I would ask that you and your officers monitor Mr. Blakeley's movements over the next few days," Lou said. "If his car heads downstate or if he leaves Charlevoix, I'd sure like to know about it."

"We don't have the manpower to do that, Lou. I suggest that his employer monitor his day to day activity. We can do a few drive-bys but that's about all."

"I understand. We'll take any help you can give us. I'll talk to Superintendent Forrest about monitoring his activity."

"Can this guy carry this out?" Lou asked.

"He sure can," Chief Brewbaker answered. "Blakeley's behavior was totally out of control and very scary. We often see this as a prelude to any major crime. In fact, most crime starts with this kind of anger toward someone."

"When I talked with Cynthia Hamm, she said that Bill would

never hurt anyone and that these outbursts of anger are his way of expressing his insecurity, but that he's not capable of carrying out the threats," Lou said. "She called it by some psychological name, I didn't record it."

"Well, you now know what has happened. Any monitoring of his comings and goings, will be appreciated," Maggie said. "We'll be in touch if anything else develops," and the conversation ended.

Brian Conway called back and told Maggie that lunch with Mr. Thompson at the Embers was set for the next day at noon.

Wednesday, November 11, Mt. Pleasant, Michigan

Lou and Maggie were right on time for lunch after long drives from Grand Haven and Battle Creek. They waited in the lobby of the Embers, a very popular restaurant which, over the years, had probably provided a meal for every family of a student at Central Michigan University. Lou and Maggie had been waiting about five minutes when Brian Conway appeared with Dick Thompson. They exchanged greetings. The hostess led them to a no-smoking table, in a quiet portion of the dining area.

After an initial round of coffee and ordering, the group set to work. "Mr. Thompson, the reason we want to talk with you is to ask about a former employee, Bill Blakeley. Have you ever heard of him? He taught special education in Mt. Pleasant in the very early 1980s and was laid off in 1982."

"Oh sure. I knew Bill Blakeley. I knew him quite well as a matter of fact. His dad, believe it or not, was a friend of mine in junior and senior high school. We were on the football team. Bill's dad was an excellent football player and all-around athlete for that matter. I wasn't very good, but my folks expected me to be on the team, so I was. Yeah, I know Bill," responded Fred.

"Do you remember when he was laid off?"

"Oh yeah. He took it hard. Got very upset and angry. I think he feared for his family. Trudy wasn't working. She had a teaching certificate, too, but they decided that she should stay at home and take care of Bryan. Yeah. The layoff news was devastating, and my heart went out to the young man. It really did."

"Talk more about his anger and reaction to the news," Lou said.

"There's not much to say. He kind of lost it, and like many people, he didn't keep his anger inside."

"Did he threaten anyone's life?"

"Yeah. He scared a few people for a couple of days, but we just took it as the initial shock of being laid off. We could all understand. He cooled. Hearing that you are losing your job, when you have responsibility for a young family and don't know what's next is not easy."

"I know. It's very difficult," Lou replied.

"I've had to lay people off over the years, and they all take it differently. You just can't predict. Some you expect to take it well, some fall apart. Others you expect a flare up, and they almost thank you."

"Almost thank you?"

"Yeah. Some want to get out anyway, and this just serves as a force to help them make up their mind. But, Bill loves kids and teaching, and he wanted to settle in a community and sink in some roots. He liked Mt. Pleasant because of the university. He could take classes and go to sporting events here. He even did some umpiring and refereeing, but the anger in his personality got in the way."

"I'll bet."

"Yeah. One time he was working a community softball league game and he called a guy out on a double play. The guy was upset at the call and they stood there nose to nose, like Leo Durochur and the man in blue, and eventually really went at it. A little shoving took place and that led to a full-blown fist fight. Because Bill is so big and strong, the other guy was taken to the hospital with a broken cheekbone. It was ugly."

"What was the result of all of that?" Maggie took over the questioning.

"Well, as I recall, he was disciplined by the community recreation director, and told that he would no longer be involved with their program."

"Were there any other examples of these angry outbursts?"

"Bill liked to drink in his younger days, and his favorite hangout was the Foul Ball Sports Tavern. Story goes that he got into a fight there after a Central Michigan University football game. Some out of town guy made a derogatory statement about people with disabilities."

"What happened?"

"Oh it was one of those, 'you want to go outside and settle it' type of things. The other guy took him up on it, and they went outside. Bill roughed him up pretty badly. You gotta either be drunk or stupid to get that guy mad. He's big and strong, and pickin' a fight with him is like taking on Goliath."

"Was that it? Were you aware of any other fights or angry episodes?"

"No. He was counseled to get some help. Trudy got scared when he got angry. He never, as far as I know, was threatening at home, and there was never any problem at school. She saw to it that he got some therapy for dealing more effectively with his emotions."

"So, he went to a psychologist or a counselor?"

"Yeah. He got some help and then there weren't anymore confrontations like I've described."

"Back to the layoff," Lou said. "So, he didn't take the news well, and became angry and threatening?"

That's right. But nothing serious, I think he went right to the doctor who was helping him. He got through the crisis. He applied for a job around Lansing. I don't know where..."

"Mason."

"Yeah. That was it. He went to Mason and this pleased him because he could be near Michigan State."

The conversation shifted to the cream of asparagus soup. Everyone commented on the wonderful flavor. The sandwiches arrived and the empty soup bowls were taken away.

Maggie brought the conversation back to the layoff. "You're very helpful, Fred. I'm fairly certain that you won't be able to answer this next question, but I'll ask it anyway. Do you recall anyone passing away around the time that Bill was laid off in 1982?"

"Oh, sure I do. My good friend, Larry Lorimer, died a few days after Bill was laid off. I'll never forget it. The reason I won't ever forget it is that I was meeting with Bill when my secretary came into my office and said that I had an important call. Bill asked if he should leave the office, and I shook my head for him to stay. I picked up the phone, and it was Larry's wife, Lucy. She was hysterical, saying that Larry had died. I expressed shock and asked her where she was. She said she was at the hospital. I hung up and excused myself from the meeting with Blakeley and rushed over. I drove right to the hospital."

"Who was Mr. Lorimer?" Maggie asked.

"He was the high school baseball coach and gym teacher. Larry was a neighbor, and we went to the same church. Lucy, my wife and I were in a dinner club together."

"How did he die?"

"Well, they said it was stroke, but I'll go to my grave doubting that."

"Because?"

"Well, I'm not a doctor, so I have no basis for my thoughts, but it couldn't have been a stroke. Larry was one of those health nuts. He was into low-fat diets before anyone ever began talking about the fat content in food. He used to brag about his cholesterol counts. He had no family history of cardiovascular problems. As you get older the dinner conversations often turn to discussions of health matters. He would talk about how fortunate he was not to have any problems. I know that we can't know if the blood in a person's body is constricted from getting to the brain, but let me say that Larry Lorimer did not die of a stroke. I've no way to prove my point, but a team of fifty stoke specialists would never convince me that that's how Larry died."

"What did the autopsy conclude?"

"There was no autopsy."

"Why not?" Lou asked.

"Lucy. She wouldn't hear of it. Larry was gone and an autopsy wouldn't bring him back," she said. Lucy didn't need or want detail. 'Let him enjoy Heaven, and we'd just have to adjust,' is what she said. An autopsy was out of the question. End of case.

"Lucy came home from a meeting and found him sitting at his desk in his study at home. He was slumped over dead. She called emergency medical services unit and the paramedics were on the scene within minutes. The medical examiner determined that the cause of death was stroke."

"Was there ever any suspicion of foul play or possible homicide?"

"No."

"Do you think there was any foul play?"

"I don't think so. I knew Larry well and we shared a lot. He didn't have an enemy in the world. There was nothing taken from their home that we know about, and so there was nothing that would cause anyone to be suspicious," Fred explained.

"Let me ask you this. Would you think that Bill Blakeley could be involved?"

"Absolutely not. Bill loved Larry. He admired him and enjoyed watching his baseball teams play. In fact, Bill Blakeley is the last person I would suspect to have anything to do with the death of Larry Lorimer," Fred responded.

"You've been very helpful, Mr. Thompson. Maggie and I appreciate your giving us a noon hour. Thanks, Brian for arranging this opportunity to help us with our work."

Before they left the Embers, Dick Thompson turned to Maggie and asked, "Do you think Bill Blakeley had something to do with the death of my friend?"

"Yes, I do. We've much more work to do with our investigation, and we're not ready to make any pronouncements or accusations, but yes, what we've been learning over the past few weeks leads us to at least be suspicious of Mr. Blakeley, to the point where we have to conclude that he may have been involved in the death of Mr. Lorimer."

"If that is what you prove, I'll be very shocked. If you have any more questions, please know that I'm always available to help you. Brian knows how to reach me. Thanks for lunch. Very kind of you to allow me to enjoy that cream of asparagus soup and the club sandwich. That will last me till dinner with my bride."

With that, Maggie and Lou headed back to their homes aware that they had uncovered a definite pattern. In each case, except Battle Creek, a school employee died within a couple of days of Bill Blakeley's layoff. It still could be all pure circumstance.

Thursday, November 12, Grand Haven, Michigan

Lou enjoyed an early morning jog along the shore of Lake Michigan. His daily ritual fulfilled more than one need. He received the exercise his body needed to stay healthy, and some solitude to think about the investigation they were conducting. Lou felt that it was time to summarize the findings and move on to the next step of the investigation.

Maggie came over to Grand Haven for a strategy session. Carol decided to take the day off given her district's adjusted time policy. She wanted to finish a quilt she was making for her niece in Parsons, Kansas who expected a baby soon.

Carol made a brunch for the three of them. She put out pancakes, juices, a quiche, and a variety of sandwich makings. They helped themselves and enjoyed small talk. Eventually, they turned their attention to the quilt and the investigation.

Late in the morning, Lou cleared off the dining room table and placed a multi-paged, scotch-taped road map of the investigation upon it. They had found, through previous work, that putting the important information in one place, and in full view, helped them see the big picture.

They made three columns. In the first, they put the victim's name, in the second they put the school district, and in the third the cause of death. From top to bottom they saw, Lorimer, Anderson, Young, Olsen, and Franklin. In Column two they saw, Mt. Pleasant, Mason, Stockbridge, Battle Creek, and Newberry. In the third column they observed, stroke, asphyxiation, insulin shock, hunting accident, and heart attack. The one incident that broke the pattern was Jack Olsen in Battle Creek because he died in a hunting accident and not by some medical cause. Also, only the Battle Creek situation was investigated by authorities. In all other instances the deaths were explainable and accepted by family, law enforcement, and medical professionals.

Maggie and Lou thought that maybe this was all a big goose chase. Afterall, the whole thing started because a neighbor, a neighbor reputed to be a bit eccentric, thought that because someone visited the Franklin home a couple of hours before Thomas died that foul play was involved. Sure, Bill Blakeley was angry. Being laid off is an anger-evoking event, and anger is a human emotion. No one has yet suspected that he ever committed murder. At least, not enough to inform law authorities. Just as they were beginning to sink their own convictions about the direction the case was going, Maggie's eyes fell on the list of victims, and she suddenly saw another pattern.

"Oh my gosh. Look at that Lou," said Maggie, a bit excited and wondering if she had hit on a substantial clue or just a strange coincidence."

"What do you see?"

"Well, look at the names. Look at the first letter in each last name. Look at the order, too."

Lou studied the list, "L, A,Y, O, F. Yeah? I don't get it."

"You don't? Oh come on, Lou."

"Lay of? You mean like lay of the land, or something like that?"

"These five letters are five-sixths of the word 'LAYOFF'."

"Oh, sure. Coincidence, pure coincidence."

"Why would you say that?"

"Well, no killer is going to plan six murders and pick a person whose last name begins with the letters in that word."

"Why not?"

"Well, for one thing, how is the killer to know, especially if it is Blakeley, that he would be laid off six times when he or she began the killings? Secondly, what are the odds that someone in a given

151

school district where Bill worked would have a medical condition that could be explainable as natural if the person died by murder? And then to also have a last name beginning with the letter of a word, pure coincidence."

"I'll grant you that it doesn't appear plausible, but you have to admit that stranger things have happened, Lou."

"Yes. I don't mean to throw out your observation. It certainly gives us a clue to who might be next, if a sixth layoff is in the future for Bill Blakeley."

Lou and Maggie continued their analysis and enjoyed a couple of chocolate chip cookies. Lou was convinced that someday some researcher would conclude that chocolate excites the brain cells to regulate inductive and deductive reasoning.

They continued to pour over their notes. All of this time they had been focusing on Bill Blakeley, his anger and his threats. He was the logical suspect.

Lou got out all of his notes from his visit to Newberry and went over them once again. Of course, how could he not have remembered Bill Blakeley's father. Bill, Jr. said that his mother and father visited the family whenever there was an occasion that called for a celebration or an event that was troubling. This would put another person, Bill Blakeley, Sr., in the towns when the deaths occurred.

꒳

At about eleven-thirty Carol answered the door bell at the Searing home, and came into the dining room, "There's a man at the door who wants to see you. Were you expecting someone?"

"No."

"He's acting nervous. My intuition tells me that you may not want to see this guy. Do you want me to tell him you're not here?" Carol asked.

"I'll see him, but give me a minute or two. Tell him I'll come to the door in a minute, that I'm on an important call. Don't have him come in."

"Is there danger, Lou?"

"Could be. If this is the guy who threatened Maggie last week, it could be trouble."

"I'll tell him you'll be a minute."

Lou immediately called the Grand Haven Police and talked to the police chief, Oliver Watkins. "Ollie? Louis Searing."

"Yes, Lou. How are you?"

"Fine, but I need your help."

"Sure, what's the problem?"

"I'm at home and a man is here to see me. It's possible that this is a man I'm suspecting of murder in the Upper Peninsula."

"Do you want me there?"

"I want you on alert. I don't want you tearing in here with lights and sirens, but I want you or your people seconds away."

"No problem."

"This is just a safety precaution. If he's the guy I think he is, Maggie talked to him a week or two ago and he threatened her, so I don't know if he'll put a bullet in our heads in a few minutes or just bring us warm greetings."

"We'll be across the street in an unmarked car. Listen, a little advice. You don't have to meet with him, you know."

"I know, but I'm going to."

"One more thing. Meet with him with some people around. It may calm him or at least keep him from acting if he knows that others are watching," Ollie said.

"Thanks for the advice."

"We'll be across the street and there in a second if you need us."

"Thanks, Ollie."

"Take care of yourself, Lou."

Lou walked to the front door, and as he approached Carol quietly excused herself and joined Maggie. Maggie and Carol stayed in the dining room but positioned themselves to be able to see the two talk.

"You wanted to see me?

"Mr. Searing? I'm Bill Blakeley."

153

"What's on your mind, Mr. Blakeley?"

"I want to have a little chat."

"You're lucky to find me here," Lou said stepping outside on the porch. He could see the unmarked car approaching from the right. Lou had no plans to go back into the house with Mr. Blakeley.

"I take a lot of chances in life and this is one of them. If you were here, fine, if not, our meeting wasn't supposed to happen. Simple as that. My boy called about a week ago. Seems you're looking into his past and asking a lot of questions."

"Can't deny that. When Tom Franklin died in Newberry, some people thought there was foul play involved, and the police there were asked to investigate and to put the rumors to rest or to make an arrest and bring some justice to the Upper Peninsula."

"Let me make this as clear and as simple as I can. My boy never hurt nobody. Understand?"

"Not exactly. He brought a little pain to a guy at second base in Mt. Pleasant, and he rearranged a guy's face outside of the Foul Ball Tavern about the same time. In addition to the physical abuse, his threats have sure given people some sleepless nights and a lot of fear. I've got proof, so don't talk to me about your boy not hurting anybody."

"I mean the murder stuff. Everyone gets in fights at some time in their life. His threats are only because of threats made against him by the school people."

"It's not normal Mr. Blakeley. People who are together don't act that way. Your son's behavior is not normal," Lou said, realizing that he was pouring some salt in the wound. Most fathers will defend their sons, and he wasn't helping himself by trying to drive a wedge between a close father and son team.

"My boy is no murderer. He has had a rough life, and through no fault of his own, he's been forced out of too many districts. His family has been affected and that's tough to take. He's a good man."

"I'm sure you think he's innocent. I expect to have that determined in a court of justice if there's enough evidence to bring a charge against him."

154

"Bring a charge against him? What are you talking about? He is as innocent as the day is long," Bill, Sr. said raising his voice.

"Mr. Blakeley, your son has been laid off five times in his career. He is verbally abusive and has threatened people's lives. In four of the five school districts, a person died within two or three days of the layoff, and you tell me that you don't think I have a reason to be suspicious?"

"You don't have any evidence, and you won't find any because there is none to find. I know my boy, and yes, he's angry and, yes, he's verbally abusive and, yes, he had some fights when he was younger, but he never committed a murder."

"Then how do you explain these deaths? You were visiting at the time of all five deaths. Did you do it?" Lou asked, realizing that he was taking a big chance with this accusation.

"Don't be ridiculous. Of course not. I resent you making an accusation like that."

"Well, I think somebody committed the murders or caused the deaths. If it wasn't you, and it wasn't your son, then someone is following your family around. Someone else is pretty upset at these layoffs, and you guys are getting the finger pointed at you. I suggest you find out who is making you and your son look like murderers, and bring the person to our attention fast. If you don't, you two are going to be paying big bucks to a lawyer who may or may not succeed in keeping you out of prison for the rest of your lives."

Bill stood on the porch speechless. After a few seconds he said, "I was in the area, and I took a chance on seeing you. I want you to know that my boy would never kill nobody. That's all."

"At this point, no evidence points definitively to anyone, Mr. Blakeley." Bill Blakeley, Sr. shook his head, frowned, and after thanking Lou for speaking with him, left. Bill, Sr. travelled north to Rudyard. He planned to share dinner with his friend, Stan Hovath.

Lou called Ollie and thanked him for having an officer nearby.

At about noon the phone rang in Chief Fitzpatrick's office. Sharon answered, "Oh hi, Lou. Calling for Mr. Fitzpatrick?"

"Yeah. Is he there?"

"You're lucky. He just got back from Zellars. We've had a rash of petty thefts lately, and he's acting like a big city cop. Never a dull moment. I'll put him on."

"Hi, Lou. How is life in the Lower Peninsula?"

"All seems about as good as its going to get."

"What's on your mind?"

"I've got an idea that I want to run past you."

"Shoot."

"Well, my best thinking on this case points to the conclusion that the deaths in the Bill Blakeley school districts are because of Bill or his dad."

"That doesn't surprise me."

"No, me neither. But, it's all circumstantial evidence and theory. We've got no witnesses, no weapons, nothing, except that it makes sense, and that has never been enough in most courts of law. Not enough to convict anyone of five murders."

"That's right. So, what's your idea?"

"I've got to get both men back in Newberry, and this is how I think I can do it. Listen and see if you agree. I propose that the school board have a recognition night and honor some teachers who have done a good job for the district. It would be stretching it a bit, but one of the honorees would be Bill Blakeley for his work initiating the special education program for emotionally impaired children. The school board should extend an invitation to the parents of each honoree. They should have a nice dinner and give each honoree a plaque."

"How does all of this help us?"

"We'll ask the parents to come to the Franklin house for a reception before the honors dinner. Be sure to tell the parents that this is a surprise and they shouldn't talk with the honoree about the dinner or their being invited. Then we'll invite Bill Blakeley, Sr. a half hour earlier than the others and emphasize the importance of being on time. We tell him to park out front. I'll be with Mrs. Cunningham watching out of her window to see if when she sees his car and him walking up to the Franklin house, she can pinpoint him as the person she saw last October 10."

"That could work."

"Then, about an hour later, we ask the parents to leave, and we inform the honorees to arrive at the Franklin house to get boutonnieres and corsages before going to the dinner. We tell Bill, Jr. to arrive a little earlier making sure there is parking in front of the Franklin home. Then once again we ask Mrs. Cunningham's reaction to seeing Bill, Jr. walk up to the Franklin house."

"It seems like a lot of work just to get two guys to park and walk up to a house, but if that's what it takes to get a good clue, let's do it," offered Fitz.

Fitz called Jake Williamson and explored the idea with him. Jake wasn't all that enthused because of the work that goes into a dinner like that, and for Jake, Bill Blakeley wasn't an issue anymore. Blakeley was gone, all was back to normal, so to speak, so why go to all of this trouble just to see if Mrs. Cunningham thinks the person walking up to the Franklin house was one of the Blakeleys?

"I won't help with this idea," Jake said. "I don't mean to be difficult, but a recognition dinner takes a lot of work and it would be phony. I'm not about to put people through a lot of work to be dishonest and honor people I don't feel deserve an honor. Please tell Mr. Searing that I have a lot of respect for him, but this idea gets a thumbs down."

"I understand and can see your point. However, if Mrs. Cunningham is quite certain that Bill Blakeley, Jr. or Sr. was the one walking up to see Thomas Franklin the afternoon of October 10, we may be about to solve five murders."

"You've got to find some other way to get those men to walk up to the Franklin home. Sorry, Fitz. I've always been on your side and will do whatever you think will help you do your work, just as you've done for me, but I can't justify this one."

Fitz called Lou back and delivered the message. "I can't really blame him," Lou said. "I'd have probably reacted the same way. I respect Jake. We'll find another way to get at this." As Lou was about to hang up, he noticed a fax message coming out of his machine. It was from the chief of police in Charlevoix. The message urged Lou to call him. Apparently he was having trouble reaching Lou.

"Fitz, gotta go. Keep thinking about a way to get Mrs. Cunningham to make some identification of the Blakeley's."

"Will do. See ya, Lou."

Lou hung up and immediately called Charlevoix. It was in the noon hour. "Chief Brewbaker? This is Lou Searing."

"Yes. Thanks for calling back. I couldn't get you via the phone, so I used the fax."

"Sorry about that. Lot's going on."

"I called to let you know that we've been keeping an eye on Bill Blakeley as time permits. He left town at about eleven a.m. I've contacted the State Police. The Post Commander in Petoskey said they would have a surveillance team involved."

"What does that mean?"

"It means an unmarked car and plainclothes officers will track Blakeley wherever he goes. They won't let him out of their sight."

"Good."

"They will also send a couple of officers over to your house to be there if Blakeley arrives."

"A lot of people just to track this suspect."

"Well, I told the commander that Blakeley was a suspect in murdering five people. There wasn't any question about their being involved."

"That's great. They'll keep us informed of his movement?"

"Right."

"Do you have any clue where he is headed?"

"No. we checked at work, and he called in sick this morning. I will call you at one hour intervals. If he's coming to see you, he would still have about a four hour drive."

"Yeah. Thanks. I'll be home all day. I'll call the police here in

Grand Haven and alert them to possible trouble later this afternoon. Talk with you in an hour."

"Yes, sir."

Lou hung up and called the Grand Haven Police Chief. "Ollie, this is Lou Searing."

"Yeah, Lou. What can we do for you today?"

"Trouble is on the way. I just got word from Chief Brewbaker in Charlevoix that Bill Blakeley is on his way south. If he is coming to see me or Maggie, or perhaps 'get us' is a better choice of words, he'll be here in about four hours."

"I know you will call the shots, Lou, but my advice is to have Carol out of the house. Perhaps you should come to my office this afternoon."

"Thanks, Ollie. I might ask Carol to go downtown for a few hours, but I'll stay here at home. I'm not one to run from anyone. I'll need you and your officers close at hand in case shots are fired. Brewbaker will be calling every hour to brief me of his progress. I'll call you when Blakeley gets in the area."

"Lou, I'll be glad when this investigation is over."

"That makes two of us. Thanks for being there for me, Ollie."

"You bet. Is this a good time to ask you to buy a couple of tickets to the police officers' dance and raffle?" Ollie asked with a hint of humor.

"Sure. You better get my money before Blakeley gets to town," Lou joked back.

༑

The State Police called in the location of Bill Blakeley on the hour, and, in turn, Chief Brewbaker called Lou to report his progress. It would soon be time for Bill to turn east or west in Grand Rapids. A turn west would mean he'd be heading to Grand Haven. An unmarked state police cruiser was positioned near a large interchange that separates east and west bound I-96. If he went on south on 131, it could mean that he may not be making a trip to see Lou.

"Lou? Chief Brewbaker here."

"Yeah. How's he doing?

"He went right on past I-96 and is heading south."

"Are the state troopers going to keep him in view?"

"Yeah. They'll stay on him."

"Curious where he might be going."

"Understand. I'll be back as soon as I hear anything important, like a destination."

"Thanks a lot, chief."

Lou was nervous since Bill Blakeley had threatened Maggie over the phone, and since Blakeley knew that Lou was suspecting him of very serious crimes. Lou tried to attend to some correspondence while he waited for the phone to ring.

"Lou. Brewbaker again."

"Where's he now?"

"He's pulled up to the Holiday Inn just south of Grand Rapids. He went into the registration area for a few moments. He got into his car, drove around to the back, parked, and went into room 207. There's only one other car in the area and the State Police are doing a computer check on that vehicle at this time. I may need to break away for a second or two to get that information. Here it comes now. The vehicle is registered to a Cynthia Hamm of Mason. Does that ring any bells?"

"Sure does. Very interesting. Now what?"

"They'll wait for him to come out and we'll see how many people were in the room with him. We aren't sure this Ms. Hamm is in the room. We only know that her car is parked near his. Room 207 is registered to Bill."

"You'll call back with more information?"

"Sure. Could be five minutes, fifteen, half hour, who knows."

Maggie and Lou weren't surprised that Blakeley could be with Cynthia Hamm. She had, undoubtedly, told Bill about her conversation with Lou. She was very supportive of Bill and was likely having an affair with him, Lou thought. There were lots of socially accepted places to meet and talk, but mid-afternoon in room 207 of the

Holiday Inn would cause Lou to leap to conclusions. After about fifteen minutes Lou's phone rang. "Louis Searing."

"Brewbaker here with an update."

"Yeah. What's happening?"

"We got a report that Bill and a guy described as six feet, 200 pounds, slim, muscular, and about 30 years old exited the motel room about five minutes ago. Bill got in his car and is driving north on U.S. 131. The unnamed man got into the car registered to Ms. Hamm and is now also traveling south on U.S. 131."

"Well, so much for an affair."

"Yeah, but who's he seeing that he needs to check into a motel for forty minutes? I mean drive all the way from Charlevoix to Grand Rapids to meet a guy in a motel for forty minutes?"

"He could be gay."

"Doubt it, but that's one explanation."

"So, now what? The troopers have both cars in view, right?"

"No, they will track Blakeley. As far as they know, the other guy is not a threat."

"They could have been meeting to plot my death!" Lou said with some trepidation in his voice.

"Request was to track Blakeley," Brewbaker replied matter of factly.

"I suggest you call Ollie and brief him. The State Police may have already done this."

"Will do."

With that, Lou called Ollie who promised to assist. Ollie said he'd gotten a call from the State Police. They were calling to brief him of their activity. Ollie told Lou, "You'll soon have a couple of plainclothes troopers on your doorstep. With your permission, they'll be in your home in the event that Blakeley does come to Grand Haven."

"Thanks for the heads up," Lou said, feeling more comfortable with protection. Lou and Ollie finished their phone conversation. A few minutes later the phone rang. "Louis Searing."

"Lou. Ollie here, Blakeley just drove into Grand Haven and is approaching Robbins Road coming north on 31. If he is headed for your home, he'll be there in about five minutes."

"Thanks Ollie. I know that. The surveillance team just called the troopers who are in my home right now."

"I asked the State Police if they needed anything from my office. They said 'No.' I indicated that I would alert my officers to stay clear of your area. I don't want a cruiser in your neighborhood by chance because it might interfere with the State Police team. You're in good hands with these guys, Lou."

"Maggie and Carol are here with me. We're not going to run. I'll see him if he wants to talk. If he's going to blow us away, well, we chose to accept this case."

A minute to two later two cars came into the neighborhood. One was Bill Blakeley's and the other had to be the unmarked State Police vehicle. Bill pulled up in front of the house and the State Police car turned around and parked in the front of a house across, and two doors down, the street.

Blakeley got out of the car and walked quickly up to the front door. The troopers were positioned in the dining room where they could peek through curtains and hear what was said and immediately intervene if needed. Maggie and Carol were in the living room. They couldn't see Blakeley, but could hear the conversation. The door bell rang. Lou waited a few seconds and then opened the door.

"Mr. Searing?"

"Yes."

"Mr. Searing, I was passing through the area and decided to see if you were home."

"Well, you got lucky. What can I do for you?"

Bill Blakeley seemed calm. Maybe he wouldn't need the police protection after all. But, then again, all that could change in a split second with a rage of anger and a violent act.

"I took a chance that I could see you. I want to do whatever I can to assure you that I'm not in any way involved with Mr. Franklin's death in Newberry."

"Explain again why you feel you need to tell me this?" Lou asked.

He felt comfortable inviting him into the house. Lou ushered Blakeley into the living room and introduced him to Carol and Maggie. This was the plan worked out with the troopers who thought if in Lou's judgement, Blakeley was not a threat, bringing him around other people would do even more to minimize the possibility of a violent confrontation. The troopers could follow every move and hear every sound.

After sitting, Bill said, "You suspected I might have been involved when you were up in Newberry a few weeks ago. I was talking with my friend, Cynthia Hamm, several days ago and she said you talked to her about me and my layoff in Mason. So, I obviously figured out that you are continuing to suspect me of involvement in murder," Bill said, remaining calm and level headed.

"Your recent call gives evidence of a very upset man."

"Yes. I guess I lost it. I get very angry at times and I say things that I later regret. I'm sorry if that blowup was threatening."

"We'll accept your apology, but it was very threatening. Life threatening to be more precise. Your behavior certainly leads one to think that you may be involved with Mr. Franklin's death."

"I can see that."

"You came all the way down here from Charlevoix to chance finding me in?" Lou asked, fishing for why he was downstate.

"No. I came down here to see someone for a few minutes, and as I said, on my way back I thought I'd take a chance to see you."

"Not trying to be nosy, but it's a long trip for a few minutes with someone."

"I'm trying to get some help with this anger problem. My son may be getting into drugs at his school in Charlevoix. I'm realizing that my anger may be more harmful to my relationship with him, and with his friends, not to mention my students. Mrs. Hamm knows a counselor who she thinks can help me. I know the manager of a Holiday Inn south of Grand Rapids. He gave me a room with some privacy so I could talk to a psychiatrist to see if he can help me. He works out of Mason with Cynthia. They're friends. As a matter of fact, his wife needed their car today, so he borrowed Cynthia's. I'm coming here directly from that meeting. He thinks he can help me and we're setting up some sessions. My insurance will help pay for the therapy," Bill explained.

"I hope you get some help," Lou said standing in front of an undeniably calm and sane Bill Blakeley.

"I think he can help me," Blakeley said. "But again, I came here to see what I can do to help you understand that although I get angry, I've been able to control it except for a couple of unfortunate episodes when I was in Mt. Pleasant. I had a fight with a guy when I was an umpire, and then I had a fight with a guy who made fun of some people with disabilities. I regret losing it in those two situations, but that's it," Bill explained.

Maggie found Bill to be very convincing. She had the feeling that if she hooked Bill up to a lie detector device, he would pass with flying colors. To listen and watch him, she wondered if he would be capable of picking up a fly swatter to put a pesky fly to sleep. Maggie cautioned herself, remembering the threatening phone call he had made to her recently. She realized it wouldn't take much for him to slip into another angry rage and possibly help one of them to an early death. She felt glad that he was getting help.

Lou wanted to get Bill on his way so that he could call off the police. "I don't mean to be rude, but I do have a meeting soon and, as you say, you took a chance on seeing me. I'm glad we were here to talk with you. I'll be very open and honest with you, Bill. We've been asked to assist in an investigation into the death of Mr. Franklin, and that's our job. If you are innocent as you state, and we don't have any evidence to the contrary, there is nothing to worry about. As detectives, we're following a number of theories and leads. Because you were laid off in a district where Mr. Franklin was a key player in the layoff decision, and because you expressed anger which you admit to, you are one of many who may have been involved. It's as simple as that. Yes, I did talk to Mrs. Hamm because you were also laid off in Mason. I wanted to talk to her about your work in Mason. So, simply put, an innocent man should have no fear. I appreciate your stopping by to assert your innocence. I repeat, we have no evidence that you are involved. I hope that makes you feel better," Lou said walking Blakeley to the door.

"Thanks for seeing me. If I can help you in your work to clear me as a suspect, I will do anything you ask. Again, I apologize to you, Mrs. McMillan, for my threatening phone call a few days ago. I know that didn't help my case."

"Apology accepted. Have a safe drive north and enjoy the colors. We don't have many more days of bright sunshine and colorful trees," Maggie said.

The four shook hands and Bill Blakeley was out the door, into his car, and on his way back to Charlevoix. Lou thanked the troopers for their presence, advice, and support. He, Maggie, and Carol were relieved that nothing happened. The troopers indicated that the surveillance team would track him out of town to be assured he was on his way to Charlevoix. Lou called Ollie and explained that Blakeley stopped for a talk and, on this day, was no threat to their lives.

⌁

Bill Blakeley, Sr. met his friend, Stan Hovath, at the Pure Country Family Restaurant. They had planned dinner around six o'clock. Hilda seated them at their usual table. Bill looked down on his luck.

"You alright, Bill?" Stan asked.

"I don't feel very good."

"Stomach upset or something?"

"I've been getting dizzy and having trouble remembering stuff."

"Seen your doc?"

"Nah. He just says I'm getting old, and I am. Got my boy on my mind all the time."

"He having problems again?"

"He's adjusting to a new school. He's having kind of a tough time, I guess. He and the family have moved quite a bit in his career, and it takes its toll, you know? My grandson, Bryan, is not taking to the new school. I think he is getting in with a bad crowd, and Billy thinks drugs are becoming a problem."

"That's bad news. That stuff can mess up a life."

"Can't mess up a life like getting laid off can, I'll tell ya that."

"You been laid off before, ain't ya, Bill?

"My whole life has been downhill ever since I got the word. I think I might have scarred Billy for life when he was about six."

"How's that?"

"I couldn't take getting laid off. I was shedding some tears, and I guess Billy was watching me. Bea told me later that he came to her and asked why I was cryin'. She told him that I'd been laid off and he asked what that meant. Bea told him it meant that I couldn't work no more, I wasn't needed 'cause there was no work to be done, or no money to pay me to do it, or something like that."

"Tough for a little kid to understand that."

"Yeah. She told him everything would work out, but it didn't. I got a check from the union for awhile, but I couldn't find more work. I didn't have no skills. I used up all my glory in high school on the football team."

"I didn't know that. Were you a ball player?"

"Yeah. I was all state, and I was wanted by Michigan State and the U of M. I had the world by the tail till the third quarter of the last high school game of the season. I got tackled. It was a clean hit with a ton of lard piled on my knee. It ain't been the same since. Muskegon Heights got a 15 yard penalty, but I got a penalty for life. Once the colleges heard I was in surgery, I was a goner, and the scholarship went to some kid with a normal body."

"Tough, tough thing to have happen, Bill."

"Yeah. It was kind of devastating. Without the money for college, I stayed in White Lake and married Bea shortly after we got out of high school. I got a series of jobs for a bit more than minimum wage and worked about twelve hours a day. Bea worked as a receptionist for a doctor until Billy was born."

"Sounds like you two were making it."

166

"Yeah. We lived in a small, run down house outside of town, but we were young and in love. I remember getting a call on a very hot day from Mr. Laughead who had a job as a forklift driver for Laughead Industries. It paid double from what I was getting on a twelve hour day, and I got some medical benefits. Thought I'd died and gone to Heaven."

"Sounds great."

"Yeah. We were lucky when Bill was born. The doctor Bea worked for delivered him for free. He knew we were scraping to get by, and he done it for us 'cause Bea was a good worker."

"Every once in awhile you hear about some nice effort like that doc you had."

"Yeah. Don't know where we would have gotten the cash to pay him. You know, all I wanted was a steady job in Whitehall or Montague, a nice family, and a chance to live a simple life. This was what was happening to me until Mr. Laughead asked to see me. He called me into his office and said, 'Got some bad news for you, son. I hate to be the one to break it to ya 'cause I like you, and you're a good worker.'

"I asked, 'What you got to tell me, sir?

'Orders are down, way down, and we got to let some men go and wait till the demand goes up, you know, more orders and more work.' I started to feel sick to my stomach, and I said, 'You mean I'm bein' laid off? Is that it?'

'Afraid so, son,' he said. 'The union will give you some money for a few weeks. We'll call you back in when we get some more work.'

"That must of been hard to take."

"I stopped at a bar on the way home. It didn't make no sense to give money to Anheuser Busch when I just got laid off, but I had to drown this feeling of helplessness. I went home and told Bea. I slipped into my chair and then it hit me. I was useless. I couldn't provide for my wife and son. That's when I lost it, and when Billy saw me cryin' like a baby."

"Ain't nothing wrong with that. That's a real blow."

Well, after that, Billy's happiness kinda dried up. We didn't have a

Christmas. We got some used shoes and clothes at the St. Vincent de Paul store. We had one meal a day, and Billy was called a lot of names at school. Being poor was ugly and humiliating. Even though he was a tough kid, it got to him, hurt him bad. He often told me that he never got over what that layoff did to me, and to him."

"Did he ever got any counseling?"

"He saw a social worker or psychologist or something in school. I guess that helped, but the kid had such anger about the layoff."

"Well, he had a right to be angry seeing what that did to his old man."

"Billy got through school. It was a miracle he didn't quit. I think two people saved him. He had a high school teacher, Miss Nichols. She was young, pretty, and took a liking to Billy. The other was Trudy. She saw him as a fine, young man, down on his luck; but, he was strong, good looking, and he played good football. He was someone she could look up to, someone to protect her, someone to love her. He gave her what she needed and that was physical and emotional attention."

"Nothin' like a girlfriend to bring a little joy into your life."

"She really turned his life around. I give her a lot of credit. She could see that Billy liked kids, and even though he had a lot of anger in him, she could see that he would make a good teacher. He's a good teacher, Stan."

"You bet he is, Bill. You're proud of your boy and you got every right to be. He went on to college then?"

"Yeah. His knee didn't get crushed, and he got some scholarship help at Grand Valley State University. He played defense, second team. Trudy worked in the book store on campus, and they loved and supported each other all through college."

"That's a good love story."

"Yeah, but because of the layoff, the kid's life was messed up and neither he nor me will ever forget what that word did to us. Know what I mean? It's devastating man. That word will haunt me and my boy till the day we die."

"You got work though, didn't ya?"

"After about ten years, I got a truck drivin' job for Great Lakes Trucking. Stayed with them for almost twenty years. The ten years from the time Billy was six to sixteen I couldn't get nothing more than part-time work. I done a lotta drinking then, too. God love Bea, and I hope she's in Heaven for sticking with me. If I'd have been her, I'd have packed up and left me. She worked for the doctor for all that time, and we got by, thanks to the doc and what little I brought in. You know, I can still hear Mr. Laughead telling me I was being laid off, and to this day, when I think back and hear him talking to me, I feel like I'm going to get sick. I can't forget what it did to me, Bea, and my boy, Billy."

"Hey, it all worked out, didn't it? I mean you got a truck driving job that lasted a long time, Bea stayed with ya till the day she died, Billy and Trudy are working, you got two wonderful grand kids, and the governor is cutting your taxes. Everything is coming up roses."

"There weren't roses in the garden when my Billy was growing up. I ain't ever going to get over it."

Hilda came to the table and apologized for taking longer than usual with the special. She explained that they had run out of the Swiss steak, and they had to call the IGA for more meat. Bill said, "That's OK. Me and Stan had a serious talk for a few minutes. We didn't notice. Did we Stan?"

"Nah, you can kiss the tip goodbye, though, Hilda," Stan said with a smile.

⌘

It was early evening. Just before Maggie was to leave for her home in Battle Creek the phone rang. "Hello."

"Lou? This is Fitz in Newberry."

"Hi, Fitz. How are you doin'?"

"Doin' just fine. Got some information that I thought you would be quite excited to hear."

"I've had enough excitement for one day, Fitz, but, what have you got? I'm going to put this on speaker phone because Maggie is here with me and I want her to hear what you have to say."

"Fine. Hi, Maggie. I look forward to meeting you. Lou has such high praise for you."

"Thank you, Fitz. I hold him in high regard, too. What's the news?"

"Mrs. Franklin stopped in my office today and she had Mr. Franklin's daily diary with her. She had been looking through it and she came across something that she thought I would be interested in."

"This is getting quite dramatic, Fitz. Do we need a drum roll?" Lou asked.

"No drum roll needed. In Franklin's diary, on the page for October 10, he writes, 'Met with Bill Blakeley. Need to reconsider the decision to layoff Bill and disrupt special education class,'" Fitz said.

"We need Paul Harvey and the 'rest of the story'! Don't tell me he didn't put a big Jr. or Sr. after the Blakeley name? All I want are two little letters," Maggie said full of hope.

"Hey, I thought you folks would be happy to hear about this?" Fitz said.

"We are," Lou replied, "Don't get me wrong, we believed one of them was with Franklin that afternoon, so this substantiates that belief. Your finding would be big news if we knew if he was talking about father or son. Assuming Franklin is writing the truth, we now know that one of the Blakeley's is lying, since each told us that he did not visit Franklin that afternoon."

"I don't think you're right, Lou," Fitz said. "Bill, Jr. said he did not visit with Franklin. He couldn't have known whether his father did unless his father told him."

"I understand what you're saying. I talked to his father early this afternoon. He was upset that I was suspecting his son. I flat out asked him if he did it. He denied any involvement. You know, Fitz, it's almost a rhetorical question to ask whether anyone stopped by, because at this point, even if we knew exactly who was in the house, we have no evidence at all to link murder to Franklin. I mean we don't even have a body, and there was no autopsy. We have no witness. We have no evidence, not even a bottle of pills, a syringe, nothing. Even if we can prove one of them was there, so what, except that it fits a pattern."

"What's your hunch?" Fitz asked.

Lou continued, "In all five cases a school district person died within the first three days of the layoff notice to Bill Blakeley. In each case, I have talked with people who knew Bill, Jr. He was very angry and made life threatening comments in all cases. Bill, Jr. says that his mother and father always came to visit with the family when they had good or bad news. If this is true, it places Bill, Sr. in the town when the deaths occurred, and we know that he was in Newberry. So, to date, there is a strong pattern of layoff, anger, and death with mom and or dad in town. On top of all of this is the coincidence factor."

"Meaning?"

"Meaning that there could be no connection whatsoever. It could just be chance that all of these people died and there's no relationship to Bill Blakeley's layoff at all. Now, my guess is that the pattern is not chance or coincidence, but like the Newberry death, we've got no witnesses, no weapons, and no evidence of any foul play. All we have is theory and what people think, which is important, but it isn't going to give a prosecutor a leg to stand on."

"By the way, Harold wanted me to mention a theory he's developed."

'What's that?"

"He thinks the murderer could be Trudy Blakeley."

"Trudy?" Lou asked surprised that she'd be suspect. "You just said that the man who visited Franklin was a Blakeley."

"Yeah, maybe Harold thinks she may be involved with either her husband or father-in-law. She was in town when the death occurred. She's definitely affected by Bill's layoff. She obviously would be very sympathetic to her husband's plight."

"Interesting. We haven't given her any thought."

"Well, it's just a theory. Harold's trying to look at all the angles."

"I guess she's not been a suspect because she didn't leave the house that afternoon. Also, Mrs. Cunningham saw a man go up to Franklin's home."

"I know. Maybe Trudy plotted and orchestrated the murder. We don't know for sure that Trudy stayed at home when her husband and father-in-law were out. She could have told whichever Bill was visiting to give Franklin the drug."

"Could have happened, I guess," Lou said quickly thinking that maybe she was involved.

"Well, as I said, Harold's just looking at all possibilities and he can't rule her out, so she's on his list of suspects. He wanted me to mention the possibility to you, that's all."

"We'll think about it. Thank Harold for the thought, will you?"

"Sure. You know, if you two get this solved, it'll make a good movie or book someday!" Fitz said.

"Yeah. I enjoy putting some of these mysteries to pen. When I was in Talkeetna, Alaska a few years ago, I went into a writers' store, The Writer's Pen. It was a specialty shop in the small town of Talkeetna. I fell in love with the place! I could see myself having a spot in the world like that right here in Grand Haven. I figured I'd work on my mysteries while tending the store. I'd have the coffee on, a sleeping cat and a lazy dog to add a little atmosphere and to give me a little company. It wouldn't be the type of store that would have bumper-to-bumper people. It would be a store that would appeal to mystery fans and to people needing to buy writing supplies and stuff like that."

"Sounds like a neat type of place."

"In my dreams, Fitz. I can see my Michigan writer friends stopping by for a visit. We could have some coffee and talk about our sleuth's cases."

"Sounds like fun. I think you should do it. I can see it now. A mystery comes up and you just put a shingle out that says, 'Gone to solve a mystery.' Then you not only solve it, but you come back to your store and write about it; sell it to pay the rent and heat, and just get into a cycle of solve, write, and sell."

"I suppose I could call them *The Louis Searing and Margaret McMillan Mysteries*," said Lou, feeling good about how that sounded. Lou had a flashback to his boyhood days when he would read the *Hardy Boys* mysteries. They saved him on more than one occasion when a book report was due. He also recalled his father who must have read just about every mystery written in his day.

"I like that. *The Louis Searing and Margaret McMillan Mysteries*. I'd read 'em."

"Of course you'd read 'em, you'd be a major character in one of 'em. You could put your grandson on your knee, point to where I talk about Chief Fitzpatrick, and say, 'Grandson, that's grandpa he's talking about.'"

"Immortalized in a Searing and McMillan mystery."

"You got it. Hey, enough of this dreaming. I'm using up the Newberry taxpayers' dollars on a phone call that sounds like we have nothing better to do. Thanks for the tip. Sorry that I'm not more excited about it, but it does add one more piece to the puzzle. So, for that we're grateful. Thank Mrs. Franklin for her help will ya, Fitz?"

"Will do. Go set up that store. Sounds like a great idea and a wonderful dream."

It had been a long day. Maggie decided to get on home. Carol invited her to stay for dinner. "No thanks, Carol. You've been kind to feed me once today. I want to get home to Tom."

"Sure. Just wanted you to feel welcome to join us for some dinner before you left."

Maggie drove her motorized wheelchair out to her customized van. She entered, strapped herself in, and pulled away with a smile and a toot of the horn. It had been quite a day. Lou and Carol waved as she pulled away.

Friday, November 13,
Battle Creek and Port Huron, Michigan

$\mathbf{M}$aggie and Lou thought it was time to talk with the Charlevoix superintendent of schools. Lou suggested that Maggie make the call. She dialed the number. "Good morning, Charlevoix Public Schools, Superintendent's Office. How may I help you?"

"This is Margaret McMillan. I'd like to talk with Dr. Forrest please. Is he in?"

"Yes, one moment please. May I tell him what this regards?"

"In all due respect, it's a personal matter."

"Fine. One moment. please."

A few seconds later Al Forrest answered.

"Good morning, Dr. Forrest."

"Good morning."

"My name is Maggie McMillan, and I, along with Lou Searing, am assisting Chief Fitzpatrick of Newberry in looking into a possible homicide involving a past member of the Newberry School Board, Mr. Thomas Franklin."

"Uh-huh."

"Our investigation to date indicates that there may, and I repeat, may, be a connection to Mr. Bill Blakeley. I want to make myself perfectly clear. He is not about to be arrested or anything like that. We're uncovering a pattern that would have him playing some role in a series of deaths, but we could be completely off base, and we don't want him accused of anything. We have no solid evidence. In fact, we have no evidence at all that he is involved. We believe we have an obligation to let you know what we know so that we can be knowledgeable about each other and hopefully support each other in this matter."

"As you can imagine, it's a bit unnerving to hear that a member of my staff may be a suspect in a murder, but I'll heed your words of caution, and I realize that there's no evidence of his involvement."

"Good. How's he working out in his new job, by the way."

"Fine. I think the family is having a little trouble adjusting to the move. Bill is doing a fine job at the juvenile detention facility. I think they're having some adolescent problems with Bryan, and Heather is getting a bit rebellious herself."

"Sounds like a fairly normal family."

"I would imagine so."

"Well, the reason for my call is to give you some information about the pattern we've discovered, and to ask that you keep to yourself what I'm about to tell you. It wouldn't be fair to Mr. Blakeley, or to his family, for you to tell others what I'm about to share. Not only that, but if you did and it got to Bill that I told you these things, he may become quite angry with me."

"I understand. You have my word."

"As you know, from Bill Blakeley's personnel file, he has been employed in a number of school districts during his twenty years as a teacher. He has been laid off in the last five districts. All the layoffs are due to millages failing, or to inclusive education, or to fluctuations in student patterns. In each case, an employee of the school district has died within three days of the layoff notice. Now again, as I said earlier, these could all be very normal deaths that just fit a pattern of coincidence, and that's why I don't want accusations made at this time. We don't have any evidence linking Bill to these deaths."

"I understand."

"The pattern begins with the first layoff, where a coach died of a stroke. Then, in Mason, a high school counselor died of carbon monoxide poisoning, which was called a suicide. Next in Stockbridge, a woman died of insulin shock. Then, in Battle Creek, a principal died in a hunting accident. Finally, in Newberry, Mr. Franklin died of a heart attack."

"Boy, that does sound like a pattern that defies coincidence."

"I agree. Now, the obvious message to you, and where you can help, is to let me know if you plan to layoff Bill Blakeley. If there are ever any such plans, then we need to work together for everyone's safety."

"Well, strange that you should call, Mrs. McMillan. As a matter of fact, I was talking to the county administrator the other day. He told me the county is thinking about taking over the juvenile detention special education class. They plan to hire a new teacher and cut expenses by several thousand dollars. He was wondering if I had a spot for Blakeley in the public school program. I have no need to hire any teachers, special or regular, at this time. The county administrator said that they planned to do this soon, and that I should be prepared to lay Blakeley off."

"Does Bill know this?"

"I would imagine so. Rumors fly pretty fast in small towns. I don't know for sure, but if he hasn't heard about the possibility by now, it will only be a matter of days. In fact, I think *The Courier* is going to do a small story on county plans for changes in a number of areas."

"You know, I'm actually beginning to feel sorry for this guy. Six layoffs in a career. He never missed a year's work. A lot of families up and move several times over a career: businessmen on the way up, ministers, military people, and university types. Everyone moves around either by choice or necessity, but I guess knowing that all Bill ever wanted was to sink some roots in a town and raise a family, my heart does go out to the guy," Maggie said.

"Yes. I agree."

"Anyway, what I think we should do is have a meeting in Charlevoix for a day or two to put our heads together and plan so that we can be sure to minimize the possibility of an untimely death if and when his notice is delivered."

"Fine. Who do you want involved?"

"Actually, the fewer the better. You obviously need to be involved, and Chief Brewbaker needs to be there, and I guess your personnel director needs to help. Do you agree?"

"Yes. I think that would be a good team. I assume that Chief Brewbaker knows what I now know?"

"That's right."

"I assume you don't want me to tell my personnel director anything about this?"

"That's right. We'll bring him or her on board when we meet together."

"Good. Thanks for your call. My secretary will arrange a one to two day meeting up here for discussion and planning."

"Yes, and please, it's critical to the investigation and to peoples' lives that this be kept quiet."

"As I said, you have my word."

"Good. Thanks. Lou and I will talk with you soon."

~☙~

Carol and Lou had looked forward to a fall get-away weekend for a long time. The annual event with friends usually took place in early October, but because of a number of conflicts and football tickets to the MSU or the U of M games, the weekend got pushed closer and closer to Thanksgiving.

The location of the gathering was known only to the organizing couple. The rules were in place; a dress up outfit needed to be packed in case the organizing couple chose a nice restaurant for the Saturday night dinner. This unknown was not Lou's style. He always felt more comfortable when he was in control of things. The annual event among friends had been going on for about a decade, and each year it had been a happy occasion. Lou grew to accept the choices of his friends.

On Friday afternoon, the organizing couple called each of the other couples and told them where the gathering would take place. The distance rule was for traveling to be no further than four hours. Then all drive, separately or together, to meet for an eight o'clock dinner. Carol received the instructions. She shouted up to Lou as he was gathering some things for the trip. "We're going to Port Huron to the Thomas Edison Inn."

"Oh good. I like it there."

Four hours later they pulled into the parking lot of the fashionable Inn. They checked in and learned that their room was on the third floor, and the view would be a great one. Carol pushed back the curtains and urged Lou to gaze out at the Blue Water Bridge spanning the St. Clair River, dividing the United States and Canada. Just at that moment a freighter moved under the bridge and cut its way south. The huge boat, so close to shore, knifed its way under the bridge and along the breakwater. It was an awesome sight.

Lou gave Carol a hug. They were glad to have some time together away from home, and a change of pace from their normal routines. Together they recalled how each year they had promised one another that they would do this get away three or four times a year, and yet, the reality of it was that every fall was the only time they found themselves off, together, enjoying being in a nice place with good friends

"We've got to slow down, Lou," Carol said.

"Yeah. You're probably right."

"You seem to be on the go all the time. You get all wrapped up in these murder investigations. I'm not complaining. I'm happy when you're happy. I just hope you aren't letting all of this get the best of your health."

"I think I'm doing OK. I'm jogging every morning, and the doc says all the tests are normal."

"I know. It's just that when we get away and relax a bit, it seems that we should do it more often."

"Well, then we'll get away more often. We'll make it a priority, that's all."

At eight o'clock Lou and Carol appeared in the dining room to join the other three couples who make the annual retreat weekend so much fun. The Simkins were already at the table and having a glass of wine. Diane and Ed went to Kansas University with the

Searings. Ed was the Kent County director of social services and Diane was a medical social worker. Across the table were the Hoeflers; Hillary and Harry. Lou and Carol got to know the Hoeflers when they were neighbors in East Lansing. The third couple was the organizing couple this year, Derek and Jane Beyer. The Beyers were teachers in Okemos, and Lou and Carol got to know them when they lived in Haslett and went to the same church, St. Martha's in Okemos.

"Hey, you guys sure picked a great place. I love it here. First class Inn, water out the window, freighters bringing some charm, and a chance to be with the most beautiful woman in the world," Lou said, smiling at Carol, and enjoying the feeling of being as relaxed as he could be.

"We agree," Harry Hoefler rose to greet them. "Great choice and great people. We've been looking forward to this weekend for a long time. We should do this more often!"

"That's what we just said when we were unpacking. Why do we put so much time between what the eight of us enjoy so much?" Carol asked.

"The vote from the Simkins made it unanimous. This is a great place to share with friends and enjoy some quality time together."

With that, Lou proposed a toast. "To a great relaxing weekend with wonderful people. May our friendship grow and may we do nothing but relax and appreciate our good fortune." Each lifted a glass and cheered knowing how lucky they were to have good friends, good health, and a couple of days to share.

"Is Mr. Searing in this party?" The joyful moment was interrupted.

"Yes. I'm Louis Searing."

"You have a phone call in the lobby."

"Excuse me, my friends." Lou walked toward the lobby, wondering if it had something to do with the case.

"Hello."

"Lou, this is Maggie. I'm so sorry to bother you, but I got a strange call from Bill Blakeley, Jr., and I thought you should know about it."

"How was it strange?"

"He said he suspected he was going to be laid off again. He thinks this is because of us. He said he couldn't take another disruption of his family and that your family would have to be disrupted this time. He said he was sorry, but it was time for the Searings to know how it feels to have their lives torn apart. Then he said something about you asking questions in various towns, and that this is the reason he is going to be laid off again. He was real mad, Lou. More obscenities and threats."

"Did he offer any specifics to his threat?"

"No."

"Well then, it's just that, a threat. He's not going to control my life."

"I know Lou, but I wouldn't take any chances. He could know you're in Port Huron, and you're vulnerable away from familiar surroundings. If I were you, I'd return to the safety of your home and the security that your police friends in Grand Haven can provide."

"Don't like to give into his demands. Carol and I are here for a relaxing weekend with good friends."

"I know you are a strong willed man, Lou, but I don't see how you can be relaxed without feeling threatening. I suggest you let him control the situation a little and come on home. There can be many other weekends."

"This man's sick. He's got to be committing these murders, Maggie! He can be kind one minute and then he turns into a raging lunatic the next. We may need to talk to a psychiatrist to see if his personality can give us some clues to this case."

"Good idea."

"Well, we'll check out and come home tonight. Thanks for your call."

"He was very angry. It was weird, Lou. It sounded like he was going to kill you. I am understanding how scared folks are dealing, with this guy. I'm sorry that your weekend is spoiled."

Lou hung up. Lou was not one to lose it, but Blakeley's saying what he did to Maggie, and ruining his weekend, was enough to bring out his anger.

Lou walked back to the table where his friends and Carol were waiting for a report. All were hoping that it would be good news. "Everything OK?" Hillary asked.

"Carol. I need to talk with you privately. Everything is alright, but I need to talk with Carol." She pushed herself back from the table and went out of the dining room with Lou. The others were quietly pessimistic. They waited for whatever was to happen next.

Outside of the dining room, Lou briefed Carol. She was visibly upset on two counts: a threat on Lou's life, and the realization that the weekend she wanted so much to enjoy was finished.

They returned to their friends, sat down, and tried to explain the situation. They were sorry to have a potentially wonderful weekend interrupted, but they all knew that Lou was an investigator, and sometimes at various points in his work, things get kind of crazy. Lou did his best to encourage their friends to get this mess out of their minds, and to go ahead and have a great, relaxing weekend. Before leaving, Lou said, "Let us assure you that we won't let twelve months go by before we all get together again. Tell you what, we'll plan the next get together. Will all of you agree to do this again soon?"

They all agreed. All rose and gave their friends farewell hugs. Lou and Carol left to pack, check out, and to drive west to Grand Haven. Lou felt determined to solve this thing, and get Bill Blakeley to a place where society would be protected from his sickness.

Before leaving Port Huron, Lou called Chief Brewbaker in Charlevoix to inform him of the call Maggie received from Blakeley. He asked for surveillance, once again, in case Bill Blakeley would head south to carry out his threat.

Monday, November 16, Grand Haven, Michigan

The first thing Monday morning, Lou called Superintendent Forrest in Charlevoix. "Superintendent's office, Melanie speaking."

"Good morning. Is Dr. Forrest there? This is Louis Searing in Grand Haven."

"Just a minute please. May I tell him what this is regarding?"

"I don't mean to be uncooperative, Melanie, but when he hears my name, he'll know what it's about."

"Sure. One moment please, Mr. Searing."

A few seconds later, Al Forrest came on the line, "Good morning Mr. Searing."

"Good morning. I doubt you are aware that Mr. Blakeley called Maggie last Friday evening."

"No, I didn't know that."

"Well, he did, and it was a very angry and threatening call, which was quite disturbing. He acted in a consistent manner to past episodes. His outbursts are predictable."

"I'm sorry."

"He said that he expected to be laid off once again. He thought this time it was because of me and my asking questions about his possible involvement in Franklin's murder. He told Maggie that he couldn't take another disruption for his family, and it was time for me to find out what it was like to have a family disruption. Then, apparently, he gave Maggie the impression that he intended to harm me."

"I'm sorry," Al said apologetically.

"The purpose of my call, however, is to find out what further plans, if any, you have for laying Bill Blakeley off."

"Well, as I told Maggie last Friday, the county probate court is thinking of taking over the educational program. If they do, they intend to hire a new teacher and save themselves quite a bit of money. As I also told you, we have no openings in special or general education for Bill if and when the county takes action."

"How did Bill get word that he might be laid off?"

"I don't know for sure. It wasn't from Charlevoix schools, I know that. The decision has not been made, no meeting with Mr. Blakeley took place, no written notice was given. There was an article in the paper about the county taking on more responsibility for their own programs, including education. I'm sure there is talk at the detention facility about all of this."

"Do you have an expected date to give him his layoff notice?"

"I have an appointment with the county commissioner tomorrow morning. I'm expecting him to give me his decision, and I further expect it to be that they will take over the special education program. I imagine that it will be in a few months. Our contract indicates that an employee needs advance notice, so if my prediction is right, we'll give him his layoff notice one week from today."

"That would be Monday, November 23."

"Maggie has not told me when we can have our all-day meeting. Did you decide when this can happen?"

"We talked about it, and the best day is this Wednesday."

"We'll be ready to go at 8:30 Wednesday morning. You will be there, and you'll have your personnel director there?"

"Correct."

"As soon as possible, please send me a list of all employees in your district."

"It'll be faxed in a few minutes. Is there anything else you need before Wednesday morning?"

"I don't think so. Is Blakeley at work today?"

"Yes, he is."

"If he doesn't come in tomorrow, I want to know."

"Absolutely."

"Thanks, Al. Maggie and I will be coming up tomorrow evening. We'll be staying in a motel, so we'll be ready to meet with you and your personnel director. What's his name?"

"Randy Richards."

"OK, you and Mr. Richards, at 8:30. You'll have a room where we can work for the day?"

"It's all taken care of."

"Great. See you Wednesday morning."

"Sure thing."

Lou called Maggie to brief her of the plans. Lou fully expected to return with the case solved. The layoff notice would be given on Monday, and by Wednesday, if Blakeley's patterns were not coincidental, a threat on someone's life would happen. Hopefully, they would catch Blakeley in the act. Which Blakeley he couldn't know for sure, but he fully expected it to be one of them.

Tuesday, November 17,
Charlevoix, Michigan

Maggie, joined by her husband, Tom, picked up Lou in Grand Haven. Tom was a good travel companion for Maggie, and often provided the assistance she needed in spite of her independent ways. Luckily he had no golf trip planned or patients needing an emergency wisdom tooth extracted.

The three headed for Charlevoix. They encountered some light snow around the Traverse City area, but other than that the drive was uneventful. They checked into the Lodge motel. It was close to downtown and the school administration building on Clinton Street. They had a vacant, accessible room available for Maggie and Tom. Lou's room was next to theirs. They also had kitchenettes, allowing them to prepare meals. Lou and Maggie decided to base themselves at the motel during the week long stay. They hoped to go home for the weekend, but planned to see how things developed.

Wednesday, November 18,
Charlevoix, Michigan

As the clock struck 8:30 a.m., Lou and Maggie entered the office of Superintendent Al Forrest. Al's secretary, Melanie, greeted them warmly and told them where the meeting would be. There was chalkboard space for plotting and planning, a telephone, a copy machine, and a fax machine. At first glance, it was equipped just the way Lou would wish it for the discussion and planning to occur.

The first thing Lou did was pick up the phone and call Chief of Police, Brewbaker. "Police Department."

"Hello. Is Chief Brewbaker available?"

"Just a minute. Who's calling?"

"Louis Searing."

"He'll be with you in a few seconds."

"OK, thanks."

"Morning Lou. What can I do for you?"

"Probably should have called you sooner, but I'll play catchup. Maggie and I are down the street at the Board of Education Administrative Offices, and we'll be meeting most of the day with Superintendent Forrest, his personnel director, and hopefully with you for a part of the day."

"Just tell me when you need me and I'll be there. I have to see the mayor about 11:00, but other than that I'll be protecting the people and property of Charlevoix for the rest of the day."

"Well, protecting the people and property of Charlevoix is what our mission is all about. Can you come over at about 9:00 and stay with us for as long as you can?"

"Sure, be right over."

"Thanks."

Coffee and donuts were delivered to the meeting room. Superintendent Forrest walked in and introduced himself. Al Forrest was a tall and handsome man. He looked distinguished and wore very conservative, stylish clothes. He looked like a community leader. Al introduced the school district's personnel director, Randy Richards. Randy was about five foot six or seven and looked to weigh about one hundred forty pounds. He was wearing a sweater and slacks, and appeared to be an easy going guy.

After introductions, Lou said, "I just called Chief Brewbaker and he will be joining us around nine o'clock. At that time, we'll lay out our work, and we can discuss how best to proceed."

"That's fine. I've scheduled the day here. I'm to give a speech at the Rotary Club luncheon this noon from 11:30 till about 1:15. I'll have to attend that meeting," Al said.

"Oh sure," Lou responded. "We're going to need a break, in fact, several breaks. Our brains need a rest, too."

At precisely 9:00 a.m. Chief Brewbaker entered the room. "How is that for perfect timing?" he asked.

"Not bad," said Lou extending his hand in greeting. This was the first time the two of them had met, though several phone conversations had been shared. Lou introduced him to Maggie. She cordially greeted him, "Let me thank you personally for all of the help you've given us. We appreciate your being there for us."

"Pleased to be able to help. Hopefully, I can continue to assist."

Chief Brewbaker was tall, thin, and looked too young to be the Chief of Police. His full head of hair was cut short. He had a thin moustache that was neatly trimmed. He either was quite an athlete, didn't eat more than 100 calories a day, or his genes gave him the right to eat while not storing fat onto his body frame.

In an effort to establish control, Lou called the meeting to order.

"Could we please begin? We've got important work to do." With that, the five sat down to hot coffee and fat-filled donuts to begin talking and planning.

"Let me begin by setting the stage for our work, and I'd like to do that with a few rules. The first rule, and, perhaps the most important one, is that anything said in this room must stay in this room. We can't have leaks to anyone; and, by anyone. I mean staff, family members, friends, it doesn't matter who. No one can hear what we talk about in this room." The three nodded in agreement, and seemed committed to honor this request.

"Secondly, we must be accessible to each other at all times. We need to know how to reach one another, and we need to commit to making sure that we will give this case 100 percent of our attention for the next several days." Once again, the men nodded and pledged support.

"Those are the only two rules: availability and confidentially. If we keep to these two rules, we'll be a long way toward solving this case."

"Now that the rules are clear, I'm dying of curiosity. What's this case about?" Randy asked.

"I forgot that you haven't been brought up to speed with this situation, Randy. We'll do that right now. First of all, is this the team? Is there anyone else who should be involved?"

Al Forrest said, "I think this will do it for planning purposes. We'll need to get additional information or involve others as we carry out whatever we decide to do. But, for now, the five of us should be it." Brewbaker nodded in agreement.

"Let's begin. Our goal is for each of us to know what the rest of us knows so that we are working from a common base of information. This may sound like a lecture, but be patient, as it's important that we all know the details. Randy, feel free to ask any questions, since Al and the chief know about what I'm going to share.

"This whole case began for us early last month in Newberry in the Upper Peninsula. School board member Thomas Franklin died of an apparent heart attack. Two days before Franklin died, Bill

Blakeley received a layoff notice. He became very angry and recruited the parents of his special education kids to fight the Newberry district to reinstate the program. That's another interesting story.

"Bill's father, Bill Blakeley, Sr. came over on Saturday morning to visit the family during this stressful period of time. A neighbor of Mr. Franklin's said that she saw a man, a tall man, go into the Franklin home before Franklin died, and at the time, Mrs. Franklin was not home. As a result of my investigation, with help from Chief of Police Morgan Fitzpatrick and retired state trooper, Harold Holcomb, we're concluding, with little concrete evidence, that either Bill Blakeley, Jr. or his father met with Tom Franklin that afternoon.

"We found out that Bill Blakeley has been with a number of school districts in his twenty-year career as a special education teacher. However, he has been laid off from the last five. In each case he was successful finding employment,which means that he was never been without a job. Those five include Newberry in 1994, Battle Creek in 1992, Stockbridge in 1990, Mason in 1985, and Mt. Pleasant in 1982.

Lou continued, "We've also learned that in each school district a person died within three days of Bill Blakeley getting his layoff notice. There was no suspicion of foul play or murder in any of them except in Newberry, where the bridge club of old ladies had a theory that the last person to visit Tom Franklin brought on his heart attack prematurely.

"In four of the five cases, the cause of death was related to a medical or mental health problem the person was having. Mr. Franklin had a heart problem, Mrs. Young died of diabetes complications, Mrs. Anderson died of a carbon monoxide poisoning, and Mr. Lorimer died of a stroke. The only non-medical death was Mr. Olsen who died in a hunting accident.

"In each case, it's believed that Bill Blakeley's father and mother, when she was living, were in the town where the deaths occurred. Bill, Jr. said that the family comes together whenever there is good or bad news. A layoff notice is bad news.

"So, I'm going to put a pattern up on the chalkboard so you can see how it fits into our case." In the first column Lou wrote the names of the people who died: Lorimer, Anderson, Young, Olsen, and Franklin. In the second column he wrote the cause of death: stroke, suicide, insulin shock, hunting accident, and heart attack. In the third column,he wrote the school districts: Mt. Pleasant, Mason, Stockbridge, Battle Creek, and Newberry. Finally, in the fifth column, he wrote the year of the layoffs: 1982, 1985, 1990, 1992, and 1994.

"Were murder investigations conducted in those cases?" asked Brewbaker.

"Not a one, except as I said, in Newberry. Even there, Mrs. Franklin and the family doctor have no suspicion of foul play. Franklin was having chest pain and numbness in his hands and arms, which are all classic symptoms of an impending heart attack. Only one autopsy was carried out and that was on Mrs. Young in Stockbridge. No family members suspect foul play that I'm aware of. I didn't speak to any family members except Mrs. Franklin, but in some communities, there's a belief that Bill Blakeley took his anger to the extreme and was involved in the deaths. This is certainly what a few people believe happened in Stockbridge and in Newberry.

"Now let me talk about Bill Blakeley, Jr. He expresses his anger verbally. He gets very angry and 'attacks' people with threatening comments. We've personally experienced a few instances of this. On two occasions he verbally went crazy with Maggie. He has a history of verbal abuse, but people generally believe this is not a problem in any school where he's worked, nor does he verbally abuse his family. At least, that's what I've been led to believe," Lou explained.

"From my talk with Al last Monday, it's my understanding that you may be laying off Bill Blakeley next Monday. Is that still correct?"

Randy said, "Yes. That's the plan right now."

"When will he get his layoff notice?" Maggie asked.

"We're planning to call him into the office late Monday afternoon to tell him, and we'll hand him the official notice at that time," Randy said.

"Who will be present when this happens?" asked Maggie who continued the line of questioning.

"When these things happen, it's usually just myself, the person being laid off and the union representative," Randy said.

"Is that who'll be there on Monday?"

"Yes. Unless we decide otherwise."

"I don't have a feeling that it should be any different. Does everyone agree?" All present nodded.

Lou continued. "Now, looking closely at the pattern we've established, Bill will get very angry and make threatening statements. He may just kinda boil inside, say nothing, and take off out of here for a fast drive or some other irrational behavior. You can't help but feel sorry for the guy."

"Is there any need for me or my staff to monitor him?" asked Chief Brewbaker.

"It might be a good idea. Nothing immediately irrational has ever happened in the previous districts, because no one knew enough to ask the authorities to keep an eye on him."

"Unless you folks think differently, we'll keep an eye on him." said Brewbaker.

"Now, Randy, this could be a very disturbing meeting, but if we've learned from the past, we know he will be very threatening, but he won't immediately act on the threats. In Stockbridge, the superintendent sent his family to visit relatives for a few days till things settled down a bit. You need to be prepared to handle a difficult scene."

"We've had some pretty upset people receive layoff news over the years. I'm not saying I'm not concerned, but I've had some experience with people getting quite bent out of shape getting this news," Randy said.

Lou added, "One thing may be in our favor. Bill is expecting to get laid off, where in the past he was not. On the other hand, this layoff news will fall especially hard, since the family just moved here and is just getting settled. It really couldn't come at a more inappropriate time. I feel sorry for the guy and his family.

"One more time," Lou continued. "The notice, verbal and written, will be given Monday afternoon. We expect he'll get very angry and act this out in some way. Then, we expect he'll call his father in Rudyard. His father will come down to see the family, and will probably arrive on Tuesday. Sometime from that point on, probably on Wednesday, there will likely be an attempt on someone's life, someone who works in the Charlevoix Public Schools if the pattern we've discovered plays out."

Al spoke first, "What can we do to protect our staff? This could be terrible."

"Yes, it could. The main purpose for the rest of our time here together is to create a plan. We need to figure out how best to protect the staff, and at the same time to catch any person who may be intending to commit murder. This will be no easy feat, since whoever it is has killed five other people with hardly any suspicion of murder." Before we go forward, does anyone have any questions about the background of this case, the characters, or what our mission is about from this point on?"

"It seems that our job as school administrators is to help you in any way we can to prepare for the layoff notice, and to give you a list of any people who may be targeted for his revenge," Al said.

Randy commented, "You know, if a member of our staff's life is threatened, maybe we have an ethical responsibility not to lay that man off. I mean, if we know that doing so could lead to murder, maybe we should find a place for him in the system. Is it really worth it, to potentially have some innocent member of our staff die over one teaching slot? We could find the money and find something for him to do. We could keep him for his remaining ten years. He may decide to move on his own, or even if he doesn't, to have him here for ten years and to keep a life from being taken would be far more worthwhile and ethical. Don't you agree, Al?"

"Got a point there, Randy."

"This is not a decision for us to make," Lou said. "We're only investigating a possible homicide in Newberry, and we've discovered a pattern. If you decide to lay this man off, our investigation indicates that someone in the school system might die, or unless I'm just dealing with coincidences, will die. So, Randy has a good point.

If you decide not to lay Bill Blakeley off, we won't be in the same position to solve this case. However, a member of your staff may not have his or her life threatened. It's up to you, but we'll need to make a decision. If you aren't going to lay him off, then we can get back home and continue to look for clues in the Newberry situation. If you are going to lay him off, you'll have what no other district has had, and that is an opportunity to catch a murderer. If Bill Blakeley isn't guilty, it would be nice if you could still find a place for him. If he is guilty, we need to put this case to rest. We could solve five murders, ranging over the past thirteen years, in one shot."

"When the meeting began, you asked if we need anyone else involved? As a result of Randy's comment, I think we should involve the president of the school board," Al said.

"Can he or she be trusted to keep all of this to him or herself. It's absolutely critical to solving this case that not a word be said about any of this," Maggie cautioned.

"The President is Lucille Vandenberg. She's an attorney in town. She knows how to keep confidences. It's part of her work. She may also be able to bring some of her legal knowledge into the case. What if we move forward, a staff member dies and it somehow gets out that we knew this was possible, yet we went right ahead and let it happen? It seems to me that the family of the murdered staff person could sue us for every penny we've got," Al said.

Chief Brewbaker made it clear that they have a moral, ethical, and legal responsibility to warn possible victims of a threat on their lives. What they do upon receiving the information is up to them, but they must let people know that their lives may be in danger.

It was nearing 11:00 a.m. and Chief Brewbaker had to leave for his meeting with the mayor. Superintendent Forrest needed to attend to some phone calls and then he had to go to the Rotary Club meeting. "It's time for a couple of you to do other things. I suggest we adjourn until 2:00 this afternoon," Lou said. "At that time, I suggest that Al invite Lucile Vandenberg to join us, if you are still going to consider laying Bill off next Monday. We all realize that you can change your mind up until the time Randy says the word, and gives notice to Bill Blakeley. Then, after further discussion, Chief Brewbaker, Maggie, and I will await your decision on whether or not to proceed. If we go ahead, there's work to do. If you decide to keep Bill in some other capacity, then hopefully all will get back to normal around here very quickly."

The five, and Lucille Vandenberg, met at 2:00 p.m. as planned. They took several minutes to brief Mrs. Vandenberg. Following the briefing, Lucille said to Al and Randy, "I'd like to discuss this privately with you. Could we go to your office, Al?"

"Absolutely. Excuse us."

The three were gone for about a half an hour. When they came into the room, Lucille was the spokesperson, "We've decided not to go ahead with the layoff of Bill Blakeley. It's not in the best interest of our staff, or Mr. Blakeley. We signed a contract with him, and he moved his family here under a trust that he would have a job. I don't believe we should fail him at this time."

"That's fine with us. We made it clear that you are making the decisions, and you know what is best for your staff, your students, and your community," Lou replied.

"Sorry to bring you two all the way up here, Lou. And, sorry to take so much of your day, Chief, but we think we're doing the right thing, and that's what is important to us," Al Forrest said.

"We'll ask, once again, that not a word of this meeting or anything said in the meeting be shared outside of this office. Our lives are not exactly sure bets at this point, and I assure you that a leak to Mr. Blakeley about this meeting or what was said would result in a very ugly scene. So, while I support your decision to not layoff, I trust you will support our decision not to disclose the meeting in any way."

"Lou, you have our word," Al said, and each person present nodded in agreement.

Maggie and Lou drove back to the motel and met Tom who was back from a long hike. The three checked out, and headed south. The next few days were relatively calm compared to all that had gone on the previous month and a half. It was good to put it all behind them for awhile.

Saturday, November 21,
Grand Haven and Charlevoix, Michigan

Lou enjoyed another Saturday morning jog along the shore of Lake Michigan with Samm scampering along beside him.

In the meantime, Bill Blakeley was calling his father. "Dad?"

"Yeah, Billy. How are ya doin?"

"Not very good, Dad. I've got wind that I might get laid off on Monday. The county wants to take over the program, and there is no opening in special education in Charlevoix Schools."

"You've got to be kidding, Billy. What are they up to now? How much crap does a guy have to take before the union will stand up to protect you anyway?"

"Yeah. I don't know what I'm going to do. We're just getting settled. The house payments have started. I'm just numb, Dad." It was obvious that it was all getting to Bill, and he had the right to be upset. This was no way to treat anybody.

"You got a contract, boy! Ain't that good for nothin'?"

"Guess not."

"I'm comin' down there Billy."

"That's OK, Dad, you don't need to come down. Maybe I won't be laid off. I just expect it to happen. I haven't been called into the office or anything like that."

"Won't hear of it. Your ma and I have come to be with you and Trudy every time there was joyful news, like the birth of Bryan and Heather, and every time there has been bad news, like these layoffs. You need me, son, and I'll be there for you."

"If you insist. I can't stop you, but you may be making an unnecessary trip."

"If you don't get laid off, I'll get to see you, Trudy, and the kids. My health is getting worse, son. I don't think I got many more trips in me."

While Lou was running and Bill was calling his father, Lucky Williams was calling Dr. Forrest. Lucky was Bill's supervisor at the juvenile detention facility. "Dr. Forrest?"

"Yes."

"Dr. Forrest, this is Lucky Williams. I'm sorry to call you on a Saturday morning. A superintendent should have some peace and quiet on the weekend."

"Good morning, Lucky. A person with the job of superintendent seems to belong to the people, and there's no such thing as a time where there's freedom from a call or a problem. It comes with the territory, I guess. What can I do for you?"

"Well, something been bothering me and I've got to talk to you about it."

"OK. What is it, Lucky?"

"Late yesterday afternoon I was talking to Bill Blakeley, and I felt it fair to warn him that he'd be laid off on Monday. I mean, I'd want to know if it was going to happen to me. Well, he just went berserk. He was making threats about me and my family. I don't scare easily, but I was scared. I was in the Marines and went to Camp Pentleton, and I never even came close to going through what he put me through."

"Are you OK now? Do you need some counseling, or protection, or anything?"

"Nothing's happened so far. I had my shotgun with me at home, and I stayed up most of the night. I sent the wife and kid to a friend on the other side of town."

"Did you call the police?"

"No, I didn't want to put the police on him. I figured it would just make him angrier, even though I don't know if that would be possible."

"So, he thinks he's going to get laid off on Monday?"

196

"Yeah. That's what I was told about a week ago, so I briefed him. I just thought he'd appreciate a little warning so it wouldn't hit him so hard. I was laid off once, and I didn't know it was coming. I took it hard. So, like the Bible says, 'Do unto others...' you know. Just trying to help him."

"I don't blame you, Lucky. Bill has a reputation for coming unglued like this, so it was predictable; you just didn't know it. I don't think it has anything to do with Lucky Williams. Thanks for calling. I'll take it from here."

"Sorry, Dr. Forrest, if I caused any harm to anyone."

"You did what was the human thing to do. Get some rest and try to relax."

Within seconds of hanging up the phone, Al called Lou. Carol answered the phone and explained that he was out for a long jog. She assured him she would have Lou call him when he arrived home. Carol jotted on a note, "Call Al Forrest at home."

When Lou came in from his run, he sensed that something was wrong. Seeing the note from Carol confirmed it. He called Al right away. Al told Lou about the episode between Lucky and Bill. Lou said, "We don't have any time to waste. I know you made the decision not to lay him off, but it's too late now if he thinks it's in motion. His pattern may already be unfolding. Trust me, we've got to plan how we'll handle this."

"I've got to get the go ahead from Mrs. Vandenberg, but I'm sure she will go along with your advice."

"Maggie and I can be there by 2:00 this afternoon. I want you to call the following people and ask them to be at the school board office by 2:00. Call Mr. Charles Fraser, Ms. Gail Farrell, Mrs. Angie Fry, and Mr. Daniel Flores. In addition, I need you, and Chief Brewbaker."

"I'll do my best to reach them. Why Chuck, Gail, Angie, and Dan?"

"I'll explain later. It'll take us a few minutes to pack and then we'll head up. Jot down my car phone number in case you need me, my number is 555-7655."

"Got it. See you soon."

✌

The drive to Charlevoix was routine. Lou, Maggie and Tom moved along at a good clip, making their way north and passing all the familiar small towns and landmarks along the way. While Maggie and Lou were driving north, Al Forrest was calling Charlie Frasure, the maintenance garage supervisor; Gail Farrell, the middle school girls' physical education teacher and girls' volleyball coach; Angie Fry, the high school chemistry teacher; and Dan Flores, a sixth grade teacher who handles the driver education responsibilities. Al explained to each that they were needed for a meeting at the school administration building at 2:00 p.m. He expected the meeting to last the rest of the day and it may even go on into Sunday. Of course, each person wanted to know why this meeting was being called. Al made it clear that the meeting was not optional, and that it was very important that each attend. No one would stay away, if only for the curiosity of what could be so important to be called to a Saturday afternoon meeting at the administration office.

Lou and Maggie pulled up to the administration building. Lou took his attache from the back seat, and preceded Maggie into the building where he found a room of strangers and the group he left three short days ago. Maggie lowered the lift in her van so she could exit. She made her way to the Administration building, entered and greeted those present.

Al introduced Charlie, Gail, Angie, and Dan to Lou and Maggie. They paid close attention to the introductions and listened carefully to what was said about each. Charlie had been with the school district for almost thirty years serving as a bus driver for many students and then moving to maintenance supervisor. Gail was one of those energetic coaches who always seemed ready to participate in a sport at a moment's notice. She was young looking and had been with the Charlevoix district for two years, coming right from Central Michigan University where she was quite an athlete in her own right.

Angie was getting on in years. She could have retired several years ago, maybe she should have, but she loved children and chemistry, and Charlevoix needed her, she was told. Dan, like Gail, was a relatively new teacher, and the only man in the elementary school. He did some coaching of the sixth grade basketball team and earned some extra cash in the summer by taking his life in his hands each day with fifteen year olds eager to get their driver's license.

"Thank you all for coming." Lou said. "Your being here is critical to helping us solve a very complex and difficult case. I'll explain the situation we face momentarily, but I must make it very clear that no word of this meeting, or anything you hear in this meeting is to leave this room. I can't emphasize this enough. I know you are human beings and what you are about to hear will be information you will want to share with family, friends, and neighbors, but please, please do not say anything. As we continue to talk, the reasons for my plea will become obvious.

"Maggie and I are licensed Michigan private investigators. We've been working with authorities in Newberry up in the U.P. A little more than a month ago a school board member died. Most are quite certain he died of a heart attack. A few think that the death was premature, even by a few minutes, and think that he was murdered. We are trying to help the police determine if the death was natural or if the man was killed."

Maggie added, "We want to make it perfectly clear at the outset that we're going to be talking about one of your colleagues, Bill Blakeley, the special education teacher at the juvenile detention facility. Do any of you know him?"

"I remember when Mr. Forrest introduced him as a new employee at an all staff meeting, but I haven't talked to him," Dan said.

"His son, Bryan, is in my chemistry class, first hour, but I haven't met Mr. Blakeley," Angie said.

Both Charlie and Gail shook their heads side to side.

Maggie continued, "I also want to say that you are going to hear some theory with no evidence concerning Mr. Blakeley. I'm certain that if he's not involved in some crime, the things I'll say about him will stay with you for a long time. Even if he's innocent, I'll feel bad that I've shared with you some thoughts that may cause you to form an opinion that isn't true. For his sake, Lou and I truly hope he's not involved, and if that is determined to be the case, I hope you can erase from your mind the accusations and opinions we'll share in the next few minutes."

"Mr. Blakeley has been laid off five times," Lou said.

"Five times!" Gail was shocked. "How could someone get a pink slip five times in education these days?"

Lou responded, "There's a reason in each school district, Gail. A millage doesn't pass, inclusive education leads to staff reduction, or a school chooses to downsize and some bumping occurs. I know this is hard to believe, but I've looked into each situation, and in each case it is explainable and makes sense."

Lou continued, "At any rate there is a pattern that we've discovered, and it goes like this. Blakeley gets the layoff notice in person and/or in writing. He gets very angry and makes serious threats that scare people terribly. Then, within three days of the layoff notice, someone dies in the school district. In four of the five cases, the person died by logical medical means. By that I mean a heart attack, a stroke, insulin shock, and suicide. In the fifth case, a principal died in a hunting accident.

"Here in Charlevoix, Mr. Blakeley was to be laid off even though he barely started because, as you read in your papers or heard via the grape vine, the county is taking over the program and wants to hire their own special education teacher, which is their right. Your administration decided not to layoff Mr. Blakeley, but late yesterday afternoon, Mr. Williams thought Blakeley was going to be laid off on Monday. In a kind gesture, he told Bill that this would happen to him. True to our prediction, Bill got very angry and threatening toward Mr. Williams. It was my advice to Dr. Forrest, that we meet and advise you of what is happening. He agreed, and this is why we've invited you here today."

"Why have we been chosen to meet with you?" Dan Flores asked.

Maggie replied, "There is more to the pattern. The first letter in the last names of the victims in the other school districts over the past several years spell the word LAYOFF. Or, it would be more accurate to say that is the case with the first five letters. The victims names so far have been Lorimer, Anderson, Young, Olsen, and Franklin."

"So, since all of us have last names that begin with 'F' we are the possible next victims, right?" Gail concluded.

"Yes, that's why you are here. Let me repeat that we expect you to be safe and we're here to help you plan for the next few days. You may wish to leave the area and visit a friend or relative in some other city."

Dr. Forrest interrupted, "If any of you choose this option, you will not be charged with sick or vacation leave. We want to support you with your decisions."

"This is the first opportunity we've had to be ahead of the game, so to speak," Lou said. "There has been no suspicion of murder in the other districts at the time of, or immediately after the layoff. So, in this instance we hope for your assistance in preventing a crime from happening."

"Are we in any danger?" Angie asked.

"I'd be lying if I said 'no,' but, I am very certain that you're not in danger if you do exactly as we suggest," Lou answered with authority.

"Well, if we decide to stay, what are we supposed to do?" asked Charlie.

"Several things. Now, listen. In one school district, a woman was diabetic, lived alone, and had a routine. The theory is that someone switched her insulin containers. In another case, a man had a bad heart and was visited by someone who may have given him too much digitalis. So, think if you have any medical problem that could lead to early death with the appearance of natural causes, tell us now.

"We want you to pay attention to your families. Most of the victims lived alone. The victim is not likely to be someone from a big family or someone who is always around people.

"We want you to think about hobbies that would put you in life-threatening situations. Hunting and boating are examples of activities that would be quite popular in Charlevoix. Stay away from those things for awhile.

"We will give a picture of Bill and his dad to each of you. If you see them anywhere that seems strange, call me or Chief Brewbaker immediately."

For the next couple of hours, each potential victim developed his or her profile so that Lou, Maggie, Chief Brewbaker, and Al could try to be a step ahead of the murderer. If there was a murderer.

♫

Meanwhile in Rudyard, Bill, Sr. called Stan and asked to meet him for coffee at the Pure Country Family Restaurant. At 4:00 p.m. the two men met at their regular table. Within a few minutes of sitting down a couple of hot cups of coffee arrived without them even asking. Some things are just expected, and coffee is expected when Stan and Bill are together.

"What's on your mind, Bill?"

"Billy's been laid off again."

"You gotta be kidding me?" Stan was shocked.

"He called and told me it wasn't for sure, but his supervisor told him it was going to happen on Monday."

"Are you going down there to see Billy?" Stan asked.

"I don't know. He said it wasn't necessary. He hasn't had the meeting yet. I still don't feel real good. I might, and I might not. You know, Stan, when I get thinking about Billy getting laid off, my heart kind of takes off, and I feel like I'm gunna throw up."

"You gotta take care of yourself, my friend. I know this is real upsetting for you, but Billy's got his own life. He and Trudy will make it. You gotta let it go, Bill."

"I can't. The memories hurt. Billy hurts. My heart hurts. I'm not saying like a broken heart, I mean it really hurts. I gotta get home."

"Let me take ya to the hospital, Bill. You don't look good."

"Nah. They'll just tell me to get some rest. The worst place for a person to go is to the hospital."

"Listen to me. You gotta get some help. We're going in, I'm taking over. You aren't thinking clearly. We'll take your car. Give me the keys, Bill."

Bill reluctantly gave Stan his keys. It was as if he was giving in, but then again, he really thought this might be it. What difference did it make when you think you're going to die?

They got in Bill's car and headed to the hospital. Bill asked Stan to pull over to a mailbox; he had a few bills to pay. He wanted to get them in before the five o'clock pick up, otherwise he would miss the final payment date and have to pay a finance charge. Stan did as asked.

The hospital was in Sault Ste. Marie and the drive was about thirty minutes. The men didn't talk much enroute.

Bill was examined by the doctor on duty who ordered a series of tests. The doctor kept Bill overnight but didn't think there was a life-threatening situation. Stan was standing next to Bill's bed. "Shoulda never let you talk me into coming to this place!" Bill was angry.

"You had no choice. You looked bad. I couldn't have lived with myself if you would have gone home and passed away. A friend takes care of a friend. Your insurance will cover this. Enjoy the nurses care and have a couple of meals. They won't be as good as what we get at our restaurant, but what do you expect?"

"I feel like a prisoner in here."

"Relax. We can play cards for awhile. You watch some TV when I leave, and then get some sleep. They'll serve you breakfast in bed, and I'll have you home for the Packers-Lions game."

"Thanks for being here for me. That's what I try to do for Billy."

"No problem. I'm glad to help. Do you want me to call Billy?"

"Yeah. Don't alarm him. Tell him I won't be coming to see him, but ask him to call."

"Sure. I'll go down to the lobby right now and call. When I come back, we'll play some cards."

Stan got Billy's phone number and placed a call from the pay phone in the hospital lobby.

Trudy answered, "Hello."

"Trudy?"

"Yes."

"This is Stan Hovath, a friend of Billy's dad in Rudyard."

"Is everything OK?"

"Yeah, I think so. Is Billy there?"

"Not at the moment. Can he call you?"

"Yeah, maybe that would be good."

"Everything's OK with Dad. That's what you said, right?"

"He's in the hospital now, but he'll be fine. The doc thought he should stay overnight and have some tests, that's all."

"I'll have Bill call. How can he reach you?"

"We are at the hospital in the Soo. His dad is in room 402 and the number here is (906) 555-4557. When do you think Billy will be back?"

"Soon, I think. Said he had to take care of some business, but I'm not sure what that means. He's still very angry about a possible lay-off, and when he gets like this, it's frightening. It always turns out for the best, he just can't see it."

"Tough on you, and it gets to Billy's dad."

"I know it does. Thanks for calling. Say 'hi' to Dad and I'll have Bill call when he gets in."

"Thanks, Trudy."

Stan went back to the room to report that Billy was out of the house taking care of some business. He told him that Trudy was sorry he was in the hospital and that Billy would call when he arrived home. With that out of the way, they played some cards and waited for the phone call that didn't come. Bill, Sr. couldn't understand why Billy didn't call. He worried about him, but eventually got some sleep.

ॐ

Late that same afternoon, in Charlevoix, the team was about to conclude its intense session of personal profiles. Before they left, Lou gave them another lecture. "Let me go over the procedures we're going to use. If you are going out of town, please let us know where you will be so we can check in with you on occasion. If you're staying in town, please listen carefully to these instructions. In the event that you suspect any problem, do not try to intervene in any way. Always call Chief Brewbaker and follow his advice. Call me if you don't need police intervention but want to share anything you hear, see, or suspect. Everyone has my number at the motel, my car phone number, and the number of the administration building. If for some reason you can't reach me, try to reach Maggie.

"Don't do anything out of the ordinary that would subject you to danger. Do not hunt, boat, fly, or hike. Do not open packages. Do not eat any food other than what you prepare. Lock your house or apartment. Don't let anyone, no matter what the conditions, into your home or car. Do not be alone unless it's absolutely necessary. These conditions will only last a few days if things go as we suspect they will.

"We don't want you to be overly alarmed. You should be very confident and feel secure that you are prepared. Again, if you have any questions, call me or Maggie. Do not hesitate to do so. Maggie or I will call each of you every evening to discuss the day and to hear any observations or perceptions you have. Are there any final questions?"

"If you write a book and have it published, will we get any of the royalties?" Angie asked with a chuckle.

"Royalties?" Lou said with surprise and a chuckle. "You'll probably all get parts in the movie and one of you will walk away with an Oscar for best supporting actor or actress in a drama."

Maggie said, "Let's hope that nothing happens. We couldn't be happier if this pattern turns out to be coincidence, and no one is threatened."

Trudy was feeling guilty about not telling Bill that his father was in the hospital. Just as Stan tried to take care of Bill, Sr., Trudy was trying to take care of Bill, Jr. A human can take only so much stress before flipping out completely. The layoff, plus Bryan's drug problem, plus Bill's dad in the hospital was more than Trudy could, in good conscience, put on her husband. She didn't tell Bill about the call; later she would beg forgiveness. Her mind was reeling, and she could say she lost the slip with the phone number on it and was embarrassed and afraid that Bill would get angry with her. She could outright say she never got a call from the Upper Peninsula and let fate take its course, but she felt she knew she should tell Bill about his dad. She would, but when it was the right time. This didn't seem to be a good time.

〜

Al Forrest invited Lou, Maggie and Tom to his home for dinner. The Forest's eldest son was a dentist in the Chicago area. As Tom was an oral surgeon in Battle Creek, he had a chance to talk about his profession before Maggie, Lou, and Al began pouring over the staff profiles, trying to outwit one of the Blakeley's.

"The two people who seem to fit the pattern are Angie or myself," Al said.

"Why is that?" Maggie asked.

"Well, Angie is up in years. She has cancer, but many don't know it. She lives alone with her cat, Buttons. She lives in a year-round cottage on Lake Charlevoix. The area is pretty desolate, as most people board up their cottages in late September or October. She has only one sister who lives in Tacoma, Washington. Her sister is quite elderly herself, so no one would be suspicious of a murder or expect a lot of investigation."

"That all makes sense. Now why you?"

"Well, like Tom Franklin, I'm an influential person in the system who is partially responsible for laying him off. I established his trust by encouraging him to apply, and then in a matter of weeks, I turn around and lay him off. If anyone is targeted, it would have to be me. I live on a winding road with many steep hills and sharp turns. It wouldn't take much tinkering with my car and I'd probably find myself going over the cliff in a freak accident of brake failure. I'm asthmatic, and an evening without my inhaler would cause me to die for lack of air."

Lou enjoyed the evening dinner with Maggie, Tom, Al, and his wife, Susan. While they sipped their after dinner coffee, the three continued to pour over the information provided by the team. At about nine-thirty, they thanked the Forrests' and drove to the Lodge Motel in downtown Charlevoix.

Sunday, November 22,
Charlevoix, Michigan

As the Blakeley family gathered together to eat their traditional Sunday breakfast, which usually consisted of pancakes made by Heather or Belgian waffles made by Bryan, Trudy decided that she had to tell Bill about his father. She would take whatever the consequences were for not telling him last evening.

"I have something important to share with the family," Trudy said. "Last evening, Grandpa's friend in Rudyard called to say that Grandpa was in the hospital."

"What's wrong?" Bryan asked. Bill sat in his chair looking stunned.

"He didn't feel very good and his friend, Mr. Hovath thought he should be seen by a doctor. After talking with Grandpa, the doctor thought some tests were necessary and he wanted Grandpa kept in the hospital overnight," Trudy reported as factually as she could without being an alarmist.

"Why didn't you tell us last night?" Bill asked.

"Honey, with all the stress you're under at the moment, I thought you could handle the news better this morning," explained Trudy.

Trudy was very surprised to hear, "You're probably right. It has been quite a week, and it doesn't look like the storm will end anytime soon."

"I think you should call him to see how he's doing. In fact, I told his friend that you would probably call last evening, but that was before I thought it best to delay giving you the news. Your dad may be concerned that you haven't called. Please tell him that it was my fault and that you called as soon as you heard he was in the hospital."

"Dad will understand. I'll call after breakfast." Trudy breathed a sigh of relief. He could have gotten very angry and stormed out, but for some reason, he took it well. She couldn't predict anymore, but she was thankful he was supportive of her decision to delay the news. Just then the phone rang.

Heather answered, "Hello."

"Bill Blakeley please."

"Just a minute please. Dad, phone's for you."

"Hello."

"Mr. Blakeley?"

"Yes."

"This is Mary calling from the hospital in Sault Ste. Marie. I'm sorry to have to give you this message, but your father passed away this morning." Bill sat down and didn't say a word, sort of like when he sat in the personnel director's office and heard that he would be laid off.

"Mr. Blakeley?" No response.

Trudy could tell that something had happened and it wasn't good. She asked, "Bill, what's the matter?"

"Dad died," was all he said. He handed Trudy the phone. Then he walked into the living room, sat down, and cried while Bryan and Heather looked on.

Trudy talked into the phone, "Hello."

"I'm sorry to have to be the one to give you the news, but ...."

"I understand. What happened?" asked Trudy.

"The doctor believes it was a massive heart attack. There was no pain. The nurse went in his room to check on him, and he was dead. Do you want an autopsy performed?"

"I can't answer that now. I'll have to ask my husband, but he's very upset with the news at the moment. I'll have to call you back," Trudy explained.

"I understand. We'll need some decisions soon."

"We'll come right up. We'll be there in about three hours. Do we come right to the hospital?"

"Yes, that'd be fine."

Trudy hung up after getting directions. She went into the living room to console Bill. He was beginning to get control of himself. Bill seemed close to the breaking point. The family decided to go to Rudyard. Bill called his supervisor and told him the news. "If they are going to tell me I'm laid off, they'll have to wait until Tuesday," he concluded. "It's possible that I'll quit before I give them the chance to lay me off. It is also possible that my family and I won't come back to Charlevoix, period."

Lucky Williams called Dr. Forrest and relayed the news about Bill's father's passing away and Bill's comment about maybe quitting his job or not even returning to Charlevoix. Both couldn't get over how much bad luck could come to one family.

Al Forrest called Lou at the motel.

"Hello."

"Lou. This is Al. Hope I didn't wake you up?"

"Oh no. I've been out for a six mile run, had breakfast, and am still going over the profiles. What's on your mind?"

"Lucky Williams, Bill Blakeley's supervisor, just called and said that Bill's father died in Rudyard. The family is going up there, and he won't be back until at least Tuesday."

"You've got to be kidding!"

"Don't think so. It happened."

"Well, there goes one of the two people on my list of perpetrators. If Bill, Jr. isn't killing these people, then this case is history."

"I just thought you would want to know. Do we call Angie, Gail, Don, and Charlie?" Al asked.

"No. Not yet," Lou responded without giving it any thought. "He could come back on Tuesday or Wednesday and carry out some threat or add another to the list of people who had to be sacrificed for his being laid off."

"Are you going to call them and brief them?" Al asked.

"Sure, I'll do that. What time is it? Nine-thirty? I'll wait an hour or two and then bring everyone up to speed."

"Sounds like a good idea."

"Let me begin with you, Al. You said yourself that you might be a potential victim, and I would suggest that you may be right. Be very careful for the next few days. Be suspicious of everything, take absolutely no risks, and do nothing that would be out of your routine."

"I'll be careful."

Lou called Maggie and asked her to come to his room when she could. She came right over and Lou told her of Al's news. They waited a couple of hours and then called Charlie, Angie, Gail, and Dan. Lou told each what he had said to Dr. Forrest. "This could be all over now that Bill Blakeley's father has died. First of all, he has not been laid off yet. There has been no meeting with him and no written notice. Second, his father will not be coming to visit, so if the father was doing the killing, that is out of the picture, and Bill will be gone to take care of arrangements for his father's funeral. So, on the one hand, I say relax, on the other, I say be very diligent."

Lou reminded them that each could still be a victim. "Be very careful, do not take risks, and stick to a routine. Eat only food you prepare. Go nowhere alone." Each promised to be careful and to call Lou or Maggie if for any reason they suspected something.

The rest of the day was uneventful. While Charlevoix is a colorful and interesting city, Lou and Maggie thought they needed to be next to a phone for quick action. They didn't leave the motel. Lou watched the NFL on TV. Maggie wrote letters to some friends. Tom went off for another long hike and hoped to get some unique nature photos.

When the game was over Lou read a William Kienzle mystery. "Father Koesler sure can solve those crimes," Lou said to Maggie. Lou often thought of himself as the Father Koesler of special education. In many ways, the Catholic church and special education are alike. Both have rules and procedures. Both have a hierarchy of characters. Both have acronyms and a vocabulary all their own.

Both have "penalties" for not staying in line with authority. Lou thought that if he could meet Father Koesler, he would like him. After all, they both cared about people, had analytical minds, and enjoyed solving problems.

The phone rang. It startled Lou. He answered, "Hello."

"Mr. Searing?"

"Yes."

"This is Lucky Williams. Mr. Blakeley's supervisor at the detention center."

"Oh yes. How are you?"

"Fine. I talked to Chief Brewbaker a few minutes ago, and he said it was alright to call you."

"No problem. What can I do for you?"

"It's not so much what you can do for me, as what I can do for you."

"What's that?"

"Well, first of all, I'm taking some risks in talking to you. Can I trust that you won't tell anyone what I'm going to say?"

"Sure, but I will share it with Maggie. We work together to solve these cases."

"That's fine, I trust you. Anyway, I went into Bill's classroom after he made threatening comments to me. I found a folder on top of his desk, and inside was detailed information about Mrs. Fry."

"Mrs. Fry, the high school chemistry teacher?"

"Yes."

"What information was there?"

"A lot of it is basic; address, family members, job, hobbies, interests. Then it gets a little strange, because he has also written medical information. It says that Mrs. Fry has cancer, for example."

"Does the folder have a title?"

"No."

"Is the information hand written?"

"No. It's typed."

"Does Bill have a typewriter in his room?"

"No. He has a computer."

"But, the information is clearly typewritten and not from a computer?"

"Yes. It's typewritten."

"Have you seen any other things he has done that have been typed?"

"No. But, I don't know if he has a typewriter at home."

"Can I see the document?"

"I guess so. I'm not sure the folder is still on his desk. I can meet you at the detention center, and we can take a look."

"I'll come right over. Where is it again?"

"Northeast of town. Go north on 31, and turn right on the Boyne City Road. Go about a mile and it's on the right."

"See you in a few minutes, and thanks Lucky."

"No problem."

"By the way, why is your name Lucky? That isn't the name your parents gave you is it?"

"No, my name's Harry. I was supposed to be laid off about ten years ago, and the school board changed their mind. I got to keep my job. Some friends said I was a lucky guy, and for a few days, people around me called me 'Lucky.' It just stuck."

"Makes sense. See you soon."

Lou suggested that Maggie remain at the motel in case anyone called. He drove to the detention center, met Lucky, and went into Bill's classroom. On his desk was the folder, and inside was the typewritten information about Mrs. Fry. "Do you have a copy machine in the building so I can make a copy of this?"

"Sure." Lucky took the page and went to the office to get the requested copy.

While Lucky was gone, Lou looked around Bill's classroom. On the desk was a large lesson plan notebook. He opened it and looked at the previous Friday's plan. Bill had noted that Lucky had mentioned a possible layoff on Monday. He had also written, call Dad and Cynthia. There was a phone number after each name.

Lou turned the pages. On Monday, which would be tomorrow, he had written: "May be laid off today. Look into State Police

213

Academy." On Tuesday he had written, "Someone will have to pay for this happening to me."

Lucky returned with the copy that Lou wanted. "Anything else I can do for you?"

"Look at this lesson plan notebook, Lucky. Look at what he's written into the block for last Friday, for tomorrow, and Tuesday."

Lucky read it, turned to Lou and said, "This looks like a lesson plan for murder."

"That's just what I was thinking. By the way, Dr. Forrest told me that Bill made very threatening statements to you."

"He sure did. He's pretty scary."

"In all of his statements, did he threaten anyone else?"

"No, it was all directed at me."

"Do you see that as strange?"

"I did at the time. I was thinking, 'Hey, don't kill the messenger.' I was trying to make this ugly experience a little better by giving him some indication that it might happen. I wish someone would've done that for me ten years ago."

"Once again, no comments about harm coming to anyone else?"

"It all happened so fast, so threatening. He was very angry. He may have said that someone would have to pay for this or something like that."

"Thanks for calling and giving me this information."

"No problem."

"What happens now? Is he due back soon?"

"I don't know. When a family member dies, a person can be gone for three or four days. It's hard to tell. I know he won't be back in town tomorrow. He could be at work on Tuesday, but I can't imagine that he would be here. With all that's going on, I wouldn't be surprised if we didn't see him period, but if we do, I'd bet my money that it'll be at least a week."

"Thanks. Let me have your phone number in case I need to call."

Lucky gave Lou his number and walked him to the door. They shook hands, and Lou drove back to the motel. He took the typewritten report from his pocket and placed it on the desk in his room.

Maggie and Lou studied it very carefully. They read, "Angie Fry is a 69 year old, high school chemistry teacher. She lives alone in a year-round cottage on Lake Charlevoix, 144673 Pinecone Drive (approximately two miles out of town on the eastern side of the lake). She has a cat named 'Buttons'. She has a sister who lives in Tacoma, Washington, her only known living relative. She attends the Methodist Church. She is active in issues for senior citizens. She has an unusual hobby of collecting cookie containers. She drinks coffee, soft drinks, and wine on occasion. She enjoys having students pay her a visit when they are home from college, for holidays, or weekends. Mrs. Fry has cancer, but it is not known by many, and she has received treatment for it. Her workday schedule is consistent. She arrives at the high school at about 7:30 in the morning. She stays at the school all day and returns home at about five each day. Almost every day after school she has an activity. She likes shopping, volunteers for hospital auxiliary, or visits friends in the nursing home. She is in her church choir and goes to choir practice on Thursday evenings. She rarely drives at night. Her best friend at school is Mrs. Hyzer, the geometry and trig teacher. Her best friend outside of school is her neighbor, Mrs. Flowers, who watches the house like a hawk when Mrs. Fry isn't home. They seem to look out for each other. Mrs. Fry has taught in the Charlevoix district for 36 years. She has received many community awards, and her pride and joy was receiving the Michigan Chemistry Teacher of the Year Award in 1979."

"Very interesting profile, and one which someone would need if planning to kill her," Lou said.

"It looks like she's the targeted person, Lou."

"I think you're right."

Lou called Al Forrest and Chief Brewbaker and asked if they could come to the motel for a short briefing. Both were at the motel inside of fifteen minutes. Lou shared the typewritten report he had received from Lucky Williams. Lou also told them what he had seen in Blakeley's lesson plan book with particular attention to the Tuesday comment about somebody having to pay for the layoff. Ironically, the layoff that wasn't to happen.

Dr. Forrest said, "I have to share what I did and I realize that I may be botching things up, but my heart said I had to do it, so I did. I reached Bill Blakeley in Rudyard, and I told him, on behalf of the board of education and the staff, that we were very sorry to hear of the death of his father. I told him that he was not being laid off and that he would be working for Charlevoix for as long as he wished. I told him to take the week off to get himself together, and that we would pay the expenses if he needed counseling as a result of all of this trauma. I also offered to provide any costs beyond their insurance for Bryan to get help with his drug problem."

The three others in the room appeared to be stunned, yet there was a sense of well being about the kindness Al Forrest showed. "That's a very compassionate thing to do," Maggie said. "How did he respond?"

"He was very thankful. Trudy got on the phone and was also thankful."

Chief Brewbaker brought the three back to reality, "What does this do to our investigation?"

Maggie responded, "I think we should bring the four people back together to explain what has happened since yesterday afternoon. I'm still very concerned with this information about Mrs. Fry, and I think that it's possible that something could happen. We've uncovered a lot of incriminating evidence and I don't want us to drive home and find out tomorrow, or Tuesday, that someone died mysteriously. So, we'll plan to be here at least through Monday."

"Sorry, but I had to do what I thought best, and that means to help a teacher I brought here."

"No apologies needed, Al," Lou said. "We're proud of you, and I hope I would have done the same thing. Thankfully, you have your priorities in place."

Late Sunday afternoon Al called the four teachers whose last names began with the letter "F." He asked them to be at the Administration Building in a half hour for an important meeting. They were all at home and agreed to be there. Charlie made Al promise that the meeting would be over in time for him to get home for *America's Funniest Home Videos*. In return for the promise, Al asked Charlie to pick up Mrs. Fry, which he was pleased to do.

At about five o'clock Sunday afternoon the seven people were gathered in the board meeting room of the Charlevoix Public Schools Administration Building. Al and Lou thanked the group for coming on such short notice. Lou addressed the group. "We've asked you to come here this evening to brief you on the events of the last twenty-four hours. Some of you may have already heard what's happened.

"Bill Blakeley's father died very early this morning in Sault Ste. Marie. Bill and his family have gone up there. Dr. Forrest called Bill and expressed sympathy on behalf of the board, and staff. He promised Bill that he would not be laid off and told him to take a week to get himself together. I want to say, before all of you, that I admire the very kind thing he did. I trust you are thankful to have a leader who acted in such a compassionate manner. When we drove up here we had a theory that either Bill or his father was committing murders, and they were part of a pattern that seemed quite obvious to us. Bill, Sr. is dead now and is quite incapable of carrying out a murder early next week. Bill, Jr. has no reason to take out any revenge on this district that has just shown him great compassion and support. It's highly unlikely that he would murder anyone. Besides, he won't even be in town.

"I was informed of and found that some information about you, Angie, was in a folder on Bill's desk at the detention center. It was a one-page report that told all about you. I don't want you to be concerned, but it looks to me like you may have been targeted."

"What was in the report?" Angie asked.

"Just a lot of information about you. If it would make you feel better, I'll share it with you. If it'll disturb you, I'll keep it to myself."

"No, I'd like to see it, or I'll be curious."

Lou took it from his valise and handed it to Angie. She read it and said, "I think I can explain this. Last week, Wednesday, I was interviewed by a teacher in the middle school. Her name is Anne Austin. She said she was on a committee with an elementary teacher and a special education teacher. This committee was asked to get information from a few of us old timers for some type of recognition at our annual holiday party. All of this is what I told her. My guess is that she wrote it up, typed it, and shared it with the members of the committee. I guess Bill was the special education teacher on the committee."

"Well, that seems to take care of that," Maggie said.

"Is there anything else for us to do?" Dan asked.

"I guess not. It looks like we're at an impasse. Thankfully, it seems that no murder will take place in Charlevoix. Now I'm thinking that maybe all of the past murders were not murders at all, but just coincidental deaths around the time Bill was laid off. Or maybe it was Bill, Sr., and murder is no longer the issue. I guess we'll just pack up and head home. But, before we leave, I have a couple of things to say. First of all, for Bill's sake, please honor your commitment of silence from yesterday, and do not share a word of this weekend. It would simply not be fair to Bill or his family to have terrible, untrue rumors out there. The man has gone through enough already. Secondly, don't put your guard completely down. For the next few days, please be very cautious. It can't hurt to be very aware of your activities, and call Chief Brewbaker if you suspect anything. It's better to err on being overly cautious than to err by thinking something isn't worthy of attention. It's time to get back to families and whatever we have left of the weekend. Thank you for your work with us yesterday and today," Lou concluded.

With that, all seven disbanded to their homes. Maggie, Tom, and Lou decided to stay overnight at The Lodge motel. They were tired, and snow was expected.

218

Monday, November 23, Charlevoix, Michigan

Lou got up early, read the *USA Today*, and went out for his morning jog. The air was cold, crisp, and refreshing. It took about five minutes for his body heat to stay within his running outfit and to keep him protected from the elements. While he was running, he had the intuitive feeling that he should stay in Charlevoix for most of the day. It was nothing that he could put his finger on. If something was going to happen, it would happen today, and even at that, the chances were slim to nil that anything would happen.

Lou showered, and went with Maggie and Tom to Judy's restaurant for a hot bowl of oatmeal with unbuttered toast and a small orange juice. A healthy meal would get him off to a good start. Maggie had tea and a bagel. After breakfast, Lou suggested that they drive out to the Charlevoix-Emmet Intermediate School District office. Lou wanted to see if he could pay a visit to Ed Keller, the director of special education, and a friend of his. Ed and Lou shared a strong interest in special education history. Since he was in the area, he thought a short visit would be appropriate. Maggie and Tom agreed, and they drove out to the office on the chance that Ed was in and could see them.

On their way they passed an ambulance with its lights flashing and the siren blaring. When they arrived at the intermediate school district building, they were shown the way to Mr. Keller's office. They were greeted with firm handshakes and smiles. Lou introduced the McMillans to Ed.

"What brings you up to God's country, Lou?"

"We're up here investigating a possible murder connection. It's special education related and connected to other parts of the state. One of our prime suspects is in this area, so we needed to get up here to do some work."

Ed's secretary came into his office and said, "Sorry to interrupt. Dr. Forrest has just died. Thought you would want to know."

"Oh my God. What happened?" Ed asked.

"I don't know. He was in his office this morning and Melanie found him there dead."

"Heart attack? Stroke? What happened?"

"All I know is what Melanie said when she called. The ambulance came and took him to the hospital, but he appeared to be dead when the paramedics arrived."

Maggie, Tom, and Lou listened to all of this before Lou said, "Ed, I'm sorry, but we have to leave. Talk to you again soon."

"Is this news related to your investigation, Lou?"

"I hope not. Talk to you later."

They drove straight to the Charlevoix Area Hospital with the goal of convincing Mrs. Forrest that an autopsy should be done. To date, only one autopsy had been done on the previous five victims, and it was critical that one be done at this time. Thankfully, after talking with her, she conceded to have the autopsy done. Susan Forrest realized that in the long run it would give her peace of mind to know why he died.

They drove over to the Administration building. Chief Brewbaker was there overseeing the activity at the scene of death. Lou and the chief looked at each other and instinctively believed that Blakeley had broken through their plans for all potential victims to be cautious. "What happened, Chief?" Lou asked.

"I got a call that he was slumped over at his desk. His secretary found him when she went in to get some papers. There was no indication that he was not feeling well when he got to work this morning. There was no panic, no cry, no evidence of any interaction with anyone."

The mood in the building was somber. Mr. Forrest's office was sealed off so no one could enter without Chief Brewbaker's permission. A couple of officers were taking photos and combing Al's office looking for any evidence of foul play or any evidence of a motive for Al's death.

The secretaries were emotionally upset. Maggie made a point of immediately talking with Dr. Forrest's secretary, Melanie Marrison. "Mrs. Marrison? I'm Margaret McMillan, and I've been working with Dr. Forrest for the last several days on the matter related to Mr. Blakeley. He may have mentioned that he's been in touch with me?"

"Yes. He did. This is so terrible."

"Yes it is. He was a fine man. I could tell he was a compassionate leader from the short time I knew him."

Melanie started to cry.

"I know you're upset and I'm sorry to be asking questions so soon after you've had this traumatic experience, but I must learn as much as I can, as quickly as I can."

"I'll try to help."

"Try to go over the morning as you remember it, and give me as much detail as you can."

Lou, Maggie, and Chief Brewbaker listened as Melanie provided her memories of the morning.

"He came to work a little late which isn't typical. He arrived about eight-twenty. He was in a good mood and was friendly, which is like him. He went into his office and did paperwork. He dictated a few short letters and all seemed very normal. He met with Mrs. Walker, our high school principal, for about fifteen minutes. You may want to talk with her. They were talking about the new suspension policy."

"We'll need to see her when we finish here. Had he had anything to eat or drink?" asked Lou. Chief Brewbaker had already conducted interviews with the secretaries, but he understood Lou and Maggie's need to inquire.

"Vickie brought in some cookies and most of us had one."

"Did Dr. Forrest have one?" Maggie asked

"Yes. He had two and maybe three. He really enjoyed chocolate, and chocolate chip cookies were his favorite."

"Everyone chose these cookies from the same plate?"

"Oh yes. Every Monday one of us brings in something sweet to start the week."

"Did he drink anything with the cookies?"

"Yes, I took him coffee twice."

"You all drank from the same pot?"

"Yes. It's a coffee club arrangement."

"Are any cookies and coffee left?"

"Yes. I think so."

Maggie knew the detectives would confiscate anything that would give a clue to possible poisoning for analysis by the State Police Crime Lab.

Maggie's questions continued. "Then what happened?"

"I took his mail in to him and..."

"Did you open all the mail?"

"Yes. I read it, date stamped it, stapled the envelope to the letter or enclosed information, and then I'd take it all in to him."

"What was his mail this morning?"

"Oh, I don't remember all of it. There were some items from the State Department of Education in Lansing. There were some letters of interest from perspective teachers looking for jobs. There was a personal letter from another superintendent asking for a letter of recommendation for a job out of state. There was one very nice gesture. A former student sent him a tea bag with a note telling him he hoped he would enjoy the tea. You see, Dr. Forrest was a connoisseur of tea, and often people would send him tea from all over the state, nation, or world for that matter."

"Did he drink the tea?"

"I don't know. He keeps a hot pad in his office. He could have heated some water and used the tea bag."

Maggie continued with the questions. "Did he get any threatening phone calls or any phone call that seemed different or out of the ordinary?"

"No. There were very few calls this morning."

"Tell me what happened just before you found him?"

"After his meeting with Mrs. Walker, I took him his mail, and he said he had some important work. He didn't want to be disturbed unless you called. I remember that. He closed the door, and about forty-five minutes later I needed to talk to him. I called him on the phone, and there was no response. I knocked on his door, and again no response. I walked in and found him slumped over on his desk." Melanie once again became emotional, and Maggie apologized for asking her to recall this difficult scene. But she needed the information.

"I went over to him and could see that something was terribly wrong. I went out to the other offices and asked for help. One of the secretaries who has had first aid training went in and called 911 from his phone. The ambulance came within minutes and the workers tried to revive him, but I don't think he responded. They took him from his office and went to the hospital."

Chief Brewbaker showed the note to Lou. Lou read outloud, "Dr. Forrest. I know how much you enjoy tea. I purchased some very good tea during a recent trip to Japan and thought you would enjoy a cup. I have been away from Charlevoix for several years, but still have fond memories of being a student there under your fine leadership. Enjoy my gift to you. Sincerely, Larry."

"Can I see the envelope it came in," asked Maggie.

Chief Brewbaker handed her a business-size envelope. The address was typewritten to Dr. Forrest, Superintendent, with the correct address. There was no return address. She looked at the postage stamp. While she couldn't make out the post office by city, she could read most of the zip code. The fourth number was not clear. Maggie stated what she could see, 497_0."

"What is the zip code of Charlevoix?" Lou asked.

Melanie said, "49720."

"Can you read the fourth number?" asked Lou as he handed the envelope to Melanie and Chief Brewbaker. Each said it looked like either an eight or a two.

Turning to Mrs. Marrison, Lou said, "Please give me your phone book."

Melanie went to her desk, picked up the phone book, and handed it to Lou. He looked in the front for Michigan Zip Codes; and, when he found the right page, he looked for the zip code of Rudyard. He saw 49780.

"The Rudyard zip code is 49780," Lou said. "If the tea was poisoned or drugged, it was in an envelope that was mailed from Charlevoix if the fourth number is "2" or from Rudyard if the fourth number is "8." Bill, Jr. lives in Charlevoix and Bill, Sr. lived in Rudyard. This case isn't closed after all."

Lou thanked Mrs. Marrison for answering their questions under the stress of the morning's crisis. He turned to Chief Brewbaker and said, "My guess is that the autopsy and the lab analysis of the tea will show that Al was poisoned or drugged in some manner that quickly led to his death. The tea was sent by Bill, Jr. or Bill, Sr. and the clue to this lies in the fourth digit of the zip code on an envelope sent to Al. If the fourth number is a "2," the envelope was mailed right here in Charlevoix. If the fourth number is an "8," the envelope was sent from Rudyard."

"Ok, but how do you know it came from Bill or his father.? Maybe it was mailed by Trudy or someone else in town or in Rudyard."

"The pattern. The pattern."

"Yes, but his father wasn't in town, he died, remember?"

"Yes, but he died on Sunday morning. He could have mailed the tea in an envelope on Saturday."

"Bill, Jr. could have mailed it on Saturday, too. Or, Trudy could have mailed it."

"That's true. Any of them could have. But Al called him on Sunday and gave him assurance that his job would be there for as long as he wanted to work in Charlevoix. He promised to pay for counseling for him and for his son's drug program. It seems to me that when he received that news, which Al said made him very thankful, Bill, Jr. would have told Al not to drink the tea. I mean, why would you kill a person who did not lay you off, and who pours out his heart to you and your family."

"With all of the emotion surrounding his dad's death, he could have forgotten he sent the tea. Or, once again, Trudy could have sent the tea."

"Would you forget that you were expecting a person to die on Monday when you sent the death package?" Lou asked.

"No, I guess I wouldn't," admitted Chief Brewbaker.

Maggie asked, "What happens now?"

"Now we need to wait for the State Police Lab to give us a report, get the autopsy report, and find out if a technician at the lab can put a high powered microscope on the zip code to give us a definite '8' or '2,'" answered Brewbaker. "Then we'll have enough evidence to make Bill, Jr. a suspect, or to get a search warrant for both Blakeley homes where we may find some more interesting information. My main concern now is that Bill, Jr. and family may be cleaning out the home of Bill, Sr. and destroying papers and things that they believe aren't worth keeping. We'll need to contact and visit with the sheriff in the eastern U.P."

"I agree," Lou said. "I definitely think they need to be warned and asked to keep an eye on the activity. Maggie and I will head up there. We might find out something that will bring some closure."

"I'm going, too," Brewbaker said. "This case is under my jurisdiction now that a Charlevoix citizen has died. Since the father is a suspect, I'll go up there and investigate, and I predict the State Police Crime Lab in Grayling will be going on site as well."

Lou pondered over an idea for a few seconds and then said, "You know, if Bill leaves this district, takes a job in another school district, and gets laid off, everyone whose last name starts with 'S' should be sequestered somewhere far and away from their school district."

"I know what you mean, but no, I think it has ended right here," Maggie responded. "If the murderer is Bill, Sr., the case is closed, and people in six communities will have some piece of mind. If the murderer is Bill, Jr., or Trudy, well, then there will be a trial that will bring a lot of people and attention to the Charlevoix County Courthouse. Finally, if father and son, or wife and husband conspired to commit these murders, the same trial will be held and it will be quite sensational. I'm kinda hoping that it will be Bill, Sr. so that Bill, Jr. can get on with his life. I really don't think Trudy is involved. I never have. But, investigators don't get to finish the script. We just go where the clues lead us and solve the mysteries."

"So, are you and Maggie going to Rudyard from here?" asked Chief Brewbaker.

"I need to talk to the high school principal. She was the last person to see Al alive, and I want to make sure she doesn't have information that we've overlooked. Then, yes, we're driving up to Rudyard to see what we can find up there. I'll be in touch with you along the way."

"As soon as I finish with the State Police, I'll be going up there."

"Maggie and I really appreciate you working with us, Chief," Lou said.

"See ya, Lou. We got one shocked and saddened community here, and the rumors will be spreading fast."

"The three of us will bring closure to this situation quickly. We're very close to solving this thing."

Maggie and Lou stopped in at the high school and talked with the principal. They didn't learn anything new. She had talked with Al that morning, and he seemed very normal.

Maggie, Tom, and Lou checked out of the motel and headed for Rudyard. As they drove along they tried to plan how they wanted to orchestrate this visit.

They didn't want to confront Bill Blakeley, as it might set off a rage, especially with the emotion of his father's death. Bill really didn't need Louis Searing and Maggie McMillan in his life at this time. On the other hand, six people had died, and this case needed to be solved. There was no question in their minds that the Blakeley family was involved. They decided to contact the sheriff in Chippewa County and to seek his advice. They needed to know the whereabouts of the Blakeley family, the funeral home, and the location of

Bill's father's house. They wanted to talk to any close friends of the deceased Blakeley, too.

"Maybe a meeting with Bill, Jr. would be beneficial for all concerned," Lou thought outloud. "Maybe this is the best time to face this thing and get some answers. A man should be allowed some grieving time, but six people may have given their lives to murders and their families deserve answers."

They decided that they would pull into Rudyard and do what they needed to do. If paths crossed, so be it. They'd handle the situation as it presented itself.

They continued north on I-75 after crossing the Mackinac Bridge. Maggie drove about thirty miles and exited at the sign for Rudyard. She turned west, and only had to go about two miles until they saw the welcoming sign to Rudyard, a town named after the famous English writer, Rudyard Kipling. Chief Brewbaker had called them on the car phone, as promised, and told them he was in Rudyard already and was meeting with Deputy Sheriff Mike Moody. "You must have had your siren on, chief. You got right up here," said Maggie.

"I'm just doing my job. I feel obligated to solve the death of one of our finest citizens. This is Officer Moody. These folks are Lou Searing, Maggie McMillan and her husband, Tom. Lou and Maggie are investigating a series of murders over the past many years, and unfortunately the most recent is in my city."

"Pleased to meet you folks."

"We're not planning to be here long. We do need some information from you, and then I think we'll be pretty much on our own," Chief Brewbaker said.

"Help you anyway I can, Chief. What do you need?"

"We understand there is a funeral being planned here."

"Bill Blakeley. He died yesterday morning. The funeral is tomorrow morning. Visitation is going on this evening at seven."

"What time is the funeral?" Maggie asked.

"Ten o'clock. The burial will be at the cemetery west of town, and then the church will have a luncheon for family and friends."

"How do we get a search warrant?" Lou asked.

"You need to convince me you need one, we fill out the paper work, meet with the Magistrate or the Prosecutor in Sault Ste. Marie to explain it, and then if we get it, we can search the home."

"Let's work on the search warrant," suggested Lou. The four began constructing the facts and a description of what they felt they needed to look for. They needed to establish the probable cause standard. Each felt the facts would pass that test.

Deputy Sheriff Moody described the premises. He was familiar with the Blakeley home. The items that Maggie, Lou and Brewbaker wanted to look for included; diary, photos, handwriting samples, chemicals, school directories, typewriter, stationery. Once the paper work was complete, Deputy Moody called the Magistrate in Sault Ste. Marie and explained the four investigators would like a few minutes of his time to request a search warrant. They implored that time was of the essence. Permission was granted for a visit with the Magistrate and the four drove up to the Soo. The Magistrate welcomed his guests and immediately reviewed the paperwork. There were a few questions about some of the experiences Lou and Maggie had down-state. Deputy Moody was glad the two were along to explain. The search warrant was issued and the four returned to Rudyard.

Lou thought it would be a good idea to talk with someone who might know the deceased Blakeley. Mike Moody said that the best person would be Stan Hovath. He was Bill's only good friend. They shared meals in the Pure Country Restaurant. "Stan would be the only one who might have any information about Bill Blakeley," Moody said.

The five went to the home of Stan Hovath. All of the traveling was done in Maggie's customized van. They decided that having five people descend on a man's home might be a bit unnerving so Lou and Deputy Moody made the initial contact and Chief Brewbaker joined after the explanation for the visit was given to Stan. Maggie and Tom would stay in the van.

They knocked on the door late in the afternoon. Stan opened the door. "Mr. Hovath?"

"Yes. Something wrong, Mike?" Stan asked. Everyone in town knew Deputy Moody, and all referred to him as Mike.

"Stan, we've got some people who would like to talk with you for a few minutes. This is Lou Searing, a private investigator from Grand Haven. It seems your friend Bill Blakeley may be involved in some criminal behavior downstate, and we'd like to chat about him for a few minutes."

"Well that can't be. Bill never did nothing wrong in his life. Sure, I'll talk to anybody, but Bill wouldn't do anything against the law."

"There are more than two of us. In the van are the Chief of Police from Charlevoix and a private investigator who works with Lou."

"Sure, come on in. House is a bit cluttered. I wasn't expecting company today. I'm getting ready to go to the funeral home for the visitation."

"Well, we'll only be a few minutes."

Chief Brewbaker entered the home. The group sat on chairs and the couch in the living room. Deputy Moody began, "Stan, we have reason to believe that Bill may have been involved in some murders in schools where his son was teaching."

"Absurd. Not Bill. Never hurt a soul. Looking at the wrong man. I'm certain of that."

"Well, you may be right. The Chief and the private investigators here don't have any evidence to prove that your friend is involved, but enough has happened that he is clearly a suspect."

"Well, go ahead and ask your questions. I'll help even though you're wasting your time."

"Stan, tell us about your time with Bill prior to taking him to the hospital," Lou began.

"Well, we met at the restaurant in town, and he didn't look good. He told me about his son being laid off and it really bothered him. Anyway, I told him he should go to the hospital, but he said that he didn't need to. I insisted because he didn't look good. He was thinking about going to see his son because he thought he would be laid off from his job on Monday. Guess that would have been today, come to think of it. He resisted but finally agreed to go to the hospital."

Lou continued, "You two just went out to the car and drove straight to the hospital?"

"Yeah. I drove his car. On the way to the hospital he asked me to drop some mail in the mailbox at the post office, and of course I did. He said he needed his bills mailed so he wouldn't have to pay penalties."

"Do you remember the size of the envelopes?"

"Let's see. I think I threw about six or seven envelopes in the box. A couple of them were business size, I guess, and the others were smaller envelopes."

"So it was Saturday evening, you were on the way to the hospital and Bill, Sr. mailed some letters, six or seven, in white business-size and small envelopes?"

"Right. He asked me to look at them to make sure they were addressed correctly. Sometimes, in his old age, he'd forget a zip code, or the city, or something."

"And, did you look at the envelopes?"

"Yes. One was to Chicago. One was to Sears. One was to Marquette, Michigan. I think I saw one to Sault Ste. Marie, and I do recall one of the business-size envelopes addressed to someone in Charlevoix, Michigan. Probably going to his son, Billy. Billy lives in Charlevoix."

"Did you see Billy's name on the envelope?"

"I don't remember. Maybe it wasn't to Billy. I think it was."

"Then what happened?" Chief Brewbaker questioned.

"We got to the hospital. The doc checked him out. I sat out in the waiting room, so I don't know what happened with the examination. The doc came out and said Bill should stay overnight for more tests."

"Then what happened?"

"He was put in a room. I called Billy. He wasn't home so I talked to his wife. I told her about Billy's dad. She said she would tell Billy and he would call yet that night. He never did. That really bothered Bill. Kinda sad, he never got to talk to his son one last time. The two of them were close."

"Then did you go home?"

"No, we played some cards and talked for awhile. Then I went home. The next thing I know the phone was ringing Sunday morning and this lady says that Bill died."

Lou then asked, "Did Bill ever talk about any of his activities when he went to visit his son?"

"No, he would simply say that he'd gone to visit his son and family. We didn't talk much about what he did while he was visiting."

"Did he ever seem angry or nervous before or after a visit?" Lou continued.

"He was pretty upset with his son getting laid off. We had a talk once about this lay off stuff. As a young man Bill got laid off and it really had an effect on him. I listened to him tell the story about getting laid off, and the impact it had on his family. I could tell it was a traumatic experience.

"But, no, he didn't seem nervous or particularly angry. I mean, he was not happy about what his son had to go through, and what his family had to go through. He was always putting down the Michigan Education Association. He didn't think the union was doing enough to protect his son. I do recall that."

"So, Bill never said or did anything that would lead you to believe that he might have been involved with killing anyone?"

"Oh no. He'd come back from a visit, and we'd go to Pure Country and eat meals together. We'd play cards, watch sports on TV, stuff like that. I think you've got the wrong guy here, folks. I really do."

"Well, we might. That's our job to check out all kinds of possibilities."

"Anymore questions? I've got to get ready to go to the funeral home for the visitation."

"Anymore questions, Lou, or Chief Brewbaker?" Deputy Moody asked watching for reaction. Both men shook their heads from side to side.

"Stan, we have a search warrant for Bill's home. I know that his son and family are there now. We don't mean to be insensitive to the family and the funeral home visitation, but we need to get into the house as soon as possible to search for any evidence that may clear your friend or substantiate our suspicions. I'm telling you this so you'll understand if Bill and the family are late for the wake."

Stan nodded and shook his head from side to side as if in disbelief.

"Thanks for talking with us," said Chief Brewbaker.

Stan nodded and got up to show the four to the front door.

They got back into the van. The three briefed Maggie, and then Lou said, "That set of envelopes that Stan dropped into the mailbox enroute to the hospital could very well have contained that letter to Al with the poisoned teabag. At least we now know that Bill, Sr. did put things in the mail from Rudyard on Saturday."

"What time is it?" Maggie asked.

"It's five-ten," Chief Brewbaker replied.

Deputy Moody said, "I think we should go right to the Blakeley home and conduct the search."

"Isn't that a bit insensitive with the funeral home visitation coming up in an hour and a half?" Lou asked.

"Perhaps, but I think we've got to get in as soon as possible, and we do have the warrant from the Magistrate."

Maggie suggested the search be conducted while the family is at the funeral home."

"My way of doing business is 'knock and talk.'" Moody said.

"I agree," Brewbaker nodded.

"Peace at all costs. If we break into the home while the family is at the funeral home, that will incite Bill, and we don't need that. We'll just go to the house and talk this out. We have the search warrant and I'll call a couple of officers from the sheriff's office to meet us there for support."

"Ok, let's go," Lou said.

Enroute the plan was discussed. Deputy Moody suggested that he concentrate on keeping Trudy and kids calm. Chief Brewbaker would sit at a dining room table with Bill, Jr. Bill would not be allowed to wander through the house as the search was being conducted. Lou, with help from Moody, would do the search, as carefully as possible, so as not to contaminate any evidence if they did

232

find what they were looking for. Nothing was to be disturbed from its source without photographing it first. Maggie and Tom would remain in the van and monitor activity outside the house.

At approximately five-thirty the van pulled into the Bill Blakeley's driveway. The home was a two story country farm house. It needed paint and the landscape was in need of attention. The grass was long, the bushes untrimmed. Some screens were missing or torn.

Chief Brewbaker and Deputy Moody got out of Maggie's van and approached the front door. They knocked. Lou waited back at the van. A few seconds later, the door was opened by Bryan who just stood there.

"Hello, son. Is your dad here?" Deputy Moody asked.

Bryan didn't say anything. He turned and said, "Mom, couple of policemen are here asking for Dad!"

Trudy came to the door. "What's wrong?"

"We need to talk to your husband, ma'am," Mike Moody said.

"He's in the bathroom getting ready for the funeral home visitation for his father. Why are you here?"

"We've a few questions for your husband, and then we need to look around the house here. That's all."

"Well, come in. I'll get him."

The two entered the house. A county sheriff's vehicle pulled up into the drive and Lou got out to meet the two officers and to explain what was happening.

Bill heard a car door close and he looked out of the bathroom window to see who was stopping by. He saw the county sheriff's cruiser and Maggie's van. He had seen that large, customized van when he had stopped at Lou Searing's home a week to two ago. He also recognized Lou talking to the officer's.

He knew his dad kept a hunting rifle in his bedroom along with a box of cardridges. It was there for protection because he lived alone in the country. He also used it for hunting. Bill felt ready to snap once again. The feelings were back, those same feelings as when he'd get a layoff notice. He simply had to put an end to all of the harassment that had been going on for weeks.

Trudy came up to the second floor bathroom, "Bill? Some police-men are here to see you."

"I'll be down in a minute. Tell them to wait a minute!"

"Ok." Trudy went downstairs and told the men that he'd be with them in a minute. She offered them some coffee. Both declined.

Bill quietly left the bathroom, went into his father's bedroom closet, and got the rifle and the ammunition. He returned to the bathroom, locked the door, loaded the rifle, opened the bathroom window, and positioned the rifle so that the cross hairs were right on the chest of Lou Searing, who was standing in the driveway between the sheriff's cruiser and Maggie's van.

Bill began to squeeze the trigger. With his heart beating in anger, he felt some justice in putting away the man who had been accus-ing him and his father of killing people. The quickest way to stop this harassment was to put him out. Just as Bill was pulling the trigger to the point where the hammer would strike the cartridge sending the bullet into Lou's heart, Bill's dog charged Lou. Lou stepped back instantly to sidestep the German Shepard who was intent on attack-ing this stranger on private property.

The shot rang out and the bullet tore through Lou's left arm and proceeded into the back right side of Maggie's van. She instinctively unbuckled her restraints in the driver's seat, and with Tom's assis-tance, rolled her chair back from the windshield. Lou stayed on the ground clutching his left arm. The officers in the vehicle exited and scurried around to the back using the cruiser as a shield from any further shots.

Moody and Brewbaker heard the shot. They both drew their weapons and immediately told Trudy and the kids to take cover. Moody ushered them into the garage and told them to get behind a pickup truck and not to leave under any circumstances. Trudy pleaded with Moody to let her talk to Bill, but Moody felt that pro-tecting her at this point was more important. Once Bill was isolated and could be talked to, then maybe, Trudy would be called upon to intervene.

Moody and Brewbaker quickly figured out that Bill was holed up in the upstairs bathroom. He was for all practical purposes captured. There was no escaping from the bathroom window as there was a twenty foot drop to the ground. The bathroom door was closed and it would be covered until Bill came out of his own volition or by some use of force.

While Brewbaker kept watch of the bathroom door, Moody picked up the phone and called the County Sheriff. He briefed him of what was happening. A shot was fired from the Blakeley home. Moody told them that Lou was down but he didn't know the extent of the damage. Lou could be dead, injured, or faking a hit. He had no way of knowing. He asked for reinforcements and for a suicide prevention team to be brought in.

Deputy Moody then went upstairs and tried to make some contact with Bill. "Bill, listen to me. Come on out before someone gets hurt."

"You're trespassing on my dad's property! I'm sick and tired of being harassed by police and detectives! I've been laid off because of Searing, and I've had it, you understand?"

"Yeah, I do. I can see where you're justifiably angry, Bill. You've got every right. But the way you're handling this is getting you into big trouble. Can't you see that?"

"Yeah, got Searing down and lot more cartridges beside me."

"Listen Bill. You're backed into a corner and haven't got a chance of getting out. Killing people isn't going to help you."

"Why you here?"

"We've got a search warrant to look through your dad's home. We believe that he may be involved in killing people in the school districts where you've been laid off."

"That's crazy. He never killed anybody. It was me. You want me to admit it. Ok, you got your confession. Now you happy? I did it! Now since I just admitted to a bunch of deaths, what's a few more. If you keep bothering me, I may put this barrel in my mouth and save the citizens the cost of a trial!"

Deputy Moody decided not to continue the conversation. He shouted out the door for the officer to call the Blakeley home and he gave him the number. Maggie had also shouted to open the back of her van so she could talk with them and plan next steps.

An officer opened the van and entered.

"How's Lou?" was her first question.

"It's a pretty bad wound. We've gotta get him to a hospital. He's losing blood."

"Well, get him in here and we'll take off. Have your buddy cover for me and I'll be outta here."

The officer and Tom helped Lou get into the van. He told his partner to cover for Maggie as she slipped behind the wheel and backed out."

No shots were fired and Maggie was able to get away. She took off down the road back to Rudyard and out to I-75 and toward Sault Ste. Marie. She contacted the hospital with her cell phone. A team would be waiting when she arrived.

How you doing partner?" Maggie asked.

"Hurts bad. Got no feeling in the arm. I'm losing blood."

"Maybe I ought to hook up to an EMS vehicle and have them do some first aid and then hurry you into the hospital."

"Sounds like a good idea. Gotta have something for the pain."

Maggie got on her cell phone and requested an EMS vehicle. She noted her position on the highway and in a matter of minutes she learned that an EMS vehicle would meet her at the exit where M-28 meets I-75. She turned off, and Lou was quickly put onto a stretcher. He entered the ambulance where he got quick and fine treatment for the massive wound in his left arm. Maggie followed the ambulance as it sped toward Sault Ste. Marie with sirens and flashers in full operation.

Back at the Blakeley home, Moody and Brewbaker had asked Trudy to come into the house and to talk with them about trying to get Bill to calm down. They told her to talk to him calmly and to try to get him to come out without the weapon. She agreed.

"Bill. Bill, honey. Please come out. I need you, the kids need you. You're a good man, and you're going through a lot. Please come out and let's get our lives back together. Please honey. I love you."

There was silence. Bill didn't respond.

Trudy tried again, "Bill, honey. Can you hear me?"

"Yeah. I'm just so sick and tired of all of this crap. I'm tired of all the accusations, all the stuff we've had to go through. I'm tired."

"I know honey. I am too. Please come out and hug me, and let's start again. Please. For me and the kids, Bill. All we've got is each other, now."

Trudy had been told by Deputy Moody that Bill had confessed to killing the people in previous school districts and that when he was out, by choice or by force, he'd have to be taken in and booked, but that he'd get help to deal with the trauma. Trudy didn't believe Bill's confession. She told Moody that he was covering for his dad, that was all. She was sure he was innocent. There was no question that he'd have charges filed against him for shooting Lou Searing, but that was all she thought he was guilty of.

The bathroom door opened, Bill walked out, handed the rifle to Brewbaker and gave Trudy a hug. He was then arrested for the attempted murder of Lou Searing. He was read his Miranda rights, and chose to have a lawyer present before any questioning.

Bill was handcuffed and taken to the county sheriff's cruiser. He was taken to the county jail and booked.

Lou and Maggie were contacted at the hospital in the Soo. Deputy Moody was on the line. Maggie took it. "Maggie? How's Lou?"

"He's in surgery now. Very nasty wound. The doctor didn't know if the bone was shattered or if the bullet just tore through muscle. The doc said he'd be in surgery for about 45 minutes, and its been about a half hour now."

"Has Mrs. Searing been notified?"

"Yes. I talked to Carol a few minutes ago. She's coming up. She was pretty shaken, but once she was assured that the wound wasn't life threatening, she was better. She's coming up with Lou's son, Scott, who lives in Grand Rapids. The company will be good for both of them I'm sure. What happened at the farm house?"

"Trudy talked him into coming out and giving up the weapon.

We arrested him for the attempted murder of Lou. By the way, he confessed to all the killings."

"Is that right. That's a surprise."

"Well, Trudy thinks he is just covering for his dead father. She admits he fired at Lou, but she's certain he had nothing to do with killing anybody."

"I tend to agree. My buck was on the father and still is. What did you find in the search? Anything?" Maggie asked.

"We're going back for that. First we needed to get Bill in custody and follow all the legally required procedures."

"What's happened to the family?"

"The minister of the church who is burying Bill Blakeley was an angel sent from heaven. He took Bryan and Heather with him after they were assured by their mother that all would be fine. Trudy went to be with Bill and the kids went with Reverend Nichols. They are pretty shaken up by all of this, but the Reverend is very good with helping kids in a crisis, and they'll be alright."

"The funeral home? What's happening there?"

"I stopped over and got ahold of Stan Hovath. I told him the basic details of what happened. He said he would keep things to himself for the time being and would try his best to be the family representative in greeting the mourners saying that circumstances made it impossible for the family to be present this evening. When pressed he would simply say, 'The family's having trouble with all of this, as you can imagine.'"

"The farm house? What's happening there?"

"We'll be going back after things settle here and complete the search. I wish Lou and you could be with us since you know best what you are looking for. We'll do our best and go back with you tomorrow if things don't surface as expected. Reverend Nichol's church leaders will provide housing and meals for Trudy and the kids. I'll let them back into Bill's home to get personal belongings and their car."

"How can I get in touch with you to let you know about Lou's surgery?" Maggie asked.

238

"Just call the Chippewa County Sheriff's office and ask to be put through to me."

"Sounds like everything is under control. This isn't the way we expected this drama to end, but we don't deal the cards I guess."

"Well, it isn't over yet."

"Right. There's more to the story I'm sure."

"Tell Lou we're thinking of him. I'm sorry he took the slug. Guess in retrospect we should've been more cautious. After all, Bill was a suspect in all of these murders. We should have anticipated a crazed reaction. Guess it's a lesson for next time."

"Pretty costly lesson. We're pretty lucky he'll be alright. Guess we should thank that dog for scaring Lou a bit. If he hadn't quickly moved, we may be having this conversation from the morgue instead of the emergency room."

"Don't even think about it. Will talk with you soon."

"Thanks for calling."

✧

Back at the County Building, Bill and a lawyer were present when Deputy Moody questioned Bill about Lou's shooting and his confession in the farm house. Bill admitted to firing the shot that severely injured Lou. He also said that it was time to end all of this curiosity about the people who died in his previous school districts. He said that he was the one who killed the six people. When asked for details he was reticent to give any. In fact, he couldn't put forth any information. He didn't know who he had killed, and he couldn't recall how he had killed them. He said he didn't know how Al Forrest had died. However, the police had a signed confession that he had in fact killed six people and had wounded Lou Searing. It was enough for the Prosecuting Attorney to charge Bill Blakeley with all of the murders.

That same evening, Bill Blakeley appeared before Judge Isaac Buck in Sault Ste. Marie. The preliminary findings caused the judge to decide against bail and to hold Bill Blakeley in the county jail.

They would proceed to trial. Bill's condition was determined to be such that he was a threat to the public and therefore held in custody.

The reports were filed. Chief Brewbaker and Deputy Moody drove out to the Blakeley farm home to conduct the search. They took two officers with them and entered the home.

After about 15 minutes of looking in drawers, and in two desks, it was Chief Brewbaker who came upon the information they were looking for. "Got something here, Mike," the Chief said.

"What you got?"

Chief Brewbaker was in a room that seemed to be a den. It looked to have been a bedroom at one time. The room had a desk with numerous drawers. In addition was a file cabinet made of wood. It was a four file drawer and stood beside the desk. The second drawer was open when Mike came around the corner.

"Here is a notebook, or I guess you'd call it a diary Look here. It has a detailed plan for killing one person in each school district. Here is Lorimer in Mt. Pleasant. Here is a detailed description of how he carried out the murder. Look at this, here is a school directory and every employee with the last name beginning with "L" is highlighted. Then there's profiles noting specific vulnerabilities. This book is the same for all six districts."

"This looks like very incriminating evidence."

Brewbaker called the officer over for photos of the diary in the drawer and then a few pages where the detail was provided. They picked up the diary and placed it in an evidence bag.

Moody opened another drawer and found a small chemistry lab and a book entitled, *Death Made Easy*. The book had highlighted sections which described how to kill and make the death appear to be a stroke, a heart attack, or suicide. Off to the side were the names of the victims. There was even a chapter on killing during hunting season, giving specific directions for stalking humans and what precautions to take so that shots appear to be accidents involving hunters.

"Listen to this," Brewbaker said. "He killed a Mrs. Anderson in Mason by making her drink alcohol at gunpoint till she was almost unconscious. He got her into her car and turned on the ignition in a closed garage. Then here is the account for the murder of the woman in Stockbridge, a Mrs. Young. Says here he removed the insulin from her bottle and replaced it with U500 insulin which he notes is five times her normal dose and would lead to her death."

"How did he know about these people?" Moody asked. "Seems he'd need a lot of detail about their lives to plan such detailed murders so that they all look like obvious deaths."

"Not only that, but he was incredibly lucky. I mean, no one sees him, no one happens by, no one suspects anything," Brewbaker realized that it all surpassed chance.

"Until Newberry," reminded Moody. "Lou said some old lady down the street thought the guy there didn't die without some help."

"Let me see that diary, Mike. I'm curious what he has for Al Forrest." Mike handed him the diary and Brewbaker turned to the last murder. He read, "Al Forrest is the next victim. He collects tea from throughout the world. Teabag with arsenic injected into it was mailed on Saturday, November 21, from Rudyard. Hopefully, he'll open the envelope and use the tea bag on Monday, November 23. This will be revenge for hurting my son by putting him through the pain of a layoff."

Moody asked, "What does that last paragraph say?"

Brewbaker read it silently first and then read, "Says, 'the killings are complete. The revenge has finally been carried out to perfection. No son of Bill Blakeley will go through what I went through in my life without my seeing that a price is paid for bringing this disturbing news to my beloved son and his family. Following the death of Al Forrest, I shall destroy all of my materials and diaries leaving behind not a trace of involvement. Six perfect killings. It's the price schools must pay for hurting my son. As I write this, an investigation team, Lou Searing and Margaret McMillan, are asking questions, but there is no evidence; nothing beyond the circumstantial. No court will convict, because there are no witnesses, no autopsies, no weapons, no motives beyond the ridiculous observation that six people would die following a layoff notice. Each victim has the first letter of their last name designed to spell the word layoff. I had no idea that Bill would have to endure this hell beyond a time or two in his life. Once was enough to ruin my life and to bring misery to my boy in his formative years.' Strangely, he signed it, Bill Blakeley."

"He didn't get to destroy the evidence that incriminated him. The heart attack, the trip to the hospital, and death took him away from getting rid of the evidence we needed to solve those six murders in Michigan. The son he tried to save could have been convicted if we didn't find this stuff," Deputy Moody said, proud of their discovery.

"Got to take our hats off to Lou and Maggie. They solved this thing and led us to find this incriminating stuff. Too bad they are not here to see the end of the case," Brewbaker remarked.

"The son had nothing to do with the six murders," Moody concluded.

"It doesn't look that way. It looks like he was defending his father, and why wouldn't he? Looks like they were close, and had a bond related to adjusting to layoffs."

"The bond of father and son is strong, and Bill was even willing to help his dead father by taking the rap for these deaths," Mike concluded.

"Looks that way. We need to find handwriting that matches this diary in order to have evidence that Bill senior wrote this and not Bill junior or someone else."

" I saw some handwriting in the family photo album on the coffee table in the living room."

The two looked at the hand writing. The match was very obvious. They, along with the officers who accompanied them, finished taking their pictures, documenting what they found, where they found it and then they placed it into evidence containers for review and analysis by the State Police Crime Lab. They locked the house and went back to Sault Ste. Marie.

کے

Maggie was in the recovery room when Lou came back into consciousness. "What's going on?" Lou asked.

"Well, you're coming back into the land of the living. Your arm had a fracture and quite a bit of muscle damage. The doc says that in time you'll be good as new. They had to put a pin in your upper arm to hold the two pieces of bone in place. The muscle should repair with therapy. No major nerves were damaged, just bone and muscle. Doc says you were a lucky guy. I think you owe your life to that dog."

"Yeah, looks that way. Is Carol here?"

"She and Scott called a few minutes ago from Traverse City. They should be here around midnight. The surgeon and I talked with them and assured them that you'd be better in time. The surgery was very successful. They sounded relieved. You may have quite a job convincing Carol that the next investigation needs your attention. It also looks like your golf game will take a rest for awhile."

"What happened with the search of the Blakeley home?"

"You're not even fully conscious and you want all of the news. I got a call from Deputy Moody. They found a diary, chemicals, and a confession of sorts that he and he alone carried out each of the murders. He was planning to destroy all of the evidence once Al Forrest died, but he never made it home to carry out that plan."

"Where is Bill now?"

"He's being held in the county jail because the judge determined he was not safe out in public. I think the evidence will show that the only crime he committed was attempted murder in shooting you."

"I'll not file charges as long as he gets therapy for the anger. Isn't going to do anyone any good to put a family man in prison. He's good with kids, and I've got a feeling that he'll get some good help and get his life together."

Tuesday, November 24,
Rudyard, Michigan

Deputy Moody received a call from the Michigan State Police Lab in Grayling. The fourth digit in the zip code was an eight meaning the envelope was mailed from Rudyard. Since Bill, Jr. wasn't in Rudyard when it was mailed, it added to the evidence that Bill, Sr. was the murderer. The lab also reported that the tea bag had arsenic in it. The hand writing was indeed that of Bill Blakeley, Sr. There was no question that Bill Blakeley, Sr. killed six people.

Early in the afternoon, there was a meeting between Maggie, Deputy Moody, Chief Brewbaker and the Prosecutor. Also present was the attorney for Bill Blakeley. The three presented their evidence, as well as the report from the State Police. The evidence was overwhelming that Bill Blakeley, Sr. was the guilty one. Since he was deceased, the Prosecuting Attorney directed the case be closed and that the law enforcement officials in the six towns should be notified of the findings in the case.

Also, Bill, Jr. was interviewed by a court appointed psychiatrist and found to be very disturbed given the events of the last few months, but he was determined to be sane. He admitted that he had no knowledge of the deaths in the school districts that had hired him. He simply couldn't stand to see his father accused of killing anybody. Bill recalled that his father seemed to ask a lot of detailed questions about his school colleagues, but he thought he was just interested.

The Prosecuting Attorney ruled that Bill be held in the county jail until a plan for rehabilitation could be presented to Judge Buck and put into action. Bill's attorney agreed.

⌇

Maggie made it a point to call Chief Fitzpatrick, Wanita Fuller, Cynthia Hamm, Dick Thompson, and Elizabeth Beller to explain what had occurred in Rudyard, and to bring closure to the thirteen year saga. Cynthia Hamm couldn't believe that Bill would shoot anyone, but she admitted that she was wrong. She asked Maggie to give Lou her best and to apologize for doubting his instincts.

Lou called Rose O'leary and explained what had happened and that the case was closed. He promised to take her to dinner the next time he was in Lansing. The meal would be on him, and he'd leave a more substantial tip. He was thankful to be alive, and felt he owed her a detailed explanation of the investigation.

Wednesday, November 25, Newberry, Michigan

The following day, the headline in the *Newberry News* read, "Tom Franklin Murdered: Rudyard Man Guilty."

Mrs. Cunningham and her bridge playing friends met on Wednesday because the next day was Thanksgiving. The first hand was dealt, and the conversation began with Mrs. Cunningham, "Tom Franklin was murdered. I trust each of you remembers my saying that they would eventually find this to be what happened. Mr. Searing called to thank me for being so observant. He meant 'nosy,' but he was kind enough to say 'observant.' He also said that he told Mr. Fitz that our hunch regarding how Mr. Franklin was murdered was right on the money. He said he was calling to give credit where credit was due."

Wilma Wriggley smiled and gave the signal for the others to say in unison, "Guess she was right." All of the ladies in the bridge club smiled and gave her credit for her prediction.

Mrs. Cunningham accepted her friends round of applause and said, with a gleam in her eye, "My next prediction is that we'll see a woman President of the United States at the beginning of the next millennium."

Edith Presley said, "You're batting a thousand Mildred, but I don't think I'll tell Jim of your prediction. He just might find it newsworthy. Please pass the cookies and bid."

246

Thursday, November 26,
Thanksgiving Day
Grand Haven, Michigan

Lou Searing was getting adjusted to losing the use of his left arm. He and Carol, joined by their children and families, had gone to Thanksgiving Mass at St. Patrick's Catholic Church in Grand Haven. Each had much to be thankful for. Lou offered a silent word of thanks for a charging German Shepard who perhaps was an angel disguised as a dog. Who knows?

On his knees Lou wished a good future to the Blakeley family. He thought of two widows, Marian Franklin and Susan Forrest, who would have a lonely Thanksgiving holiday today. Each had strong family ties and a solid faith that would help. He thought of how appreciative he was of the men and women who work in law enforcement. They do a marvelous job of risking their lives to keep communities safe. He thought of parents of children with disabilities and how frustrating it is when programs and services change or are taken away when they seem so needed. He was thankful for special education teachers and administrators who daily provide quality programs for tens of thousands of children and youth with disabilities. He was thankful for Carol and her love and the love of their two children and their families. He was thankful for Maggie and her ability to think through all aspects of a case.

After the church service and before dinner, Carol and Lou took a long walk on the Lake Michigan shoreline behind their home. They walked hand in hand, and they enjoyed Samm chasing sticks thrown along the beach.

In the Searing home, their daughter Amanda and husband Joe, son Scott, his wife, Patti, and their son Benjamin were putting the final touches on a Thanksgiving dinner. They had encouraged Carol and Lou to get out of the house and share the beauty of the Lake Michigan shoreline. Carol and Lou took them up on their offer.

"Got a lot to be thankful for, Sweetzie," Lou said giving Carol's hand a squeeze.

"Yes we do. I'm thankful you're OK. Kind of scary to get that phone call. Please tell me that was your last investigation. That was my prayer when I was on my knees next to you in church this morning."

"As much as I love you, I've got to do what brings me joy, and that is helping people figure out what happens when emotions go beyond reason. I'll be careful, very careful, but I've got to keep doing what I love to do."

"I know. I was being selfish, but I guess there's nothing wrong with wanting the man I love to not be in harms way."

"I love you for it. You know that. Let's go join the family, and continue being thankful for all of our blessings."

Lou and Carol walked along the cool beach to their home. Samm was beginning to slow down and seemed ready to call it a day, too. The blue sky, the cool breeze, and the sparkling water were refreshing, but it was time for a family meal and a nap.

Epilogue

↬ Bill was cleared of any criminal charges in exchange for seeking intensive therapy for his anger. His recovery went well and he seemed to be a new man.

↬ Bill, Trudy, and the children left Charlevoix. They weren't comfortable in the town where everyone knew Bill's father had killed a beloved superintendent. They moved to a small town in southeast Iowa.

↬ Trudy worked in an Iowa public school system, and Bill left his teaching in Michigan. He liked children and continued to have an interest in young people who had trouble with the police and the courts. He became a parole officer and was actually quite effective in setting some kids on the right path.

↬ Bryan received some good counseling and got his life on track. He graduated from high school and received a full athletic scholarship to the University of Iowa.

↬ Heather fell in love with a high school sweetheart, and against the wishes of her parents, married within three months of graduating from high school. She and her husband rented a small farm in a rural town in Iowa. They gave Bill and Trudy their first grandson.

↬ Maggie and Lou worked with the authorities in Mt. Pleasant, Battle Creek, Mason, Stockbridge, Newberry, and Charlevoix to explain and bring closure to the deaths of Mr. Lorimer, Mrs. Anderson, Miss Young, Mr. Olsen, Mr. Franklin, and Dr. Forrest.

The End

Perceptions of the Author:

Conflicts exist in life and they certainly exist in special education. The root of all conflict lies in our belief that we are all separate. We believe our senses when they tell us that we are different. When we see differences, we discriminate, judge, devalue, and hurt others. To protect us from ourselves we pass laws, develop rules and establish policies that further divide us and reinforce the belief that we are all separate from each other.

The truth is that we are all connected, and if we can see this connection, and believe it in our hearts and minds, then we will see that we are all one. In seeing ourselves in others, including people with disabilities, we will be able to love, to understand, to appreciate, and to accept.

This fictitious conflict points out the devastation that occurs when people believe they are not connected. What a different story would be told if children knew they were all one, if parents and school leaders knew they were all connected, if community leaders led from a perception of connectedness and not separateness. The story would be one of love, because once people learn that they are not separate, but are in fact one, it is impossible to harm, because you only harm yourself.

It is my fervent wish that the future of special education will de-emphasize all that separates us and will emphasize all that brings us together. Please join with me in working toward this goal. Thank you.

Coming Soon:
The Principal Cause of Death

The second Lou Searing and Maggie McMillan mystery opens with the Principal of Shoreline High School submurged face-down in his swimming pool at 11:37 p.m. This death was witnessed by a student who is quite certain the murderer is his teacher. Lou and Maggie get involved and work to solve another case. You won't want to miss the second adventure of America's premier education detectives.

You can reach Richard L. Baldwin via e-mail by sending your correspondence to RLBald@aol.com. The website for Buttonwood Press is www.buttonwoodpress.com

To order more copies of
A Lesson Plan For Murder

Phone orders: For credit card orders (Visa, MC, or Discover) call toll free 1-800-247-6553 (24-hour service)

Fax orders: (419) 281-6883

E-mail orders: order@bookmaster.com

Mail: BookMasters, Inc.
1444 U.S. Route 42
Ashland, Ohio 44805

Each softcover copy is $12.95 $ _____

Shipping and Handling:
Book rate is $4.00 for first book and
$2.00 for each additional book. $ _____

Tax: Add 6% sales tax for Michigan and
Ohio residents (for 1 book this is $.78) $ _____

Total: (for one book this is $17.73) $ _____

Please make check payable to: Bookmasters

PLEASE PRINT

Name: _____

Address: _____

City: _____

State: _____ Zip: _____

For additional information visit the website of Buttonwood Press at www.buttonwoodpress.com

Thank you!

LESSON PLAN FOR MURDER
Cover design by Eric Norton
Text design by Mary Jo Zazueta in Utopia
Printed by Data Reproductions on
60 lb. Simpson Offset
Client Liaison: Theresa Nelson
Production Editor: Alex Moore